Best Wishes

Julie No

1

ALSO BY THIS AUTHOR

Tomb Of The Lost
Spear Of Destiny
Drake's Gold

NON-FICTION

The World is Not Flat
The World is Still Not Flat

CHILDREN'S BOOKS

The Adventures Of Stella Earwax and Friends
More Adventures Of Stella Earwax And Friends

THE SPEAR OF DESTINY

JULIAN NOYCE

IT HAS SERVED US WELL, THIS MYTH OF CHRIST
- POPE LEO X -

PROLOGUE

CALVARY, JUDAEA, APRIL 3rd, 33AD

The man sat alone, lost in his thoughts. The world in front of him hazy and pink. The sun warm on his face. He sensed the weather would change soon; he could taste it in the air. The wind buffeted his cloak around his legs. He tasted the breeze on his lips, but it told him nothing. Somewhere nearby some women were sobbing, earlier they had been wailing. There were four of them, four mourners. Even though they had been wailing as one he had picked out each individual voice. Now though, their sobbing affected him even more. He could feel their individual grief.

Then their sobs were drowned out by the raucous shouts of men to his right. One man shouting louder than the others. Then the sound of click - clack as dice were thrown across the playing table. The dice were gathered up and the lone man could hear them rattling inside the leather shaker before they were ejected onto the playing surface again. More raucous applause followed as the twelve dice players shouted with excitement.

"I just need another five," the loudest man shouted. He was Atronius, a Centurion. He shook the one remaining dice in the cup longer than was necessary. Then when his colleagues could wait no longer, he launched the dice once again. It hit the far wall of the small table, bounced back across, hit the near wall and stopped in the middle, spinning very fast. The twelve players leaned in close. The dice slowed, then stopped as the twelve watched. They could all see it was a five.

Atronius jumped up.

"YES!" he roared.

Two of his friends slumped back on their small wooden stools. Most stood and shouted. The last man punched the table making the dice jump.

"That's it! Hand it over," Atronius ordered.

He held up the robe handed to him.

6

"That's it. Come to me," he said examining it, "This should fetch a good price. Hey! Longinus! I won his robe," Atronius cocked his thumb at the man on the cross.

Longinus, sitting away from the others, didn't play dice. There wouldn't be much point. Though he could trust his friends not to cheat he wouldn't be able to see the dice. No. Longinus was blind.

He hadn't always been blind. Longinus was a fine soldier. A Roman legionary whose eyes had begun to cloud over many months before. Intense bright light was also a problem for him sometimes, causing intense pain and headaches. There was a milky film across both his eyes that gave him a demonic appearance to anyone who gazed at him. His friends sometimes used his affliction to scare children to their great amusement.

Atronius lifted and held the robe.

"There we are. The robe of a King."

"Father, forgive them for they know not what they do."

"Eh? What?" Atronius said open mouthed.

The twelve Romans turned to look at the crucified man. They chuckled.

"Your father's not here your majesty," Atronius said, mocking the man on the cross with the crown of thorns on his head to the delight of the Romans present, "But your mother is."

Atronius slapped his thigh at his own humour.

The others were no longer laughing. They were staring over Atronius' shoulder. All except Longinus.

"What's the matter with you lot?"

"Behind you sir."

Atronius turned.

Strange, black clouds were forming where before there was only blue sky, building fast and billowing up and out, blocking out the sun. Longinus felt the shade fall across his face. The figure on the cross raised his head weakly to the heavens and then his head dropped to his chest. Blood dripped from his nose and chin from where the thorns had gouged his forehead. Longinus heard and felt the man's last breath as it escaped his lips. The Romans were still staring at the sky as the brooding black clouds built.

"What is happening?" one of them asked, "Sir you've served in the province longer than anyone else. Have you ever seen anything like it?"

"No, I haven't," Atronius answered.

They continued staring.

"It must be something to do with him," Longinus said nodding towards the crucified man.

"You don't believe all that rubbish do you Longinus? About him being the son of God," legionary Lucius asked.

Longinus didn't have time to answer.

"Look lively!" Atronius said, "The Tribune's approaching.

Tribune Plinius strode up as the men saluted.

"As you were," Plinius said, stopping when he saw the dice table.

"Oh. Uh! Me and the lads, sir, were just having a friendly game sir."

Plinius nodded, pleased to note there didn't appear to be wine cups present.

"Well as long as you're not drinking on duty. I don't mind a bit of friendly gambling," He looked around at the many groups of local people who had witnessed the executions. He took in the four sobbing women.

"Has there been any trouble?"

"No sir. No trouble."

"Good. Perhaps these people are starting to learn a little discipline," he studied the dark clouds above.

"There seems to be a storm brewing. I personally don't fancy a soaking today," he looked at the three crucified men for the first time. One of which was muttering to himself.

"Let's get this over with."

"Right, you heard the Tribune. Break their legs."

The first two men howled hideously as their thighs were smashed. With broken legs they would be unable to support their upper bodies and would suffocate quickly.

"I see you've left the king until last," Atronius mocked, "privileges of royalty your majesty," he said to the amusement of his men.

Longinus was standing directly under the man called Christ.

"Well? What are you waiting for?" Atronius asked.

The other Romans grinned in anticipation. Longinus blindly swinging at the condemned man's legs should be hilarious.

"There's no need to break this one's legs sir. He's already dead."

Atronius stepped towards Longinus, disappointment on his face.

"Dead! He was talking to his father only moments ago."

"I heard him gasp his last breath sir."

"Heard him? Oh, you and that sense of yours. You see with your hearing. I forgot. You should be careful Longinus. They're crucifying men for being miracle workers. Eh! Eh!" he laughed at his own humour.

The first few splashes of rain began to fall. Tribune Plinius came rushing up to them.

"Come on! What's taking so long?"

"Longinus says this man is already dead Tribune."

"Well, is he?"

"He does look it sir."

"Well why don't you find out."

Atronius grabbed Longinus' spear while Longinus was still holding it and rammed it upwards into Christ's side. There was no reaction from the still form on the cross and Longinus was looking up as Atronius wrenched the spear free. It came out smoothly and a torrent of blood and fluid splashed down into Longinus' face. He instantly sank to his knees, his hands letting go of the spear, still held by Atronius, and clutched at his eyes.

"Longinus!" Atronius said cursing at the blood that had splattered his arms and uniform.

Longinus by now had his head between his knees and he was moaning.

"It's only a bit of blood Longinus. Get up man."

A bolt of lightning flashed down from the black clouds and struck the spear. There was a large shower of sparks from the iron tip of the spear. Atronius cried out as he was thrown fifteen feet through the air and landed heavily on his back. Staring up at the sky he brought his hands up to his face. His palms were badly burned and it was agony but as he watched the pain disappeared and so did the burns. His hands had completely healed right in front of his very eyes. He rubbed his palms together but there was no pain.

"What the....?"

He got to his feet and went back to Longinus who had stopped moaning and was also staring at his own hands.

"Are you all, right?" Atronius called, "Longinus your eyes."

Longinus looked up open mouthed.

"Atronius."

"Yes."

"I can see you."

Atronius grabbed either side of Longinus' face as Longinus stood up.

"Your eyes. You no longer have that milky film over them."

Longinus, tears running down his face, turned to his comrades who were staring in disbelief. He called them each by name and they nodded open mouthed.

"I can see."

"It's a miracle."

"Look at this," Atronius said standing over the spear. They all gathered round. Tiny blue sparks danced and fizzed around the iron spearhead. Then one by one they grew smaller and disappeared inside the metal as it consumed them. It seemed to take on a different tinge, almost as if it was glowing from within.

Longinus picked his spear up. It felt exactly as it had before. As the day it had been issued to him. But he knew it had changed. As he had changed.

"My hands were burned by it," Atronius said, "And before my very eyes they healed themselves. As has your sight."

"It truly is the work of the Gods."

The Roman soldiers turned slowly to look at the figure on the cross.

CHAPTER ONE

The flashing lights from the two police cars and ambulance bounced back off the buildings as the three-vehicle convoy sped through the dark city's streets. The convoy had set out just after sundown from the general hospital and was heading back towards Mornaguia prison 14km west of Tunis. The October air cool.

The hectic rush hour traffic had calmed and the convoy very rarely had to stop. Each time they approached red traffic lights the lead police car would pull onto the junction and stop other traffic so the ambulance could continue unimpeded. The police car at the rear would then overtake the ambulance and the one that had stopped would fall in behind.

At the city outskirts the small convoy stopped at a military station and after a few words with the police vehicles they set off once again for the prison. Two jeeps with Tunisian national guardsmen now joined the procession. In the lead jeep a political prisoner was chained to the floor of the vehicle.

In the ambulance was another prisoner. A man who was handcuffed to his gurney. He was laying on his back, fully clothed, his upper body wearing a hoodie. The hood was up and covering his head and most of his face. Opposite him sat a policeman. A young recruit who tried to ignore the strange rattling sound that came every time his prisoner drew a breath. The few occasions that he had caught a glimpse of the man's chin he had seen a patchwork of scar tissue and it had made him feel sick. His prisoner had eighty per cent burns to his face, neck and hands and had just received treatment from the country's top plastic surgeon.

The prisoner turned his head slightly towards his guard who fought the urge not to vomit. It was hot in the back of the ambulance and the policeman felt a little claustrophobic. He tore his eyes away from the man on the gurney and tried to focus on the conversation the driver and co-driver were having. He forced his mind to drown out the sickly rattle and concentrated. The two in front were discussing a football match that had been televised the evening before. It had been a world cup qualifier between Nigeria and Tunisia and unbelievably, against the odds, Tunisia had forced a 1-1 draw and were currently second in the group with one match to play.

"I'm telling you," The co-driver said, "If that Nigerian defender hadn't been on the goal line that header would have beaten the goalkeeper and gone in."

"Maybe," the driver replied.

"Maybe? It would."

"It was difficult to tell. The camera angle wasn't very good."

"No. My brother has a very good television. It would have gone in and then we would be on top of our group and not second."

Tunisia's next game would be against Morocco.

"The next match will also be difficult for our team," the driver said.

"I will say a thousand prayers that they are victorious. My prayers will be heard."

"I hope so my brother, I hope so."

The policeman was listening with only half an ear. The football didn't interest him. He was very much a family man. The only thing that mattered to him was his job, his wife and two young daughters.

"Do you have the time please?" the man on the gurney asked in his strange, rattling voice.

The policeman started for a moment. This was the first time the prisoner had spoken to anyone. Tearing his eyes away from the very scarred face once again he flicked his wrist over and looked at his watch.

"It is just after eight thirty."

"Do you think you could ask them to turn the lights down."

"No."

Now for the first time the man wearing the hooded top raised his head and his guard saw the whole face for the first time. The scars crisscrossed every spare bit of skin and flesh. In places the skin was so paper thin the policeman could see the red sinews below. The eyes were different too. One was dark and the other had a whitish tinge to the iris. There was no facial hair, no whiskers, no eyelashes, no eyebrows. The skin around the lips, which were dry, around the nose and eyes was pulled tight. So tight that when the man spoke his lips hardly moved. What the guard could see of the forehead appeared to be equally scarred. Now he saw one ear which was shrivelled, the lobe burned off. The skin around the neck and throat was red and scarred and stopped where the hooded top began. The man's hands were also scarred.

The policeman tried to outstare his prisoner but found he couldn't and he looked down at his hands which were folded in his lap.

"I have just received laser treatment for my injuries and the bright lights are hurting my face. So, if I may ask again could they please turn the lights down."

The eyes held their stare. The guard glanced at them, in particular the white one again. Then he looked down at the handcuffs and moved his right leg slightly and felt the reassurance of his holstered handgun. Instinctively his fingers touched the butt of his handgun and the prisoner's eyes followed the movement. The prisoner smiled, the skin on his lips near splitting, the red flesh underneath dancing.

"I appreciate your concerns," the prisoner said. He lifted his wrists up until the handcuffs stopped them moving any further. The one closest to the guard broke the skin on the wrist and pinkish fluid oozed from the tear, "But where could I possibly run to?"

The guard was watching the sticky substance from the broken skin. Then he looked up into the eyes and nervously nodded.

"Thank you."

The policeman turned and spoke to the co-driver who looked back at him, glanced at the patient, then shrugged and flicked the interior lights switch, turning them down to a minimum.

"That's much better. Thank you," the scarred man said laying back and resting his head on the pillow. His breathing became the wheezing rattle once again. The policeman closed his eyes to try to block the sound out.

"How long have you been a policeman?"

His eyes flashed open again. He ignored the man and closed them again.

"Do you have a family?"

This time he kept them closed.

"I'm not allowed to talk to you."

"I'm sorry. I just thought a bit of polite conversation might make the journey go quicker."

"Be quiet. The journey will be over soon enough."

The scarred man remained quiet. Unseen by his guard his lips took on a strange smile.

The policeman regretted what he'd said.

'Was I too harsh on him,' he asked himself. He had had strict instructions prior to leaving to not speak to the prisoner. The man was apparently highly intelligent and dangerous, though he didn't look it. The policeman felt a certain pity for him.

"I've been a policeman for two years. I'm twenty-seven and yes, I have a beautiful wife and two adorable daughters."

"Then you're a very lucky man," came the reply.

The prisoner remained silent and when it was obvious that he wasn't going to say anything else the policeman closed his eyes again, not to sleep but to offer a silent prayer that the infinite would always watch over his family.

The convoy moved on through the desert. Occasionally they would pass a dwelling and see lights from within. The colours of their flashing lights reflecting off walls and buildings. Once they passed a line of camels heading in the opposite direction. Their headlights picking out the large, lumbering beasts being led by their masters. The sky was clear and stars twinkled, the full moon giving the sand a ghostly glow.

The man on the gurney lay in silence. The pain in his face starting to ease. He looked out of the side window of the ambulance at the moon. It's light soothing to him. Natural light was agonising to him. The scars on his face, neck, head and hands from burns he had sustained three months before.

Before his injuries he had been a tall, proud man. A German count and billionaire, a collector of rare artifacts and antiquities. His most recent expedition had been to recover the sarcophagus of Alexander the Great, once held by the Germans in World War II, it had been lost at sea when the British had torpedoed the German's freighter carrying it. Found seventy years later by a multinational team of archaeologists he had attempted to buy it from them. His money rejected he had taken it by force only to find out that it was in fact not Alexander's sarcophagus. In a brutal battle on his ship, he had been blown overboard in an explosion and pronounced dead. On the mortuary slab his very faint pulse had been detected. He had been treated until he was well enough to be detained in prison awaiting trial and possible extradition to the United States. The laser treatment for his injuries he was paying for himself.

He listened for a moment to his guards breathing which was getting deeper. The man was falling asleep. The scarred man moved his wrist with the broken skin to ease it and the cuff dragged the arm of the gurney and woke the policeman again. The policeman leaned closer to his prisoner to check the bonds and saw they were still locked. He looked ahead out of the windscreen. In the light from the headlights, he could see the road they were travelling was long and straight with hills ahead. In the far distance a glow on the horizon. Lights from the prison. Not much longer. Maybe five more kilometres.

He detected a strange sound which wasn't part of the ambulance. As he listened it got closer and closer, then was suddenly very loud. He saw the ambulance crew leaning forward and looking into and up in a door mirror each. The policeman was about to rush into the cab when he realised what the sound was, as a Russian Kamov Ka-50 'Black shark' attack helicopter flew low over the convoy. It kept pace with the ambulance for a few moments and then accelerated ahead over the lead police car, gained five hundred feet and flew over the approaching hills.

In the lead jeep the officer in charge was telephoning through to the barracks they'd not long left. There had been no mention of air support on his itinerary. It would be typical of General Ben Rashid Al-Din to do this without telling anyone and for a moment he dreaded questioning the General.

The girl on the end of the telephone said.

"Hold please while I put you through to the General."

The officer swallowed hard and then replied.

"No. Forget it. I don't want the General disturbed."

He rang off.

'It must be above board' he said to himself but also out loud.

"That helicopter must also be heading for the prison sir," his driver said.

"Yes," the officer replied, "It might not necessarily be for us, but it must be for the prison. There's not much else out here. Just nomads and ruins."

He glanced back at his chained prisoner who just stared at the floor.

The convoy entered the hills. The road winding and twisting as it climbed. The lead police car pulling away from the much heavier ambulance. The road became a double bend as the hills closed in on both sides. As the lead police car moved further ahead while maintaining its original speed a searchlight suddenly beamed on dazzling the driver as it picked up the police car. The Kamov helicopter was hovering twenty feet above the road in the narrow pass. The noise from its engine deafening. The driver of the police car put his arm up in front of his eyes, blinded by the intense light as the twin 23MM cannons on the Kamov spluttered into life. The bullets tore up the road as they raced towards their target. The cars headlights disappeared first in a shower of glass as both front tyres burst and bullets slammed into the two policemen inside the car killing them both instantly. Flames were pouring out from the bonnet and front wheel arches of the car as it exploded. The explosion throwing it twenty feet into the air. The helicopter some distance away jinked as the police car crashed down onto the road completely ablaze.

The ambulance rounded the bend and the whole convoy screeched to a stop. The helicopter flew over the vehicles and turned side on to the tail police car and destroyed it with a single anti-tank missile. Now the narrow pass was completely blocked.

The soldiers in the jeeps jumped out and took cover behind the ambulance the one vehicle they guessed would not be attacked. Inside the lead jeep the political prisoner was frantically pulling on his chains anchored to the floor. Not sure if this attack was to free him.

Another anti-tank missile hit the last jeep and it exploded into the air and came down on its roof.

The soldiers opened fire at the helicopter, and it lifted and moved out of range.

"Cease fire," the officer shouted, "They're not going to attack the ambulance."

There was a burst of gunfire from the surrounding hillside and the man next to him dropped dead. The officer swung around. He saw dark shapes descending on them.

"They're on the hillside!"

His men opened fire on the hillsides as the men descending took cover behind scrub and rocks.

"Cease fire! Cease fire!"

The guns fell silent.

"You have attacked Tunisian national forces. This is a deliberate act of terrorism. Throw down your weapons and give yourselves up."

The hillside waited in total silence. The whirring of the rotor blades nearby. Then a voice from the hill.

"It is you who is surrounded. Throw down your weapons. No one else will be harmed."

One of the Tunisians opened fire on the voice. A single shot from a Dragunov sniper rifle took him in the throat, blasting his blood against the side of the ambulance. He dropped to the road dead.

"Hold your fire!" the Tunisian officer shouted.

"This is your last chance to throw down your weapons."

Another shot from the Dragunov and another soldier dead.

"You will not get away with this!"

"You are being covered from an elevated position. You are compromised. There is no escape!"

The Tunisian officer opened fire. The hillside lit up with return fire and only stopped when the last soldier fell dead. The only sounds other than the Kamov helicopter were the men on the hillside reloading their weapons. Slowly they came down to the road.

Inside the ambulance the policeman guarding the prisoner had his face pressed against the small square window. He could see the burning police cars. The ambulance crew were cowering in their seats. A wicked sound of machine gun fire came through to them as a Tunisian national guardsman was put out of his misery.

The policeman inside the ambulance backed away from the double doors at the rear of the vehicle as he heard footsteps stop outside.

"Stay as you are and you won't get hurt," the scarred man ordered.

Suddenly the doors were yanked open and he went for his gun. A single shot took him in the head and his brains splattered the interior.

The scarred man looked into the dead eyes.

"Stupid fool."

The front doors were now ripped open and machine guns covered the ambulance crew as they raised their hands.

Former KGB agent Anatoly Petrov holstered his Glock 19 handgun.

"He has the handcuff keys," the scarred man gestured towards the policeman Petrov had just killed. Petrov searched the body, found the keys and unlocked the restraints. The scarred man rubbed his wrists, the broken skin sticky with fluid. Petrov stepped down into the road and made way for the scarred man.

Count Otto Brest von Werner stepped carefully down onto the road. His private army of men saluted him.

"Welcome back sir," the Russian spoke.

"Thank you, Petrov. Any casualties?"

"No sir. My team is all accounted for. Your ship is ten miles off the coast."

Two black hawk helicopters flew in low over the hills and landed in the road. Petrov gestured to Von Werner.

"If you're ready sir."

"Yes Mr Petrov. Take care of the vehicles."

"Yes Sir. And them?" Petrov asked, nodding towards the ambulance crew. Von Werner looked at them both. They were on their knees in the road, their hands on top of their heads, guns still trained on them. They were clearly petrified. Von Werner considered killing them.

"They were only doing their job. Let them go."

"Yes sir," Petrov made a motion with his hand and the guns were withdrawn. The two ambulance men got to their feet, mumbled their thanks and fled into the night.

Von Werner watched as his men set explosives on the remaining jeep and the ambulance.

"There's another prisoner here sir. Shall I let him go?"

"Why hasn't he escaped already?" Petrov asked.

"He's chained to the floor."

Petrov looked at Von Werner who shrugged and headed for the first Black hawk. The prisoner began screaming and frantically pulling at his chains as the last of the men got into the helicopters and they lifted off and headed North for the Mediterranean. Von Werner looked back at the huge fireball that lit up the night sky when the vehicles exploded.

Major Al-Assad surveyed the carnage on the mountain road. His special forces team were scouring the debris for clues. Of the police cars and ambulance there was nothing left. They were completely burned out. Just skeletons and ash remained. The jeeps, one on its roof, were twisted hunks of metal. In the lead one, were the charred remains of a human still chained to the floor. A forensics expert examining the remains. The teeth on the corpse were completely bared.

"As quickly as you can with those results," Al-Assad said to the forensics team working on the corpse. They were scanning their samples into a laptop.

"Yes sir. Do you want DNA scans on all casualties?"

"No. Not necessary. Our man was heavily scarred on the face and hands. None of the other dead match those injuries."

A lieutenant approached Al-Assad.

"Sir we've got another body. This one was in the back of the ambulance."

"The condition of the body?"

"Beyond recognition sir. He's also been shot in the head. We did find a standard issue police handgun."

"And the ambulance crew?"

"Unaccounted for."

"Is it possible they were completely incinerated?"

"Possible but unlikely. My guess is they escaped or were taken hostage."

"Why take the ambulance crew hostage and not the policeman. He would be worth more as a ransom."

"Because he was armed. Maybe he pulled his gun on them. That was probably the reason for killing him."

"Maybe. Well, whatever happened here we need to find the ambulance crew and where the ambulance came from. I want names, addresses. Find them."

"Yes sir."

A forensics expert got Al-Assad's attention. Al-Assad looked at the laptop screen.

"None of the DNA samples match Von Werner."

Al-Assad looked at the neatly lined up dead. A team nearby

examining bullet casings.

"How sure are you?"

"One hundred per cent."

Al-Assad's lieutenant came running up holding a field telephone.

Al-Assad frowned.

"It's the General sir."

Al-Assad reluctantly took the handheld.

"General Al-Din, it's bad news sir, we've lost him."

CHAPTER TWO

LONDON, ENGLAND

Peter Dennis poured himself another cocktail while trying not to spill any. He was leaning forward in the limousine to make sure he didn't splash any of the red liquid onto his white shirt.

"Would you like one?" he asked the girl opposite.

Marine archaeologist Natalie Feltham shook her head while holding her flute up.

"No thanks. I've still got most of my champagne left and you'd better not have too many of those in quick succession. I don't want you slurring your speech all night."

"Hey that's what Limos are about. Drinking in the back of them. It was good of Jim to put it on for us."

"He wanted us to arrive in style."

"That we'll do. You look sensational tonight."

"Oh, thanks and I don't usually. Is that what you mean."

"What! Of course, you do. You always do," Dennis replied eyeing up a shapely ankle, "That dress was a good idea. It is stunning."

Natalie was wearing a long, ankle length, sleeveless, black dress, with a long split down each thigh. The neck of the dress was gold. She was also wearing gold, strap heels. Her long blonde hair was held high on her head with pins. Two long strands of hair hung down, prettily, either side of her face.

"You don't look so bad yourself, but your bow tie is a little crooked."

He leaned into her.

"Straighten it for me."

While she did, he sneaked a quick kiss.

"Oi! Cheeky! You'll smudge my make up."

Then she laughed.

"What?"

"You've got my lipstick on your lips. Come here."

She wiped it off then became serious.

"I love you."

"Love you too," he replied, "And I love this car. Fancy a quickie?"

21

"What? No! The driver might see."

Dennis shrugged.

"And besides there's not enough time. Kinky bugger."

Dennis smiled.

"There's plenty of room."

The car turned a corner and Natalie saw the British museum ahead.

"Too late. I think we're here," she said as the car passed under a huge banner and stopped at the bottom of the steps. The door was opened and Natalie and Peter put their drinks down and she stepped out first, onto the red carpet and into a sea of press photographers and flash photography. Dennis stepped out and the chauffeur wished him a good evening, closed the door, got back into the driver's seat and moved off slowly past a television camera getting ready to start shooting. In front of the camera a beautiful reporter with Asian features.

"Three. Two. One. Go," the cameraman clicked his fingers at the reporter.

"Good evening and a very warm welcome from the British museum in London on this the opening night of the exhibition of what is perhaps the most important exhibit in the Christian world, the 'Holy lance' sometimes referred to as the 'spear of destiny' the mysterious Roman spear that supposedly pierced the side of Jesus Christ while he lay on the cross. I'm Kim Nguyen reporting from a star-studded occasion where the world of archaeology meets those of politics, film and stage as a host of stars pay tribute to this, the first exhibit of its kind here at this magnificent building for many years. The museum was founded by Sir Hans Sloane in 1753 who exhibited his own collections, a museum which currently holds the Elgin marbles and the controversial Rosetta stone, requested by Egypt for its return to its rightful country. Never before has an exhibit such as this, the 'holy lance' graced this the most famous museum in the world. On loan from its home in the Schatzkammer, Vienna, Austria the spear was once in the hands of Holy Roman emperors, Adolf Hitler and the American General George Patton. One of the world's truly great treasures it will be here on display for the next two months...." she glanced sideways and caught sight of Natalie and Dennis as they made their way along the red carpet towards the foot of the steps.

Dennis was admiring the six huge Roman fire baskets on stands blazing, merrily away, twenty feet high across the front of the museum at the top of the steps at the entrance. The excitement in Nguyen's voice quickened.

"Here come the renowned journalist Peter Dennis and the very beautiful marine archaeologist Natalie Feltham, hitting the headlines earlier in the summer, for the failed search for Alexander the great's sarcophagus. Natalie, Peter can I get a word," Nguyen called as they got to her.

Dennis smiled into the news camera.

"Can I ask you about your involvement tonight?"

"Hi Kim. Yes, it's a truly great turnout tonight for the exhibition."

Dennis stopped to put his hand up to a group of journalists he recognised.

"Now Mr Dennis you wrote an article on the spear," Nguyen said, holding up a copy of 'the country' magazine's latest issue. A photograph of the Holy lance on its cover, "How convinced are you that this may be the spear which pierced Christ's side, that it has magical powers?"

"I think the magic, Kim, is in what people believe. It has brought so many here tonight. The exhibition will be sold out every day and night for two months. That's the magic it holds."

"Some say that the lance doesn't resemble a Roman spear at all. That's it's quite possibly a hoax."

"Well, if it is a hoax, we'll have enough experts here tonight to prove it, one way or the other."

"That wasn't really an answer."

"Look Kim. It's been added to over the Millennia. The Roman soldier Maurice lived four hundred years after the crucifixion when he carried it into battle. It contains a Roman nail from Christ's cross for goodness sake. What more proof do you want."

"I have all the proof I need Peter. Here in this beautiful article, you've written," Nguyen said holding up the magazine again, "And speaking of beautiful, I must say Natalie you are looking exceptionally stunning tonight. Tell me what's it like to be with the most handsome, eligible, bachelor in journalism."

Natalie leaned into the microphone.

"It's an adventure Kim."

Nguyen smiled as the couple moved on down the line of photographers and reporters.

"There you have it," she said into the camera, "Hoax or not. It will be hard to convince this couple. Just three months ago they were involved in a kidnap plot when their search for Alexander's sarcophagus ended also in a hoax. The sarcophagus never found, waiting perhaps to be discovered as the 'Spear of Destiny' once was."

"I take it you know her," Natalie said looking back at Nguyen who was staring after them, microphone held nonchalantly across her chest away from her mouth, one eyebrow raised back at Natalie.

"Yes."

"How well?"

Dennis too looked back at the television reporter who was smirking at him.

"I used to date her. Hey look it's the Mayor of London and his wife."

Natalie stared after him as he continued down the line of extended cameras and microphones.

Inside the museum waiters dressed as Roman legionaries were moving amongst the milling crowds with trays of champagne and vol-au-vents. Dennis looked up at the impressive, tessellated glass roof of the great court.

"What an amazing building."

Natalie nodded. In the centre of the floor space was an area roped off. Men in dark glasses and suits patrolled nearby. Security for such an important night.

Dennis grabbed a glass of champagne from a passing waiter and a handful of vol-au-vents. The look from Natalie suggested she wasn't impressed. He stuffed one of the small pastries into his mouth.

"Hm! Prawn."

"What are you doing?"

"Soaking up the alcohol a bit."

"I told you not to drink too much on an empty stomach. You know you can't handle it."

"I'm fine. I'll make this my last glass until the speeches are finished."

"Well, they're about to start," Natalie said as the select few press photographers rushed forward as Sir Nigel Phillips, director of the museum, took to the lectern. He adjusted the microphone to his mouth and as everyone turned to face him all conversation stopped. The only sounds now were the whirring and clicking of cameras.

"Mr Mayor, ladies and gentlemen, honoured guests, esteemed members of the press, may I extend to you a very warm welcome from the Great court of the British museum on this the opening night of 'The Spear of Destiny' exhibition."

The blue cloak covering the glass case with the spear inside was pulled down rapidly to reveal the Spear for the first time. There was a burst of flash photography as a generous round of applause erupted from the hundreds of guests.

"Well, there it is," Dennis said craning his neck.

Natalie turned to him as he continued looking over the heads of people in front.

"You mean you've never seen it?"

"No."

"But you've written an article on it."

"The power of the internet babe."

Natalie smiled as she shook her head.

"You are such a cheapskate...." she stopped as they received dirty looks from people nearby.

"And now ladies and gentlemen if I could direct your attention to the large flat screen televisions around us," Phillips said, extending his hand towards one of many large televisions suspended from the ceiling.

"Wow! Dennis said, "Now that is a tv. Must be a fifty-five-inch screen."

The lights were dimmed in the great court as the screen came to life. Clever lighting around the court brought in set the mood with changing colour sequences.

The screen was dark and then the spear of destiny appeared as the narration began. Everyone watched the seven-minute video in silence and as the lights came on the screen went dark.

Another round of applause and then Phillips spoke again.

"Ladies and gentlemen, I, the Vice Director and everyone

involved with the museum would like to thank the Austrian ambassador and his staff and the Austrian government for their generosity in lending us, this, one of the most Holy relics in the world. Mr. Ambassador thank you," Phillips led the round of applause, "And now," Phillips raised his glass of champagne to the crowd, "Enjoy the party."

Phillips shook hands with the Austrian ambassador and began greeting his guests.

"I thought the video was rubbish," Dennis said.

A partygoer nearby turned to him.

"You have a better version?"

"I do."

"And you are?"

"Peter Dennis, journalist, I wrote an article on the lance."

"I see and that makes you an expert."

"I'd like to think I know a bit on the subject."

"So, do I. I'm the actor who narrated the short documentary." Dennis cringed.

"If I've offended you, I'm sorry."

"I'd like to hear your version," the man's wife said.

"So would I," said another.

"Ok. Well...." Dennis began to his new audience," The spear was originally a Roman legionary standard issue spear belonging to a Roman legionary called Gaius Longinus. Longinus worked with his legion in Judaea until his eyesight began to fade, it sounds today like he had cataracts, but of course the Romans would have no way of dealing with this affliction, anyway, sorry I'm going off the point...."

"No, it's very interesting," one listener said, "please continue."

"So, Longinus is almost blind and ends up only able to perform light duties and one day he gets a task which for him would be life changing, he's asked to assist in a crucifixion. Now it's a Friday and the Jewish Sabbath was Saturday so the executions had to be finished by midnight so the Roman tradition was to break the crucified's legs, unable to support the upper body any longer the condemned would suffocate and die within fifteen to twenty minutes. When it came to Christ's turn the blind Longinus told his centurion that the man was already dead. To prove it Longinus or his centurion thrust the spear into Christ's side emitting a flow of blood and water, St John 19;34,

The blood splashed Longinus' eyes and he was cured. '*This truly is the son of God*' he declares and is converted. Shortly after this he leaves the army and travels the province with his spear telling all he meets his story. Arrested for his faith he angers the Governor and has his teeth and tongue ripped out before he is beheaded and the spear disappears from history.

It reappears some time before 286AD and is carried by a black Roman commander called Maurice during the reign of the emperor Maximian. Maurice's entire legion, known as the Theban because they were conscripts from Egypt, of six thousand six hundred men were all Christians. This was extremely rare in ancient Roman history. The army was strongly pagan and remained so until the emperor Constantine. Anyway, the Theban legion led by Maurice, Candidus and Exupernis based in the east was ordered to Gaul, that's France today, to assist with rebels in Burgundy. In Burgundy the legion was joined by the emperor and once the rebel uprising was quelled the emperor ordered the killing of all civilians. Horrified at these instructions the Christian legionaries refused. The emperor was furious and ordered the legion to be decimated, that being every tenth man to be put to the sword, six hundred, as an example. The rest of the legion were not moved by this and soon the Rhone flowed with the blood of the entire legion. This whole event occurred in Aguanum, Switzerland. St Moritz in Switzerland is named after Maurice."

Dennis took a sip of his champagne. As all good story tellers, he gave his audience time to ingest his knowledge. He noticed the actor whose name he didn't know was actually listening with great interest. When he was sure they were ready for him to go on he continued.

"Next the spear passed to the Roman Emperor Constantine who carried the spear into battle against the rival Emperor Maxentius on the Milvian bridge over the Tiber in Rome. Losing the battle Maxentius fled with his army and the bridge collapsed and Maxentius drowned. His body was recovered and decapitated. Constantine became the sole ruler of the West. Founding the city of Constantinople on the older city of Byzantium Constantine kept the 'holy lance' or as it is now known the 'spear of destiny' there.

During the reign of the Emperor Otto III in Constantinople,

sometime around the year 1000AD a Roman nail was added to the spear. In 1084Ad holy Roman Emperor Henry IV added a silver band. In 1350 Charles IV added a gold band over the silver one. In 1424 Sigismund had relics including the lance moved to Nuremburg.

When the French revolutionary army in 1796 approached Nuremburg, the city moved the collection to Vienna, Austria. Many Kings, Popes and Emperors added to it until we end up with what we see today.

The Holy Roman empire was disbanded in 1806 and the treasures remained in the custody of the Hapsburgs.

In 1912 Adolf Hitler saw the spear in the museum in Vienna and from that moment he became obsessed with it. Some say that the only reason he invaded Austria in 1938 was to capture the spear. Hitler kept it in St Catherine's church in Nuremburg for six years believing the ancient legend that whoever owned the spear could not be defeated and held mystical, magical powers. He truly believed that his Nazi forces were now invincible."

Dennis paused again to allow his audience to catch up.

"Then on April 30th, 1945, Hitler and Eva Braun committed suicide as an American Lieutenant Walter William Horn took possession of it. He gave it to American General George S Patton. The rest of the story you all know from the vignette. It was returned by the Americans and today resides back at the Hofburg museum in Vienna, Austria."

Dennis looked at Natalie.

"What do you think?"

"My head's buzzing, trying to take it all in."

"Well, I'm sure some of you have some questions you'd like to ask me about the spear and I'll look forward to answering them but if you'll excuse me for a minute, I need to use to use the bathroom. Too much to drink," Dennis said.

"That was fascinating," the narrator said, "They didn't include half of that knowledge for my part. I must get a copy of that magazine. Are you, his wife?"

"No. Peter and I are a couple. We're not married."

"Oh, I see. He's a journalist isn't he."

"Yes."

"And yourself?"

"I'm an archaeologist."

"Archaeology? That's wonderful," the narrator's wife said, "all adventure and treasure finding. What an exciting life you must lead."

"Yes, it must be a bit Indiana Jones," the actor cut in.

"It couldn't be further from the truth," Natalie replied, "But they are great films aren't they."

Dennis was just drying his hands under the air dryer when his I-phone began ringing in his pocket. He fished it out, frowning at the display. It was his editor, Tom Rogerson.

"Hi Tom, what's up?"

"Pete. Sorry. I know you're at the premiere…."

"That's no problem," Dennis knew the phone call must be urgent.

"Pete, I don't know if you've had a chance to see the news, but Gaddafi's been killed."

"Which one?"

"What do you mean which one?"

"Well, the whole family is called Gaddafi…. Oh! You mean 'the' Gaddafi."

"Yes, I mean 'the' Gaddafi, Muammar."

"What happened?"

"He was caught by rebel forces. There was a NATO air strike on a convoy he was travelling in and he and others with him had to abandon their vehicles and they took refuge in a drain and were caught. I'm a bit sketchy about the incident to be honest Pete so I've sent the Sky news link to your phone. I know it's Friday night but when are you next in the office? Is Nat with you?"

"Yes, she is. I'm in the toilet and as for the office, I did have plans for the weekend. Wouldn't your usual newspaper reporters cover this event?"

"Yes Pete, that wasn't why I was ringing you. I want you to do an article for 'the country' focusing on the impact these events will have on others' lives. Like the one you did after Saddam's fall. You know the sort of thing. Look I'll let you go so you can get back to that gorgeous woman. I just wanted you to know so you can keep up with events in Libya over the next few days. Enjoy your weekend, I'll see you Monday."

The line went dead.

Dennis checked his e-mails, saw the Sky news link, saw that the Sky news report on anytime was fourteen minutes long, put the I-phone back to its screensaver, reached for the door handle, stopped, got his phone out again and quickly found the Sky news link.

"Fourteen minutes," he said as the report began to load, "Natalie is going to kill me."

Outside the museum the VIP's had long since finished arriving and some of the news crews were packing up. Many of the reporters were now sipping coffee and hot chocolate on this chilly, late, October night.

Kim Nguyen was talking to her camera crew, their equipment on the ground in favour of hot drinks when she heard the first parp from the Roman cornicen.

"What the hell is that?" her cameraman put his coffee down and hoisted the camera onto his shoulder when he saw the legionaries that had rounded the corner. Nguyen was frantically thumbing through the multi-page programme looking for Roman re-enactors.

"I don't remember seeing anything about this," she said, "Are you filming?"

"Absolutely," Tom, the cameraman replied.

"Live from the British museum," Nguyen began reporting, "A group of Roman soldiers are advancing towards us and the museum in what appears to be a surprise spectacle put on by the organisers who have managed to keep it quiet from us," the camera flashed back from the legionaries to Nguyen, "I have the schedule here in my hand," she said holding it up for the watching world, "And there is definitely no mention of re-enactors in it. What else will surprise us this evening. Kim Nguyen reporting from the British museum."

Nguyen moved out of the way for the camera as the Roman re-enactors swept past her, about turned at a command from their officer, clearly a centurion, and marched towards the steps followed closely by the media with cameras and reporters giving chase.

As they passed Nguyen she noticed the centurion, who was the

30

only one of them not carrying a shield, had a strange bulge under his tunic. It seemed ridiculous but she imagined it to be a gun. Not a handgun but possibly a small machine gun, a 'what were they called '? She tried to find the words in her head.

"That's it! A sub-machine gun."

She started to call out to her cameraman Tom when she realised the centurion was looking in her direction. She couldn't see his face. They were all wearing shining masks that completely covered their features. She involuntarily shuddered. The masks had a chilling appearance. She shut her mouth and looked at the ground until she felt he'd looked away. Now she studied the legionaries and though they all carried shields she was sure they had similar if not the same strange lumps under their tunics. She grabbed Tom's arm as he was filming, pulling him off balance and forcing the news camera off focus.

"Kim! What are you doing?" he said, knowing they could edit out any bad film.

"Tom. Stop filming. Have you stopped?"

"Yes Kim. What's wrong?"

"Keep your voice down," she said, "I know this sounds ridiculous, but I think these men are armed."

"Yes, they were," he replied, "With swords and spears. Their attention to detail is very good."

"I don't mean that. I mean I think they're carrying guns. Under their tunics."

"Guns?"

"Yes guns," she said, glancing around to make sure no one else was listening. Tom was watching the re-enactors' disappearing backs while searching for an answer.

"Perhaps Um! Perhaps they're police."

She raised an eyebrow at him.

"Since when have the Metropolitan police doubled as actors?"

"Well ok not them then but maybe they're security people who came with the spear. Austrian police or something."

"Possibly. But remember there was no mention of it in the schedule."

"Do you think something's going down? Kim you really do have a wild imagination don't you."

"I guess I spent too long dating Peter Dennis. I know one thing

31

though."

"What's that?"

"We need to try and get inside in case I'm right."

At the museum's entrance the security guards in their black suits with earpieces saw the small band of Romans approaching. The head of security moved into their path and spoke into his headset to his supervisor who was sitting in front of a bank of television monitors.

"Yes, I have them on visual," the supervisor said, "Wait for instructions."

He frantically flipped through his clipboard. There was no mention of a detail of Roman soldiers. He was watching them on the largest screen. They were very close to the entrance of the museum. On the other monitors he could see the guests now turning towards the approaching actors.

"Sir I need a decision," the head of security said into his earpiece.

The supervisor could see Nigel Phillips on one monitor craning his neck for a better view of the approaching legionaries.

"Sir I need your decision."

Now everyone in the great court was watching through the doors.

"Let them in," the supervisor ordered.

The glass doors were opened and the Romans marched in.

"Good show Nigel," the mayor of London congratulated him whilst clapping his hands.

"Thank you, sir. If you'll excuse me…."

Phillips rushed up to the nearest security guard.

"I haven't ordered this! Who let these people in."

"My supervisor sir. They must have clearance!"

"Clearance! Clearance from whom….? Then Phillips saw the Austrian ambassador nodding his way and smiling. Phillips smiled back as the realisation hit him.

"Ambassador Schmidt has organised this as a surprise for us. That's fine! I wish he'd told me but that's fine. I'll thank him after the performance."

Inwardly seething, Phillips put on a smile and joined in the applause as people moved away from the centre to allow the actors access. They marched in through the doors and stopped at a command from the centurion. Then at another command they turned and marched to various positions around the room. The centurion came on alone, people moving further back out of his way.

"Their attention to detail is amazing," someone near Natalie said.

"All except the masks," she replied, "Roman legionaries wouldn't have worn them. They weren't standard issue and were mainly worn by cavalry and usually only for exhibitions for re-enacting famous battles, especially Greek or Trojan."

"Oh!"

A girl moved forward with her mobile phone to video the centurion who deliberately kept his back to her. He paced around the glass pedestal holding the exhibit. Then quick as a flash he hoisted up his tunic and pulled out a semi-automatic machine pistol as did his men. He sprayed the ceiling of the great court as glass rained down. It happened so fast that the armed security guards didn't have time to draw their weapons.

Peter Dennis, still inside the restrooms, still watching the Sky news clip, looked up at the door as he thought he heard gunfire from outside. Then he heard the screaming from the guests and he rushed to the door, opening it a crack.

"Stay where you are! Nobody move!" one of the Romans was saying, "And nobody will get hurt!"

Outside the museum it was pandemonium as the gathered crowds panicked and ran at the sounds of gunfire. One of the security guards near the main doors went for his gun. The Roman nearest him shot him at point blank range with his MP5 machine pistol. At this range the bullets entered the man's chest, exited his back without slowing and smashed the glass doors behind him, to the screams of those inside.

"Now everybody calm down!" the centurion shouted, "There's no need for anyone else to get hurt."

From the crack in the door Peter Dennis tried to see what was happening. He could see Roman uniforms and then he saw Natalie who was looking his way. For a moment their eyes met. The Roman nearest the toilets saw her look and he turned with a puzzled frown as the door closed silently. The legionary next to him nodded and the first man cocked his gun and moved to the door. He pushed it open slowly and entered the toilets. There were

33

taps and basins on one side, stand up urinals against the far wall and four cubicles, each of which had their door closed. The man with the gun looked at the signs on each door. That all showed 'vacant'. He pushed the first door open firmly.

Empty!

The next two were also empty. He pushed open the fourth and Dennis threw himself at the man, knocking the gun out of his hands to slide across the tiled floor, and hammered his fists into the man's face. They both crashed to the floor. The Roman hindered by the thickness of his costume.

Dennis knocked his man aside, turned over, got to his feet and groped for the machine gun. The Roman grabbed Dennis' legs and pulled the journalist back down. Dennis turned over onto his back and kicked the man hard in the face breaking the nose. The Roman legionary scrabbled at Dennis' legs and Dennis managed to kick him away and reach the gun. He threw it up into the air, spinning it, caught it and brought it crashing down against the man's temple knocking him unconscious to the floor. Dennis shouldered the gun, pulled the man who was heavier than he looked into a cubicle and locked the door from the inside, climbed up onto the cistern, over the partition and dropped to the floor. The smears of blood on the floor he could do nothing about. He went back to the main door and opened it a crack, again.

Near the main doors of the museum Nguyen and Tom sneaked inside. Their feet crunching on the broken glass. The Roman nearest them fired warning shots into the ceiling.

"No moving!" he ordered, not realising they'd come in from outside.

They froze at his words and when he turned away from them Nguyen spoke.

"Where's the camera?"

"Silence!" the man turned and brandished his gun at them.

Tom nodded towards the plaza. Nguyen saw the camera laying on its side outside.

"I left it running."

The man with the gun advanced on them angrily. Tom threw his hands up.

"Sorry."

"Keep quiet!"

Then the Roman peered outside. The square in front of the museum was deserted. He could hear the distant sound of sirens drawing closer. The centurion heard them also. He drew back his arm and smashed the glass instantly setting off the alarm on the pedestal. The Austrian ambassador started to go forward and received the barrel of a gun under his chin.

"Now don't be a hero."

The centurion took the spear firmly in his right hand, turned with it, thanked ambassador Schmidt and strode from the museum. He handed the 'Spear of Destiny' to one of his men who shoved it into a holdall and the rest of his men followed backwards out of the museum. The last two fired bursts of machine gun bullets over the heads of everyone and left.

Two police cars screeched onto the plaza, blue lights ablaze and officers jumped out but had to dive for cover behind their open doors as the men dressed as Romans opened fire. One policeman was hit in the face by bullets that splattered through the car window. He slumped to the ground bleeding profusely, his partner frantically calling for backup on the police radio.

Peter Dennis came rushing up to Natalie with the machine gun over his shoulder. A woman near him screamed and he swung round on her, his finger to his lips.

The security guards all had their guns out now and one of them pointed his at Dennis.

"Put your hands up!"

"Relax," Dennis said, "I'm one of the good guys."

The guard lowered his gun.

"Are you all, right?" Dennis asked, cradling Natalie.

"Yes. Yes. I'm fine."

"Have they hurt anyone?"

"They killed a guard and they've taken the spear."

Nguyen and Tom ran up to them.

"Peter, are you playing the hero?" Nguyen said, nodding at the gun he was carrying.

"Kim! What are you doing in here?"

"You know me, Peter. I'll do anything for that blockbuster story."

Three black Range Rovers roared onto the plaza and screeched to a halt. The Roman re-enactors ran to them, still firing at the police. The centurion got into the first one.

Peter Dennis took the machine gun off his shoulder.

"I'll be right back!" he shouted to Natalie.

"Where are you going? It's dangerous!" she shouted back.

Nguyen watched him go.

"Still got it then Peter," she said admiringly.

"Excuse me!" Natalie cut in.

Nguyen enjoyed the look she received from Feltham. Was it jealousy.

"Oh, don't worry love! I'm last year's model."

A Metropolitan police helicopter swept in low over the museum and over the plaza. Its searchlight trained on the black Range Rovers which now sped off as more police cars arrived.

Peter Dennis sprinted out to where the Range Rovers had been. He could see they had no number plates as they reached the corner and split up, going three separate ways.

"Put down your weapon and put your hands on top of your head!"

Dennis heard the order and turned slowly to see a dozen armed police officers trained on him. Dennis held the machine gun up as high as he could, his fingers well away from the trigger and then slowly lowered it to the ground. Dennis went down on his knees and placed his hands on his head with a smirk on his face.

It was going to be a long night.

CHAPTER THREE

Peter Dennis sat quietly at the table in the interview room at South Kensington police station. A mug of hot coffee in front of him. Standing by the door was a uniformed police officer who hadn't moved in fifteen minutes.

Dennis stared at him. The man still not moving, staring stonily ahead. After a few minutes he lowered his gaze and met Dennis' eyes for a few seconds and then resumed his staring at the wall opposite. Dennis rolled his eyes and sighed with boredom. Apart from the policeman, the steaming coffee, the chairs opposite and the tape recorders there was nothing else in the room to focus on. Dennis stared at the policeman again who sighed through his nose and moved his feet slightly which Dennis took as a sign of irritation. Finally and extremely bored, the journalist put his hands behind his head, his elbows pushed out at right angles, and rocked back in his chair until it was on two legs. He stared at the ceiling while blowing out his breath.

There was a click and the door opened. A tall man in a dark suit and a very attractive, short haired, woman, also in a suit entered the room. The man carried a large folder which he placed in the middle of the table.

"And about time too."

"Mr Dennis. Sorry to have kept you waiting. I'm detective Inspector Mark Jones and this is detective Sergeant Rachel Harding of the Metropolitan police."

Dennis smiled at the female, then said.

"You haven't introduced the goon at the door."

Jones, who was in the process of sitting, stopped dead in his tracks.

"Mr Dennis this is no laughing matter and may I remind you that you are under caution."

"Yes. Yes. I had my rights read to me. I have seen the movies. Have I been charged?"

"Not yet. I would like to remind you Mr Dennis that you were arrested at the scene of an armed robbery where a security official was murdered and when arrested by armed officers you did have, in your possession, an illegal firearm...."

"Which wasn't mine," Dennis cut in.

"…. Which is a very serious crime," Jones continued, "However for the moment let us just say that you're helping us with our enquiries."

DS Harding broke the seal on a new audio cassette and placed it into the recorder.

"If you're going to start recording everything I say, then I demand a solicitor. You told me I was helping with enquiries, nothing more. Now if you've dusted that gun, you will find that mine aren't the only prints on it. In fact, come to think of it, if it wasn't for me, you wouldn't even have a suspect."

"Ah Yes," Jones said pulling the folder to himself. He opened it and turned a few pages, "The man you beat up in the toilets…."

"Beat up! He was a bloody terrorist!"

"Terrorist?"

"Armed robber then! Don't tell me he has rights."

"He has the right to prosecute you for grievous bodily harm."

"Now you're taking the piss."

"He is in a hospital bed with a broken nose."

"And you're telling me I can be done for it."

Jones didn't answer. Harding was looking at the coffee.

"What's wrong with this bloody country. I overpowered a gunman who had a semi-automatic machine gun, part of a larger group who held a party of people at gun point, including a foreign diplomat and the Mayor of London, who shot a security guard and left a policeman, one of your own, in a critical condition and I'm the bad guy. Well do you know what? I've had enough of this shit…."

Dennis suddenly slammed his chair back and went for the door shouting.

"Get me a solicitor and my free phone call."

The uniformed officer moved across the door, blocking it. Jones hadn't moved. He kept his eyes on the empty chair in front of him.

"Mr Dennis please return to your seat and sit down."

"Are you going to move?" Dennis said to the officer blocking his way. The man just stared ahead. Dennis thought about assaulting him.

'Surely that will get me taken back to my cell'.

"Mr Dennis. Sit down please."

Suddenly the fight left Dennis. Slowly he returned to his chair opposite the two detectives.

"What's his name anyway?" Dennis asked.

"Who?"

"The piece of shit I knocked unconscious."

"So far, he hasn't spoken. He refuses to answer any of our questions."

"Is he here in the station?"

"No, he is in the hospital receiving treatment for his injuries under police guard."

"Giving him the five-star treatment, I hope. That's the trouble with this country these days. The bloody criminals get more rights than the poor bloody victims. You should let me have five minutes with him. I'll get his name out of him."

There was a knock at the door and both Jones and Harding turned to look at the small re-enforced square window. The door opened as Jones got to it and he talked quietly with the person outside who handed him another folder and a large plastic bag with something heavy in it.

Dennis was staring at Harding who found it difficult to hold his gaze. She had found his behaviour unruly and disruptive, almost childish but at times she had found it difficult not to laugh at his attitude. There was something sexy about him she decided.

"Mr Dennis we really would appreciate you helping us with our enquiries."

"I will if your boss has stopped being a dick."

Harding did allow herself an embarrassed smile.

"He has his way of doing things. I have mine."

"The good cop, bad cop routine eh! Like I said. I've seen the movies."

Harding continued the smile as Jones re-took his seat. He placed the new folder on top of the other one and put the bag on the table.

"Mr Dennis has decided he would like to help us with our enquiries."

"That's provided of course, there's no more talk of me being prosecuted for making a citizen's arrest."

Jones nodded at him.

"I'll see what I can do."

"Not good enough! I want a guarantee."

"Very well. You have my word."

Dennis smiled his best smile.

"How can I help?"

Jones pushed the plastic bag towards Dennis.

"Can you tell me what this is?"

Dennis leaned forward for a closer look.

"I'm no expert but I'd say it's a Heckler and Koch MP5 semi-automatic machine gun."

"The one that was in your hands when you were arrested."

"It's not mine."

"Yours were the only fingerprints found on it."

"That's not possible. The gunmen weren't wearing gloves."

"No. The man in the hospital had a thin layer of latex on his fingertips which was removed by doctors at the hospital."

"Clever."

"How did you learn about firearms?"

"I did a training exercise some years ago with the SAS. I could tell you all about it but then of course I'd have to kill you," Dennis grinned, winking at Harding, "Also from the movies."

"Mr Dennis this is no joking matter. Luckily for you this weapon has not been fired recently."

"Well like I said it's not mine."

"We must assume then that it belonged to the man you knocked out in the lavatories."

"Well of course it belonged to him. I went to the party in a tuxedo. Hardly room to hide that is there?"

"We'll get to the party in a minute. First," Jones said, opening the new folder, extracting three large photographs, rotating them and sliding them over to Dennis, "Do you know anything about these?"

Dennis looked over at the three separate images. Each of a different Range Rover. Each car was black.

"These photographs were caught by the police helicopter. We've analysed CCTV footage, but these are the clearest images we have. Can you tell us anything about these vehicles?"

Dennis looked at each of them again. They were simply plain, black Range Rovers with no distinguishing marks.

"Sorry no. Nothing. They didn't have number plates."

"That's quite all right Mr Dennis. Now to help us with our enquiries detective sergeant Harding will need to record our conversation, merely to record anything that we may miss but might get picked up later. This is, you understand, merely to help us if we were to get a conviction.

Dennis nodded.

"Ok. I understand."

Harding inserted the previously opened blank audio cassette and pressed record.

"Interview beginning at eleven fifteen pm with detective inspector Mark Jones and detective sergeant Rachel Harding both of south Kensington police station of the Metropolitan police. Would you state your name and age please."

"Peter John Dennis. I'm thirty-eight."

"Thank you. Mr Dennis you understand why you're here tonight?"

"I do."

"For the record Mr Dennis was arrested by armed police this evening outside the British museum at around eight forty-five pm in possession of an unlicensed Heckler and Koch MP5 semi-automatic machine pistol. Mr Dennis is this weapon owned by yourself?"

"No."

"Can you tell me where or how you obtained it?"

"I've already told you where I got it."

"Could you tell us again please for the recorder."

"Where do you want me to start?"

"If you could begin with the events of your evening."

Dennis reached for his coffee and took a swig, then putting the mug back, he began. He told them about arriving in the Limo with Natalie, briefly mentioned the conversation with the actor he offended and the phone call about Gaddafi with Tom.

"I was watching the news clip when I heard gunfire from the exhibit. I opened the door slightly and saw men dressed as Roman legionaries with machine guns, similar or identical to the one on the table."

"That will be the Heckler and Koch MP5 currently exhibit 'A'," Jones said for the benefit of the tape recording.

"Yes."

41

"What did you do next Mr Dennis?"

"Well as I said I was with my partner Natalie and I saw her across the room, she saw me, but one of the gunmen came towards the toilets, I think he noticed her looking, and I hid in one of the cubicles. I could hear him opening all the doors one by one and when he opened the one, I was in I sprang at him. I knew I had one chance and surprise was essential. We fought, but thankfully I was able to overpower him. I'm just glad he was wearing that heavy Roman toga which hindered him. I managed to get his gun, the one you've presented to me in that plastic bag, and I ran outside with it as they escaped."

"And what did you intend to do with the gun?"

Dennis shrugged.

"I have no idea."

"Did you intend to use it, to hurt any of them, to kill any of them."

"No, I don't think so."

"You don't think so."

"No."

"But they'd threatened you, threatened your girlfriend," Jones looked down at his paperwork searching for the name, "Natalie. That must have made you angry."

"Angry?"

"Yes. I mean, "Jones continued, "You must have wanted revenge on them. They'd already killed a museum security guard and then came after you after having threatened your partner. You must have been a little angry. I mean who wouldn't."

"Well, I wasn't. I don't know what I intended to do. I wasn't thinking straight. But revenge wasn't part of it."

Jones stared at Dennis for several moments.

"Very well. And you're unable to give us any clues about the vehicles they used. Three black Range Rovers without number plates."

"No. I've already told you there was nothing unusual about them."

"Is there anything else you can think of that may help us in our enquiries?"

Dennis was tempted to mention Nguyen and her cameraman just so the police would bring them in for questioning. He found himself smiling at the thought. She wouldn't thank him for it. He liked Kim and decided against it. The police no doubt took names of everyone and knowing Nguyen she would probably come forward anyway.

Jones and Harding cross questioned him for a further hour when the detective inspector thanked him and formally ended the interview.

"Am I being charged?" Dennis asked.

Jones shuffled his papers into a neat pile.

"No Mr Dennis. You are free to go. DS Harding will take you to the duty sergeant where you can collect your personal items. Thank you for your help. We may need to question you further so please stay in the local area."

"I know. I know. Don't leave the country right," Dennis said, extending his forefinger as if it was an imaginary gun.

"Goodbye for now Mr Dennis."

Harding opened the door for him and he waited for her to accompany him. At the duty sergeant's desk, he signed some forms and collected his personal effects, phone, keys and watch which he put on his wrist, thanked the sergeant and followed Harding to the door with iron bars and waited while the officer with the keys opened it. Dennis walked through the door and turned.

"Cheers Darling," he said to Harding as the door was slammed and locked, then whistling down the corridor he was let out of the police station by another officer and stepped out into the cold night air. Natalie was waiting at the top of the steps for him. A taxi waiting below. He smiled and went straight to her. She threw her arms around him and kissed him hard on the lips and then pulled away. He was about to say "Wow! Did you miss me?" when she slapped him hard across the cheek.

"What was that for?"

"Don't you ever play the hero again!" she replied before turning and heading down the steps towards a grinning taxi driver. Dennis rubbed his very warm cheek and followed silently after her.

CHAPTER FOUR

Peter Dennis threw himself into his chair at his desk. It was Monday morning and the rush hour traffic had been horrendous. The small clock on his desk was showing 09.15. He'd intended to be in at 09.00. It didn't matter though. Dennis worked whatever hours suited him.

He glanced across at his editor's office and saw the door was closed and the office empty. Rogerson was probably also stuck in traffic. Dennis had tried, in the past, to use public transport but found he preferred to be behind the wheel stuck in traffic getting frustrated rather than being stuck on a tube or bus in the same traffic. Rogerson on the other hand had never desired to be squashed in, like a sardine, into a carriage crammed with total strangers. Besides he liked to look out of his top floor window a dozen times a day at his Aston Martin parked in the street below.

Dennis flicked the switch on the bottom of his computer monitor and waited for the screen to come on. It had been three days since the exhibition, the spear being stolen and his arrest. He and Natalie had spent a quiet weekend at his London apartment and ignored all calls. The moment his monitor came on he regretted it. 228 new e-mails and 142 messages in his spam filter. He opened the spam folder and ran his eyes down the list of the first fifty and without opening any of the messages he clicked delete. He cleared the rest and then emptied the trash bin before opening his e-mail folder and running his eyes down the first fifty of them as well. Four he opened and read with interest. There were some from friends and family, jokes no doubt, and he moved them to a different folder to read later. Then bored he quickly scanned the remaining e-mails and finding nothing of interest, he deleted the entire lot.

His mobile began ringing and he turned it over to see that it was Natalie calling.

"Hi babe."

"Sorry to disturb you. I know you've probably just got in but did you leave without having any breakfast?"

"Yes. I'll get something later."

"Well, I was wondering if we could do lunch."

"Lunch?" Dennis said, looking at the mess on his desk.

"If you aren't too busy. It's not a problem if you are."

"I'm a bit snowed under love…. Um…. I'm just trying to think…."

"Well, what if I bring lunch to you in the office. How does that sound?"

"Good idea. Yes. That will be much better for me."

"Ok. How about twelve o'clock. What do you want?"

"Twelve is fine. I'll be here all day. Oh and bring me something with chicken in it. Sandwich, salad, baguette. I don't mind."

"Ok."

"Ok."

"Well, I'll see you later then."

"Yeah. Sorry babe," Dennis said, nearly dropping the phone he was propping to his ear with his left shoulder while trying to remove post it notes from all around his desk, "I'm a bit busy right now."

"Ok. See you soon. Love you."

"Love you too."

Dennis hung up. Usually, he hated doing it first. He reached down to open a drawer and rummaged for a stapler when he was hit by an overwhelming whiff of perfume. He turned his head and saw a pair of red stilettos. His eyes travelled up to black seamed stockings, to a green tartan miniskirt, white blouse and on up to bright red lipstick, beautiful eyes behind thinly framed spectacles and to long, tumbling brunette hair.

Becky!

Becky Smith! Rogerson's recently hired personal assistant and the most beautiful woman in the office, the entire building for that matter. Possibly London.

'Well second most,' Dennis told himself.

"Morning Becky."

Smith came forward and perched herself on the edge of his desk, revealing a glimpse of black suspender.

"Morning Peter."

Dennis closed his eyes and shook his head in quick succession and then looked up at her. Other men in the office were watching her.

"Is there something I can do for you Miss Smith?"

Becky placed a large box file on his desk and pushed it to him.

"This is from Tom. He said it had everything you'd need in it. Well not quite everything you'll ever need," she said, shifting slightly revealing her stocking tops to wolf whistles from across the office.

"Thank you," Dennis said, deliberately avoiding her eyes.

He opened the file and began shuffling through what was in it.

"So did you have a nice weekend," she asked in her husky voice.

"Um. Yes. Yes, thank you," he replied, looking up at her at last.

"How was the exhibition? I wish I'd had someone to go with."

Dennis looked up again from the file.

"It was invite only," he said with his best smile.

There was the sound of someone clearing their throat. Dennis peered past her to look across the office.

"Miss Smith," Rogerson called from his office door. He had just arrived and his hand was on his door handle.

Becky turned and smiled.

"Just coming Mr Rogerson."

She turned back to Dennis as she slid herself off his desk.

"See you later Peter."

He watched her go. She was deliberately wiggling her bottom. Halfway to Rogerson she looked over her shoulder back at Dennis and winked at him. He closed his eyes and shook his head again to clear his thoughts. The fact that she fancied him she had made obvious in the two weeks that she had worked there. She followed Rogerson into his office and turned again to close the door. She grinned at Dennis and he found himself grinning and nodding back. Then she turned to her boss and sat and Dennis couldn't see her anymore. He concentrated on the box file she'd given him. It contained a lot of correspondence on the current revolt in Libya and Dennis suddenly found his heart begin racing at the prospect of his new assignment. He tried to put Becky out of his mind then a thought struck him.

'Shit! Natalie's coming here for lunch. What if she behaves like that in front of her. Nat will kill her. Me too.'

He picked his phone up to ring her to arrange to meet out when Rogerson's door opened again and Becky called him.

"What?"

"Mr Rogerson wants to see you."

Reluctantly Dennis left his desk and headed over.

46

'What now?' he was thinking.

Dennis entered his boss's office. Rogerson was frowning at a newspaper front page.

"Yes sir."

"Sit down Pete."

Smith held the chair for him and leaned over it further than she needed to giving Dennis a view of her backside. He did his best not to notice.

"Thank you, Miss Smith. I'd like coffee please, Peter?"

"Yes, thank you."

She poured the cups while Rogerson continued to read the front page. Then after deliberately making sure her fingers stroked Dennis' hand as she gave him his cup she poured and placed a cup in front of the editor.

"Will there be anything else Mr Rogerson?"

"No thank you. You can leave us."

Dennis watched her go. She closed the door silently and blew Dennis a kiss through the window. He glanced nervously back at Rogerson still reading. His boss hadn't noticed.

Rogerson finished reading the front page of the newspaper he was holding, then turned it around and dropped it in front of Dennis.

"Hell of a party huh?"

It had been three days since the spear exhibition and the story was still dominating the front pages.

"I assume you've been keeping up with events."

"Yes. I've read every newspaper going."

"Good. Then you can squash some of the conspiracy theories. Dixon has been covering the story since it happened. I want you to work with him on this. Is he in the office?"

"I haven't seen him, Tom."

"Well as soon as he gets in, nab him, tell him everything you know. Everything Pete."

"Wouldn't it be better if I did the story?"

"No. Dixon has covered it since it happened. I've got Alex and Suzy in Tripoli covering the Gaddafi thing. Like I said before I want you to do an article on the impact his death will have on the country. I'd get you a plane ticket but the whole bloody country is in uproar. Apart from foreign military there is nothing in or out.

You'll just have to do what you can from here. Set up a satellite link on your laptop with Alex and Suzy. They're in a hotel in Tripoli and should be able to get wi-fi. You should find everything you need in that box file Becky has given you. If you need anything else come to me Pete. Ok?"

"Understood."

"Now tell me what happened with the police."

Dennis told his boss everything that happened as far as he could remember.

"Have you told anyone else?"

"Apart from Natalie. No."

"Good. You can tell Dixon everything you've just told me."

"Ok."

Rogerson studied his journalist for a moment.

"How are you, Pete?"

"How am I?"

"Yes, how are you? It's a simple enough question. You've been through a lot lately. The affair with Von Werner and the sarcophagus, that maniac Russian...."

"Ukrainian."

"What?"

"Danilov was from Chernobyl. Chernobyl is in the Ukraine."

"Well, it was Russia once. Look the thing is you barely got over that and then this happens. I just want to make sure my number one journalist is holding his own."

"I'm fine."

"Good. And how is Natalie?"

"She's great. No, she's terrific. Apart from...." Dennis stopped.

"Apart from what?"

Dennis wished he hadn't mentioned it.

"She met me from the police station and slapped me for 'playing the hero' as she called it."

Rogerson laughed.

"Slapped you!"

"Yeah. She had a bit of a go at me."

"But you're ok now. Both of you."

"Yeah. We're fine. I don't know why I did it."

"Well, she's right. You could have got yourself killed. I guess that's why you're the best storyteller I have. You know, always being part of the action. Getting that first-hand experience."

"Something like that," Dennis replied.

"Well, that's it for now. Let me know if there is anything else you can think of that may be relevant to a story, any story in the last 72 hours."

Dennis got up to leave. At the door he stopped.

"Thanks Tom."

"For what?"

"For caring."

"I might be your boss Pete but I'm also your friend. Grab Dixon as soon as he gets in!" Rogerson shouted as Dennis closed the door.

He made his way slowly back to his desk. There was another yellow post it note stuck to his computer screen. Before he even read it, he saw that it was Becky's handwriting and the message ended in a kiss. An 'x' with a horizontal line either side.

"For fuck's sake," Dennis said quietly, "This is a form of sexual harassment."

He looked across at her. She was talking to another girl, Ruby, a journalist, but every time she agreed with something Ruby said she nodded then glanced his way. It wasn't that he was shy or afraid of beautiful women, he'd had his fair share of them, it was just that this one looked like she could get him into trouble. Trouble with Natalie and that was something he wanted to avoid at all costs. He couldn't imagine life without the beautiful archaeologist now. Their relationship over the months had blossomed into something he'd never had before. He'd been in love before of course, many times. Been hurt many times. Did the hurting. He thought about his girlfriend now and his pulse raced like it always did about her. He glanced at his clock. 10am. She'll be here in a few hours. He noticed Becky finish her conversation with Ruby and start heading his way.

"Oh shit."

Then he saw James Dixon breeze into the office.

"Hey James," Dennis called across the floor.

Dixon placed his briefcase down by his desk and looked up as Dennis reached him.

"Well. Well. Well. If it isn't the man of the moment."

Dennis pulled up a chair as Dixon sat.

"What's up Pete?"

"Rogerson wants us to work together this morning. I've got to tell you all about what happened on Fri…."

Dixon bent his neck around Dennis' shoulder at Becky's disappearing figure as she entered Rogerson's office.

"Was that Becky I just saw in that short skirt."

"Yeah."

"What do you mean yeah! She's the hottest babe that's ever worked here."

"Yeah, I know."

"And you're telling me you wouldn't."

"No, I wouldn't."

"Bullshit!"

"Look mate between you and me she's a bloody nightmare."

"Nightmare?"

"Well, a distraction then. I think she's interested in me. Either that or she's just a tease."

"If she was interested in me, I wouldn't hesitate mate. I'd be in there so quick…. Oh shit she's coming over."

Dennis turned, saw her and grimaced. He kept his back to her.

"Oh, Peter I was coming to tell you that Mr Dixon was here, but I see you've found him."

"Yes. Thank you."

"Morning James," she said walking off while biting the end of her pencil. Dixon just nodded and waited until she was out of earshot.

"Fuck me! Damn. I wish I was you."

"No. You really don't. Look, come on forget about her. Let's get started."

Dennis flipped open Dixon's laptop.

"I need to know what you've done so far."

Dixon tore his eyes away from the brunette and opened his documents on his laptop.

"Okay Pete. This was done Friday night."

The two journalists settled down to read the computer screen.

"Ahem!"

They looked up. Natalie was standing there. A large paper bag in one hand, two cartons of coffee in the other.

"Oh hi!"

"Did you forget."

"What? Oh no! I…. what's the time?" he looked at his watch. It was just after twelve, "No. I'm…. of course not. We were just working hard and I lost track of time. This is James."

"Hi James."

"Hi," Dixon replied, then spun in his swivel chair to get something from behind, "Another one Pete?" he said quietly.

Dennis looked at Natalie who raised her hands slightly.

"Oh yeah. Right."

Dennis got up and put the chair he'd borrowed back. He led Natalie towards his desk.

"What did he mean another one?"

"What? Oh, I've no idea," Dennis replied quickly, avoiding the question.

"You look nice."

"Thank you," Natalie replied.

"Who let you in?"

"A new girl. I don't know her name. Pretty. Brunette."

"Oh her."

"Very short skirt."

"Has she? I didn't notice."

"She seems nice," Natalie said smiling as he pulled up a chair for her.

"I don't really have much to do with her," he replied. Then his eyes grew wide at his waste bin. The most recent post it note was on top of the rubbish. The kiss plainly visible. Dennis nudged the bin in under his desk and out of sight.

"Peter you're acting very strange."

"Am I? Oh no! Just got a lot on at the moment." He gestured at the paper bag. "What did you get me?"

"What you asked for. Chicken salad."

"Thanks babe," he said, unwrapping his baguette. Natalie bit into her sandwich then dabbed at the corners of her mouth.

"Yes, she's very pretty. I'm surprised you've never mentioned her. What does she do here?"

"Her? Not a lot."

"Does she have a name?"

"Um. Becky, I think. Something like that," Dennis replied taking another bite.

"I'll bet all the boys in the office like her."

"Yeah, I expect so."

"Including you."

Dennis ignored her and took another mouthful.

"Peter."

"What?"

"I said, including you."

"Not really."

"Oh, come on. She is gorgeous."

"I suppose she is. I don't have much contact with her," Dennis lied, "She's Rogerson's p.a."

"Great legs," Natalie said, watching Becky strut around the office, "I love those shoes."

"I didn't notice."

"Red stilettos. Four-inch heels."

Dennis peered over the partition of his desk.

"Oh yeah."

"And you're telling me you've never noticed her before."

"Not really."

"You're lying."

Dennis had to stop himself from choking.

"Well, you can look but no touching. They are lovely shoes."

Dennis rolled his eyes and reached into his jeans back pocket, took out his wallet, took out his credit card and handed it to her.

"You know the pin number."

"What's this for?"

"Get yourself some new shoes. My treat."

Natalie's face lit up.

"Thanks darling. I've seen a pair I like in Harrods."

His smile vanished.

"Ouch."

"You'll love them. They're very high heels."

"Yeah and a very high price too I suspect. While you're there why don't you pick some wine for tonight."

"Good idea."

Natalie finished her sandwich and coffee and got up to put her coat on.

"Are you off."

"Yes, I've got a few things to do. Thanks for the shoes."

Dennis showed her out. On the stairs they passed a man in a brown suit who nodded in friendly fashion at them as they passed.

"Gruss Gott!"

Taken by surprise Dennis managed a quick, "Good afternoon."

He and Natalie stopped to look back at the lone figure who rounded the bend in the stairs and disappeared.

"What was that? German?" she asked.

"No, I think it's a more common general greeting in Austria. Though I believe most Germans have adopted it."

"Peter I've got a strange feeling about this."

"I'm sure it's nothing. He wouldn't have gotten past security. I expect he's probably an Austrian journalist reporting on Friday's events."

"I know. You're right. I just.... after what happened to us before.... I would quite happily never hear an accent like that again."

They reached the ground floor where the security desk was.

"Hey George," Dennis called out to the guard behind the desk, "Who was that guy in the brown suit?"

"I don't know man," George replied in his heavy West Indian accent, "I've just come back from my break. Gus checked him in."

"What does it say on the log?"

"Well, it looks like Gus didn't bother to enter a name. Should I go after him."

Dennis thought about it. Gus, the other security guard, had been employed by the publishers for seventeen years and as far as Dennis knew, the man was sound.

"No leave it. He must have been given clearance. I'll ask Gus if I see him."

"Sure, thing man."

Dennis led Natalie outside. They talked for a minute and then he kissed her goodbye. She turned back once and he watched until he couldn't see her anymore. Lost in amongst the other pedestrians. Dennis returned to the office and sat next to Dixon again.

"Sorry James. Where were we?"

Rogerson's door flew open.

"Pete come in here please."

"For fuck's sake. Now what!"

53

As Dennis got closer to his editor's office he saw the man in the brown suit rise out of a chair. The stranger waited until Rogerson closed the door before, he extended his hand.

"Mr Dennis I am inspector Thomas Bauer of the Austrian Criminal Intelligence Service or if you wish Interpol. I am an Austrian police officer based in Vienna where I work and report to the minister of the interior."

Dennis shook the hand.

"How do you do."

"I'll leave you to it," Rogerson said. He closed the door quietly behind him.

"Your boss thought it would be better if we talked in here. I would appreciate it Mr Dennis if you didn't discuss what I'm going to say to you outside of this room. I am, of course, investigating the theft of one of my country's greatest treasures. A theft which has caused much embarrassment to my government."

"Look I already told the police everything I know."

"Yes, you spoke with a chief inspector Jones did you not."

Dennis nodded.

"The Metropolitan police are only interested in the gun crime committed and though they assure me they are investigating the theft of the 'Spear of Destiny' I assure you they are not."

"I don't see what I can do to help."

Bauer reached into his jacket and took out a large manila envelope. He took out a photograph and passed it to Dennis.

"The spear of destiny," Dennis said, studying the picture.

"Not quite."

"What?"

"That photograph was taken yesterday."

"Then you've got it back."

"No Mr Dennis. The one stolen on Friday was a fake."

Dennis raised his eyebrows.

"A fake. Then the real one is safe."

"No not exactly. The real one was stolen a month ago."

"From where? The Schatzkammer."

"Yes Mr Dennis. The schatzkammer."

"How come this is the first anyone has heard of it. News of that nature would have made headlines."

"No. The Austrian government managed to keep it quiet. As I

said it is of great embarrassment. Three security guards died trying to protect the real one."

"So, if the real one was stolen why would someone steal a fake. Be prepared to kill for a fake."

Bauer took another photograph from the envelope and passed it to Dennis.

"Do you know this man?"

Dennis looked straight into the eyes of count Otto Brest von Werner.

"Yes, I know him. He was, that is to say, we were involved in an incident three months ago in which he took my partner and I hostage. He was killed."

"Mr Dennis Von Werner is very much alive."

"Impossible. I saw them pluck his body from the sea."

Another photograph. This one was black and white and grainy. Dennis looked at a hooded figure, terribly disfigured, but there was no mistaking the eyes.

"Von Werner," Dennis said quietly.

"Yes. This photograph was captured by CCTV. He was sitting in the lead range rover outside the British museum. This photograph was obtained when the spear was passed to him through the window. Dennis stared at the photograph open mouthed.

"He was in prison in Tunisia. His private army broke him out on a routine journey from hospital. Several Tunisian military and police were killed. Until Friday his whereabouts was unknown. We suspect he's behind the Vienna spear being stolen."

"How did he, they, get him out of Tunisia?"

"Helicopters took him to Carthage where he escaped on his own yacht."

"And he made it home?"

"Back to his castle in Bavaria. We don't know where he is now. The range rovers were found abandoned at St Katherine docks. The fake spear was left in the boot of one of them."

"There are a couple of things I don't understand. First if Von Werner stole the real spear what did he want with the fake one?"

"Mr Dennis are you aware of the legend of the spear's healing powers?"

"Yes, I wrote an article on it."

"We can assume that Von Werner has attempted to heal himself using the spear's powers and that it didn't work. That is probably why he has stolen the fake one. Upon close inspection he will have realised the London spear was a fake. It is said that the spear only contains healing powers where our saviour Jesus Christ spilled his blood."

"You mean where he was crucified."

"Or anywhere he has spilled his blood or healed the sick. There are many legends in the bible. He travelled for most of his adult life."

"So, it could work anywhere if it works at all."

"That's correct Mr Dennis."

"I need to swot up on the bible."

"You said there were a couple of things you didn't understand. What was the other matter?

"What exactly does all this have to do with me?

CHAPTER FIVE

Peter Dennis rang Natalie's phone again for the umpteenth time. She was just entering his pin number on the chip and pin device when she suddenly realised her phone was vibrating in her handbag. She saw the caller was Dennis.

"Hello," she said, putting the phone between her shoulder and ear to keep her hands free.

"Babe where are you?"

"I'm still shopping in Harrods. I've bought some great shoes and some really nice lingerie I just know you're going to love."

"That's great babe. Listen. Sorry. I know you're excited but something has come up. Something you're not going to believe. How long is Jim in London?"

"He leaves on Saturday."

"Is there somewhere we can meet him? How about his hotel?"

"If he's there. He's giving a talk tonight at a gallery in Chelsea. Why? What's all this about?"

"Look can you get hold of him and arrange to meet him. Tell him he really doesn't want to miss this."

"Why don't you ring him."

"I've tried and besides I'm not sure how safe it is. My phone may have been hacked."

"Hacked!"

"From what I've heard today. Listen I'll explain when I see you. Get Jim. We need to meet somewhere to talk. All of us. A quiet bar somewhere if not his hotel. Okay."

"There's a wine bar not far from me. I'll get Jim to meet us there."

"I know the place. I'll see you as soon as I can get there."

Forty-five minutes later Peter Dennis burst through the front door of the pub. Natalie and Jim Hutchinson were standing at the bar waiting for him. He kissed Natalie briefly on the lips, then shook the American's hand.

"What are you having to drink? It's my shout," Hutchinson said.

"Budweiser please," Dennis answered to the girl behind the bar.

"Make that three," Hutchinson said placing a twenty-pound note on the bar. Dennis waited until the three bottles of beer had been handed out and Hutchinson had received his change before saying.

"Let's sit in that booth at the back. It's a bit quieter."

The men waited for Natalie to sit and as Hutchinson sat, Dennis threw himself into his seat and puffing up his cheeks he blew his breath out.

"You won't believe the day I've just had."

"I guess by the urgency you're about to tell us."

Dennis looked at Natalie long and hard, not sure of where to start. Then he began.

"I now know who was behind Friday night. Who stole the spear."

Hutchinson leaned closer.

"Who?"

Dennis looked straight into Natalie's eyes.

"Von Werner."

"What?" Hutchinson said.

Dennis nodded.

"It's true."

"But we saw Tunisian marines pull his dead body from the sea."

"Well, he clearly wasn't dead."

Dennis saw the concerned look from his girlfriend.

"It's all right. He won't be coming after us. He's got what he wants. He's long gone."

"Are you sure?"

"Trust me."

He reached out to grasp her hand.

"How do you know all this Pete?"

"That man in the brown suit," he said to Natalie, "He's an Austrian police inspector from Interpol. He came into the office," he continued for Hutchinson's benefit, "he had a photograph of Von Werner from CCTV. Von Werner was sitting in the front range rover on Friday night. His face is badly disfigured but there was no mistaking it. It's definitely him."

Natalie felt herself shudder.

"It's all right. He's gone."

"So, my best guess then," from Hutchinson, "is that he's heard of the mystery surrounding the spear of Longinus and that's why he's stolen it. He intends to use it."

"This is where it gets interesting. The spear from London is a fake. A replica."

"What?"

"That's right Jim. The Austrians had the real one locked away in a vault. They use replicas just in case of an incident like this."

"So, Von Werner has a fake."

"Not exactly. The London one was abandoned. The real one he stole a month ago. He killed to get it."

"Then if he has the real one, why did he take the one from the British museum?"

"Inspector Bauer, that's his name, the Austrian inspector, Thomas Bauer. He thinks Von Werner has tried to heal himself with the real one but failed. You see it only works where it is said that Christ himself spilt his own blood."

"So that means where he was crucified right! Which if memory serves me has the church of the holy sepulchre built over it. How is he going to get to the ground underneath it?"

"It doesn't necessarily mean there. Anywhere where Christ bled. It could be where he was whipped by the Romans. We need to read up on our bibles, search the internet etcetera."

"What do you mean we?"

"Bauer has asked for my, our help."

"To do what?"

"To locate where Von Werner will attempt to use the spear next."

Dennis looked across at Natalie.

"You're not saying much."

Natalie didn't know what to say. She half shrugged.

"Peter I'm an archaeologist not a treasure hunter."

"I know Nat, but Bauer believes we might be the best people for the job."

"And last time we came face to face with Von Werner he was going to kill us."

"I don't think he would have."

"He watched while his Russian thug tried to kill you, would have raped me. Von Werner was going to kill us and make it look like it was self-defence. Have you forgotten all this?"

People in the next booth were now looking their way. Dennis leaned into the middle of the table.

"We'd better keep our conversation down a bit."

"What I still don't get, is what's in it for us?" Hutchinson said.

"First, we'd be helping an international police team catch a known felon. A felon we all know and second. We'd be following in the footsteps of Jesus Christ. One of the most famous men who ever lived."

"I meant financially."

"Oh I see. Look we don't know how big this thing is going to be. First there will be a reward of one million euros for the safe return of the real spear and the apprehension of the guilty party or parties responsible."

Dennis saw their looks of concern.

"Bauer has assured me the reward will be there."

"Is he going to provide us with guns?"

"Guns?"

"Last time we encountered Von Werner he had a private army that was considerably armed, or did you assume he's just going to let us waltz in and take it back from him. Look Pete it's a lovely idea but I don't see what we can do to help. I'm certainly not putting any of my team at risk again."

"What are the risks?" Natalie asked.

"Forget it!" Hutchinson said.

"We'll have the full backing from Interpol that anything we do will not result in our being arrested or convicted plus Bauer will assist in any way possible. He already has the Israeli police on full alert in case of anything happening there."

"It's too big," the American said, "it's out of our league Pete."

Dennis sat back in his seat.

"Okay," he took a swig of his beer and put it down on the table gently, "I'm in."

"What?"

"I'm helping them."

"Pete, I think it's too dangerous. Natalie, talk some sense in to him."

"To follow in the footsteps of Jesus Christ babe," Dennis said with a gleam in his eye," just think of the untold treasures we could uncover. The very tomb he lay in. Magical. Mystical. Powers from a Roman spear used by some of the most powerful men and women in history."

"You're crazy."

"No Jim he's right. It would be amazing to hold the very spear that pierced Christ's side in your very own hands."

"Oh, don't tell me you're hooked too."

Natalie smiled at her boss who rolled his eyes.

"Jim?" Dennis said.

Hutchinson picked his beer up and downed it. He banged the bottle back down onto the table.

"Well, it appears you two have made up your minds. A million euro's, eh? I must admit we could do with the money."

Natalie and Dennis were in his studio apartment where they had been since they'd got back that afternoon. It was nearly eleven o'clock and both were very tired and on strong coffee. They were expecting Hutchinson back soon. He had text messaged Natalie to say that his talk had finished and as soon as he could leave, he would. At that time of night, the taxi journey would take less than thirty minutes. His message had been received over an hour before.

Dennis and Natalie had arrived back armed with every book they could buy or borrow from the nearest library with any reference to Jesus Christ in the index. Both having quickly showered they'd settled down to study. Both had a laptop each and had searched every link and pop up possible.

Dennis was flicking through piles of mail and paper on his table in the lounge.

"Darling, have you seen that menu for the Chinese takeaway. I'm sure it was here the other day. You can't mistake it. It's got a large golden dragon on the front."

"I think I pinned it under a fridge magnet on the side of the fridge."

"It's not here."

Natalie came into the kitchen drying her hair with a towel.

"Right, what did I say?"

He stopped searching to look at her.

"I said on the side didn't I."

"Oh yeah. Got it," he said reaching for the wall mounted phone, "What do you fancy?"

"You're not ordering without Jim are you. Do you not want to wait."

"I'm not sure what time they stop delivering."

"Why don't we just order one of those meals for three. At least that way we'll get a mixture. I don't even know if Jim likes Chinese."

"Everyone likes Chinese."

She went into the lounge and sat on the sofa whilst still drying her hair. Then she stopped.

"Oh my God."

He turned with the phone pressed to his ear. She held a book up for him to see.

"You bought a bible."

"Yeah, we'll need it."

"You bought a bible!"

"Yes. If we're researching Jesus Christ it seemed like the perfect answer."

"I suppose," she said, "but you can be the one who reads it."

Dennis ignored her as the phone the other end was answered.

"Chinese will be half an hour," he said re-joining her in the lounge, "Okay so where do we start?"

She grabbed the first book from the pile.

"Anything on Jesus Christ. Why are you looking at me like that?"

"Needle in a haystack."

"We'll need to define our searches. The internet will help."

"Okay. So what should I look for? Seriously."

"Von Werner has been gravely injured. The burns to his face, neck and hands are extensive…."

Natalie remembered back to that day standing on the 'Wavecrest' ship when she saw Von Werner's body brought back on board. She could still remember the blistered flesh. It still made her feel sick.

"If he is intending to use the spear to heal himself, we need to work out what he will do next. The legend of the spear states that whoever holds it will be invincible. I think we should start with the history of whoever has owned the spear. If anyone in history or legend has had any kind of miracle or anything unusual happen to them whilst the holy lance has been in their possession. What do you think? Is that a good place to start?"

"I don't know. I guess so. You're the archaeologist."

Dennis quickly tapped in the holy lance on google. The third link on the first page included images.

"That's our piece," he said. He clicked on the top link which was Wikipedia and began to read.

"Anything?" Natalie asked after seeing his intense concentration.

"No, it's pretty much everything I've already written about it in the magazine. There's a blue link here for St Maurice but it's something I've already read before and something about the town in Switzerland named after him. Nothing new I'm afraid."

"Why don't you try Jesus Christ."

He entered the name in the search box and clicked on the top link. Wikipedia again.

"What am I looking for?"

"Is there anything about his travels?"

Dennis checked the box of headings on the left.

"A little."

"What about his acts?"

"Acts?"

"You know, his miracles."

"Oh."

Dennis re-entered his search.

"Ah! Here we are. The supernatural deeds of Jesus Christ...."

There was a buzz from the kitchen.

"That's either Jim or the takeaway."

"I'll go," Natalie said.

She resumed her seat, empty handed.

"Now the miracles of Christ," Dennis continued as if she hadn't left, "Are put into four categories. We have exorcisms, cures, controlling nature and resurrecting the dead."

"You'll just have to go through them all."

"Here's the list. We have for cures, healing the mother of Peter's wife. Healing the deaf mute of Decapolis. Healing the blind at birth. Healing the paralytic at Bethesda. The blind man of Bethsaida. The blind man Bartimaeus of Jericho. Healing the centurion's servant. Healing an infirm woman. The man with a withered hand. Cleansing a leper. Cleansing ten lepers. Healing a man with dropsy. Healing the bleeding woman. Healing the paralytic at Capernaum. Healing in Gennesaret. Two more blind men. Shall I go on?"

"Yes, I've got one in mind we can go back to. Carry on."

"Okay. Next, we have exorcisms. Probably not what we're looking for, but I'll read them out. A boy possessed by a demon. The Canaanite woman's daughter. The Gerasenes demonic. The synagogue in Capernaum. Exorcising at sunset. The blind and mute man and exorcising a mute."

"Nothing there. What's next?"

"Resurrecting the dead. A young man from Nain. The daughter of Jairus. Raising Lazarus. The others are under nature, controlling nature. The marriage at Cana. Walking on water. Calming the storm. Transfiguration. Feeding the multitude. The draught of fishes. Cursing the fig tree. The coin in the fish's mouth…."

"That's one hell of a list," Hutchinson said joining them, "What is it?"

"The miracles of Christ."

"They're just the ones we know about."

"What?"

"They're just the ones recorded. You know from the gospels. Matthew, Mark, Luke and John. There were other miracles he performed outside of the New Testament."

"Where will I find them?"

"Try the internet. I think he performed the others when he was a child."

"Wait," Natalie said, "Go back."

"Back where?"

"Something about a man with a hand."

Dennis scanned the computer page again. Then he said.

"Under cures. The man with a withered hand."

"Yes, read that one."

"This is recorded by Mark, Luke and Matthew. On a Sabbath Jesus went into the synagogue. The Pharisees of the law watched him to see if he would perform. They were looking for an excuse to have him accused and arrested so they asked him if it was lawful to heal on the Sabbath. Jesus replied 'If any of you has a sheep and it falls into a pit on the Sabbath will you not take hold of it and lift it out. Is a man not more valuable than a sheep. Therefore, it is perfectly lawful to do good on the Sabbath. Jesus then turned to the man and said 'stretch out your hand' The man stretched it out and it was healed."

Natalie looked from Dennis to Hutchinson.

"Not much to go on there is there?" Dennis said.

"These events all occurred before the holy lance comes into the story though," Hutchinson added.

"Well keep searching," Natalie replied, "We'll find a link somewhere."

The kitchen buzzer sounded again.

"That'll be the Chinese," Dennis got up and took fifty pounds from his wallet. He returned with the food and placed it on the table, then went into the kitchen and returned with plates and cutlery. The three of them settled to eating. Occasionally, Dennis would click on his laptop.

"We'll just have to keep searching," Natalie said, "There will be something."

"It must be a cure," from Hutchinson, "The other categories don't really fit in with Von Werner's injuries."

Dennis checked every miracle of Christ that he could find. He shook his head.

"Nothing really gives us a clue."

"What about that journal Von Werner had. Have you still got it?"

Dennis jumped to his feet.

"Yes."

He went to his bookcase and rummaged through a pile of books laying down flat.

"It's here somewhere," he said moving some more. Then he found it, "Ah here it is."

He gave it to Natalie. She opened it and began flicking through the pages. Then a quarter of the way through it she stopped. Hutchinson was watching her.

"Have you found something?"

Natalie's eyes continued to move over the page she was on.

"Nat."

"There may be something here."

The two men joined her on the couch, sitting either side of her.

"Saint Helena," Hutchinson said, "Who was she?"

Dennis reached across the table for his laptop. The page in the journal was hand drawn. There was a large sketch of a shrine.

There was a detailed drawing of a woman under a domed ceiling holding a large wooden cross. Underneath the sketch were the words 'St Helena's shrine, St Peter's Basilica'.

"Is that in Rome?" Hutchinson asked.

Natalie nodded.

"Vatican City."

She turned the page. There were more drawings. Simple sketches, of pieces of rope, what looked to be a tunic, some nails which looked to be Roman, some pieces of wood and the holy lance. Under each drawing were words in German.

"Saint Helena," Dennis said, "also known as the empress Helena was the mother of the Roman emperor Constantine the great. Birthdate not known but thought to be either 246 or 250AD. Died 330AD. Famous for finding the relics from Christ's crucifixion. She found the nails and rope used to fix him to his cross. She also found the cross on which he was crucified. She found a total of three crosses and had a woman from Jerusalem, who was near death, touch each one. When the woman touched the third cross, she was cured."

"Now we're getting somewhere," Hutchinson said, "Do we know where this took place?"

"Yes. She was appointed by Constantine as Augusta Imperatrix, Greek for empress. He gave her unlimited access to the imperial treasury. She went on to build many churches. One on the site of Christ's birth in Bethlehem. Another on the mount of olives in Jerusalem where he ascended into heaven. She ordered a temple- built hundreds of years earlier by the Roman emperor Hadrian to be pulled down. This temple was built over the site of Christ's tomb in Calvary. When her men excavated the ground under the temple, they found the remains of the three crosses said to be those of Christ and the two thieves Dismas and Gestas who were crucified either side of him. Dismas went on to become a saint."

"Pete."

"Oh sorry. Getting a bit side-tracked. Anyway, after the find Constantine had the church of the holy sepulchre built. Right over the spot where Helena found the relics."

"Great," Hutchinson said, "We've got no chance of searching that."

"Now wait a minute. There's more. Helena left Jerusalem for

Rome in 327AD. She took the 'true' pieces of the cross with the nails, rope and the tunic of Christ with her. They are currently on display in the basilica of the holy cross in Jerusalem where they have been since she placed them there."

"And that's in Jerusalem," Hutchinson said.

Dennis shook his head.

"Rome."

"Rome?"

"Rome."

"Great! We've got no chance of getting to that either."

"Guys," Natalie said, "I've got something here. I've just translated this German writing Von Brest made. It's not dated but he believes that the items on this page, the rope, cross, etcetera would all have magical healing powers if used together."

"All of them. But where?"

"That's the next bit of the puzzle," Natalie continued, "Von Brest was convinced that it was the sap from the tree from which the cross was cut that contained the healing powers after it was mixed with Christ's blood. The holy lance of Longinus will have touched Christ's blood mixed with the sap. This is what healed his blindness."

"It all sounds a bit farfetched," Dennis said.

"It's the bible," Natalie replied.

"Okay. Supposing it's true where is this tree?"

Dennis quickly searched google.

"Cut down," he said.

"I knew it," Hutchinson added, "It was too good to be true."

"Herod had the trees cut down and they were used in the building of the temple in Jerusalem. When, years later, the temple was rebuilt the wood was removed. Eventually it was made into Christ's cross."

"I've just translated the last of Von Brest's description," Natalie said, "He believes that St Helena took seeds from these trees and planted them. One tree has survived to today. It stands outside of the monastery of the holy cross in Jerusalem in Rome."

"So, if Von Werner was to obtain all these relics and take them with the spear of destiny to this tree he could heal himself."

"Yes."

"And the relics he needs are in Rome?" Hutchinson asked.

"Yes."

"Then we know his next move."

"Yes."

Dennis reached for his phone.

"I'll alert Bauer."

CHAPTER SIX

ROME, ITALY

Peter Dennis, Natalie, Jim Hutchinson and Inspector Thomas Bauer all cleared customs at the Leonardo Da Vinci airport and walked out into a mild, October, Italian sunshine. A Carabinieri, Italian police minibus was waiting in a bay that displayed a sign saying strictly no parking and a picture of a car being towed. Two uniformed police officers standing guard outside the bus. As the group approached the mini-bus Bauer took out his I.D and the front passenger door opened and a man in plain clothes stepped out to greet them.

"I suspect this is my opposite number in the Vatican police," Bauer said.

"Good morning," the plain clothed man spoke in perfect English, "I am Inspector Cesare De Luca of the Corpo Della Gendarmeria Dello Stato Della Citta del Vaticano or, for your ease, of the Vatican police and of Interpol. We are concerned with security, public order, traffic control, border control, general police duties and criminal investigation."

"Thank you, Inspector. I am Thomas Bauer inspector of the Austrian police and Interpol. This is Mr Hutchinson, director of the Oceanic Archaeology Institute, his assistant and head archaeologist Miss Natalie Feltham and finally journalist Mr Peter Dennis."

They each shook hands with the Italian inspector.

"Welcome to Rome!" De Luca said flashing his strong white teeth. He gestured towards the minibus.

"Do you ever get to guard the Pope?" Hutchinson asked.

"Sometimes," De Luca replied smiling again. He opened the side door of the mini-bus and offered his hand to Natalie to help her inside the vehicle. She took the hand and thanked him, Dennis following closely behind.

De Luca proceeded to the front of the mini-bus and shouted instructions to his two men who got into the front seats, one behind the steering wheel. Dennis leaned close to Natalie who was watching the Italian police inspector through the windscreen.

"You fancy him, don't you?"

"Not really. Though he is very charming."

"Charming?"

"Yes, you know, in that Mediterranean way."

"Smarmy more like."

"What is it about foreign men that winds you up so much?"

"It's foreign barmen that wind me up the most," then he leaned in close to her pushing her against the window.

"Ooh Natalie, you so beautiful. You are my heart. I love you as much as I love me. You cannot live without me. I am your world," he joked in a corny foreign accent. He leaned over even further and pouted his lips to kiss her on the cheek. She put her hand on his face and pushed him away.

"Get off me!" she said irritated.

Hutchinson climbed in and caught the tail end of Dennis' larking about.

"What are you two doing?"

"He's acting the pratt as usual."

Bauer climbed into the minibus and last came De Luca. He pulled the door to behind him and the minibus was started.

"Our journey will take approximately thirty to forty minutes. We are heading straight for Vatican City. We have many things to run through regarding the case and I have set up a command centre at the headquarters of the Vatican police. As there are only 130 officers in the Vatican police, I'm sure you'll appreciate every effort we are making and I have assigned as many officers as I can afford to the case. My opposite number in the Carabinieri is offering as much assistance as is required hence why we are travelling in a Carabinieri minibus. These officers from the national police do not know the nature of our case and will only follow basic instructions so please be careful as to what information you divulge to them. Does everyone understand?"

They all nodded.

"As to locating our targets. All airports and ports are on full alert We know who we're looking for and they are all to be granted access without any fuss. The moment one of the suspects passports is used I will be the first to know."

"Did you say they will be allowed full access? To Rome do you mean?" Hutchinson asked.

"Yes. We aim to catch them. We have routine border patrols set up. It is merely a precaution. The main purpose is to place a stamp in their passports which once acquired means that individuals are subject to Italian law. This should not cause concern for the men we are looking for. It will be merely a hindrance to them, but they won't suspect a thing."

"You do realise that these people are extremely dangerous, don't you?" Dennis said, "They will definitely be armed and are not afraid to use their weapons. They've taken myself and Natalie hostage in the past and have killed security personnel both in London and Vienna."

"Yes, Mr Dennis everything is quite under control. The Vatican is the head of the Episcopal jurisdiction of the Roman catholic church. We take the threat of terrorism extremely seriously. We will catch these individuals responsible for the attacks in London and Vienna and any attacks they have planned for my city."

Thirty minutes later and the minibus screeched to a stop outside the police headquarters in Vatican city. De Luca opened the passenger door and jumped out turning for Natalie's hand. She smiled as she stepped out and Dennis came out next with a frown on his face. Hutchinson stepped out, greatly impressed by the two pike men guarding the entrance to the police station dressed in the traditional uniforms of red, blue and orange.

"Fantastic," he said causing the others to look around.

"What is fantastic Mr Hutchinson?" Bauer asked.

"The Swiss guardsmen."

"Oh, I see."

De Luca gave orders for the two policemen to wait for him then turned to Hutchinson.

"The Swiss guard have been the bodyguards of the Pontiff since the 16th century. These are of course traditional uniforms. You will see men in suits. They are also members of the Swiss guard."

"Their uniforms are magnificent. Where do I sign up," Hutchinson said, joking.

"I'm afraid to join the Swiss guard you must be a single male of Swiss citizenship, have completed basic training with the Swiss military, have a professional degree and be between 19 and 30 years old. Oh, and of course you must also be a Catholic."

Hutchinson let his disappointment show.

"I do have a professional degree and I am a Catholic," he said. Dennis tapped him on the shoulder.

"You're just 40 years too old my friend," he said to the others laughter.

The two guards' men saluted as they walked past.

Inside the main building it resembled more of a police station. Officers in suits were on telephones or computers. One, turned and smiled at Natalie in friendly fashion while he used a photocopier. De Luca took them up a flight of steps and through a door and stopped outside another office.

"This is the commandant of the Swiss guard, Colonel Martin Sonnenburg. You may call him Colonel or commandant. Do not call him by his name."

De Luca knocked on the door and entered the room. The commandant was a tall man in a police uniform with three gold stars on his shoulders. He turned from a bulletin wall he was looking at and fixed a large smile and sprang forward to shake hands with everyone.

"Colonel, may I present Miss Natalie Feltham, Mr Peter Dennis and Mr Jim Hutchinson."

"Welcome. Welcome." he said, "I was the chief of police in my native home city and I am a Captain in the Swiss army. I am the current commandant of the Pontifical Swiss guard appointed personally by his holiness Pope Benedict XVI. Can I get you all coffee?"

Sonnenburg picked up his telephone receiver and spoke quickly into it in Italian. Dennis caught the word 'Caffe' and nothing else. There weren't enough chairs in the office and as Hutchinson was about to ask if they could sit Sonnenburg picked up a blackboard pointer and turned to the board he was previously scrutinising.

"This is all the information we have at this time," he began.

At the top of the board was a photograph of Von Werner, before his injuries. Next to it was a copy of the photograph Bauer had shown Dennis of von Werner's scarred face in the range rover. Next to the photographs was written in black permanent marker his name, date of birth, country of residence, home address. Current whereabouts stated 'unknown'.

"If you know his home address, why hasn't he been arrested?" Hutchinson asked.

"He lives in a castle in Germany. Because he has not committed any crimes in his native country the German polizei will not arrest him without a warrant. This is being dealt with by the European court of justice in Luxembourg. Unfortunately, its rulings can take months and we must follow the procedures," Bauer answered.

"This is why I want these individuals here in Italy," De Luca added, "once here under Italian law I can arrest them."

Dennis was studying the information on Von Werner.

"Von Werner is tall," Dennis said to Sonnenburg.

"Tall?"

"Yes. I've been up close to him, very close. He is about 6ft 3in or 6ft 4in."

Sonnenburg grabbed a permanent marker and wrote the word height.

"What would that be in metres?" he asked.

"Just under two," Dennis said helpfully.

"Is there anything else about him you can think of?"

They all looked blankly at the photographs of the German count.

"If at any time any of you remember anything of relevance do not hesitate to say. Now we don't know much on his associates. He employs a small private army. Mercenaries. Mainly of eastern European origin."

There was a photograph of Sergei Danilov, underneath was written 'deceased'.

"He was on the American FBI's most wanted list. We believe that he is dead."

"He is," Dennis added.

Sonnenburg turned to look at the journalist.

"You know of him?"

"I killed him."

Sonnenburg stared at Dennis long and hard.

"Call it self-defence."

Sonnenburg turned back to look at Bauer.

"Mr Dennis has told me that he knows his way around firearms. Some training with the British army I believe…."

Dennis nodded.

"I have assured Mr Dennis that any measures he takes in assisting us will not lead to any prosecution. I have that from the director of Interpol personally."

Sonnenburg nodded.

"Good to have you with us Mr Dennis."

Dennis wasn't sure if there was a hint of sarcasm.

"These other men," Sonnenburg continued, tapping photographs, are all behind bars. Some of them in North Africa. Some are awaiting extradition to the United States of America."

"Really?" Hutchinson said, "Why is my country getting involved?"

"Four of the men on this board are wanted in connection with atrocities against American forces in Iraq," Bauer interjected, "This is why Von Werner employs them. They are military trained. He can provide them with money and a new identity. A chance they wouldn't get elsewhere."

"Then why aren't the Americans leading this hunt?"

"Believe me Mr Hutchinson they want to. Luckily for us the European court of human rights does not force us to disclose personal data on these individuals. Therefore, as much as the Americans ask the data protection act means that we don't have to tell."

Hutchinson was irked by this.

"You should let the Americans deal with it. Why they'd have had the whole case sewn up by now."

"There is no need to be offended Mr Hutchinson. We are quite capable of dealing with this situation here. As it's been said twice already, once these men pass over our borders, they will be subject to Italian law."

"Why are the Swiss guard and the Vatican involved?" Natalie asked, "I mean why not just Interpol. I thought you only guarded the Pope."

"My dear Miss…."

"Feltham."

"We have been alerted to the potential threat towards one of the holy churches of Rome Miss Feltham. In fact, one of the very holiest churches of Rome. One built on Christ's very blood. An attack on a Roman catholic church is the same as an attack on the holy father himself."

Dennis was studying the photographs of the Roman re-enactors. On its own on the board was a silhouette of a man's head.

"What's this supposed to be?

74

"That is Von Werner's new number one. We have absolutely no idea who he is but he does exist."

"Danilov's replacement no doubt," Dennis said, "Have you considered that he is probably the Centurion who took the spear."

Sonnenburg looked at the grainy, still images of the Centurion taken from the CCTV at the British museum.

"He personally passed the spear to Von Werner in the range rover, didn't he?"

"Yes."

"Do you have the footage of the Roman's arrival?" Natalie asked.

Sonnenburg pressed play on his DVD player. They all watched the large tv screen. The playback was paused and he picked up the remote control.

"This clip is from a news reel," he said pushing play.

Dennis recognised the reporter's face.

"Oh Kim Nguyen," he said as the reporter began speaking.

Natalie punched him on the arm. He smiled at her but all she did was raise her eyebrows at him. He nodded towards the tv as the camera panned around for the approaching legionaries.

"Can you stop it and run it back," Natalie said.

Sonnenburg pressed chapter search and took it back by one. The clip started again. The camera panned around.

"Just as I thought," Natalie said, "Roman legionaries marched by leading off with their left foot. Any re-enactor would have known that. These men are marching on their right feet," Natalie looked at Sonnenburg and then at Bauer. "These men," she pointed at the screen, "Are military trained."

"Great," Hutchinson said, "A private army on the streets of London. What are we up against?"

"Well, there is nothing any of us can do until we know that they're in Italy," Dennis added.

"This is true."

Sonnenburg answered the knock at the door. The coffee arrived. Behind the bearer was another man carrying a leather attaché case bearing the papal seal symbol in gold.

"Help yourselves to coffee," the Swiss guard commander gestured towards the steaming pot. The other man opened the attaché case and then left the room. Sonnenburg took out I-phones, one at a time, and placed them on his desk equidistant apart. There were five in total. Once empty he closed the case and placed it upright on the floor by the side of his desk. He then picked up an I-phone from left to right and began handing them out.

"What's this?" Hutchinson studied the phone he'd been given. Dennis turned his over. On the reverse of the case was also the papal seal in gold.

"Official Vatican phones?" Dennis asked.

"These I-phones," Sonnenburg began, "Are the property of the Swiss guard. I want you to each always keep these with you," he handed the last one to Bauer, "Even take them into the bathroom with you. Do not let them out of your sight. There is only one number entered into these devices and that number is me. I want you to telephone me the moment anything out of the ordinary occurs. No matter how trivial it may seem at the time. Are you all familiar on how to use them? Good. You cannot access anything else on these phones so please continue to use your own if you need to contact each other."

Sonnenburg pressed call on his own mobile phone and the one Natalie was holding began ringing.

"This is the pre-set ringtone...."

He let it ring until he was sure everyone would recognise it.

"Are there any questions? No. Good. If there is a problem and you feel that you are threatened or in danger the emergency number for the police is 112. If you want the Carabinieri, they speak more English than the regular Polizia then it is 113. But this is only for an extreme emergency. I always want you to only liaise with me. Are there any questions?"

Sonnenburg looked from face to face. Nobody moved.

"Very well. Now assuming that none of you are too tired I have arranged for inspector De Luca's men to take you to the church of the holy cross in Jerusalem, The Santa Croce en Gerusalemme, where a tour guide awaits you. He is one of the best guides in Roma so please make good use of his services. He is not cheap. After you have finished De Luca's men will take you to your hotel. You are staying near the Termini train station. It is not the best part of Rome but convenient for you to acquaint yourselves with the city. Once again lady and gentlemen thank you for your help. Enjoy our city."

The minibus was still waiting for them when they got outside. It was the same two police officers. They were both smoking and threw their cigarette butts down and stood on them. De Luca shouted at them in Italian and one of them looking sheepish bent down to pick them up.

"This is the Vatican," De Luca said to Natalie after he saw her obvious look of disgust. She hated smoking and smokers but reminded herself that most men in the Mediterranean smoked cigarettes.

"Where exactly is this church we are going to?" Jim Hutchinson asked climbing into the minibus. De Luca got in last climbing into the third seat in the front. He unfolded a map and taking out his pen he drew a large circle on it and passed it back to Bauer. Bauer passed the map on to Hutchinson.

"Oh, I see. Piazza Santa Croce in Gerusalemme," he said, "Where is Vatican City?"

Dennis leaned over and pointed on the map for him.

"Citta Del Vaticano," Hutchinson said, "So we are here," he placed his forefinger on St Peter's square, "And the church is the other side of Rome. How far is that?"

Dennis looked at the map again.

"It's at least three miles."

Hutchinson traced his finger in a direct line from St Peter's to the holy cross church.

"Ancient Rome is between the two points," he said, "Look the Colosseum is there. What does that mean 'Palatino'? he asked.

"Palatine hill," Dennis said helpfully, "I must say Jim for someone who is an archaeologist you don't know much about ancient Rome."

"My expertise is in Egyptology," Hutchinson replied, not offended. "Inspector," he said to De Luca, "Until we are called to help what is there for us to do?"

"Commander Sonnenburg wants you to see the church with the holy relics. You will be needed if and when any of our suspects enter Italy. Until then you are free to do as you wish."

The Carabinieri minibus pulled up as close as it could to the entrance of the church of the holy cross of Jerusalem in Rome. There were a few tourists milling about on the entrance steps and many turned in alarm at the sudden arrival of the police bus. One man, at the top of the steps holding an umbrella, was watching keenly. He descended the steps quickly as the occupants of the bus climbed out.

Natalie looked around appreciatively at the neat footpaths and shrubs that fronted the church.

"It's very pretty," she said to Dennis who nodded his approval.

"Good afternoon. Good afternoon," the man with the umbrella shook hands vigorously with everyone. He removed his Fedora to reveal a brown, bald head. Dennis also noticed the man had eyes that appeared to bulge out of his face.

"I am Luigi Alberto. Pronounced Al-bare-toe," he said helpfully, "I am to be your guide for this afternoon," he turned and gestured to the baroque styled front of the church, "Welcome to the church of the holy cross."

"Grazi," De Luca said introducing the others to the guide.

"Pleasure. Pleasure. Pleasure," Alberto said with a huge beaming smile.

"He's a colourful character," Natalie said.

"Quite the natty dresser," Dennis replied taking in the three-piece suit, khaki raincoat and despite the warm afternoon sun the silk scarf Alberto was wearing around his neck.

"We are about to go inside the church," the guide started, "The current Cardinal priest in charge of the church is Miloslav Vlk from Bohemia. He has been in charge since 1994. He has very kindly given us permission to access certain areas to the church which are currently off limits to other visitors and tourists. So once inside we need to be very respectful and so please do not, anyone, take photographs. There are a very limited number of leaflets and booklets, one of which is in English, on the church and its history. If anyone would like one after the tour, they do accept a small donation for them."

Hutchinson reached into his back pocket and took his wallet out.

"I'll take one. Does anyone else want one?"

Alberto put his hand on Hutchinson's arm.

"At the end sir. For now, you don't need one. You have something much better. You have me."

This brought a chuckle from the group in front of him.

"The church is one of the seven pilgrim churches of Rome. These are visited by pilgrims in order to gain indulgences. Four of the churches have basilicas. They are St Peter's of course, San Giovanni in Laterano, San Paolo Fuori Le Mura and Santa Maria Maggiore. The other three churches are San Lorenzo Fuori Le Mura, Satuario Della Madonna Del Divino Amore and this one. Satuario Della Madonna Del Divino Amore was added by Pope John Paul II in the year 2000. It replaced the church of San Sebastiano Fuori Le Mura."

"What do you mean by indulgences?" Dennis asked.

"Indulgences are in catholic theology. They are remissions for sins committed. They are granted by the catholic church only after a sinner has confessed and been given absolution."

"Oh, I see. Well, there's hope for me yet."

"I beg your pardon."

"Oh nothing. Sorry. Just an English joke."

Alberto's face split into a huge grin.

"You English are very good at humour. Yes?"

"Very," Dennis replied.

"The church was built surrounding part of the imperial palace of St Helena which she converted to a place of worship around the year 320AD. She was the mother of the Roman emperor Constantine who became the great. In 325AD the church was converted to a basilica and the floor was covered with soil from Jerusalem. This is why the church has the name Holy cross in Jerusalem even though we are standing in Rome. From the outside the church doesn't appear to be old. The bell tower was added in the twelfth century when the church was renovated by pope Lucius II. He also added a nave, a porch and gave the church two aisles. Santa Croce was again renovated in the sixteenth century and its appearance today comes from the Cardinal priest Prospero Lorenzo Lambertini who was the head of the church before becoming pope Benedict XIV. He connected Santa Croce to two others with new roads. The current façade was designed by Domenico Gregorini and Pietro Passalacqua. For 500 years there has been a monastery adjoining the church. Then earlier this year, in May 2011 an internal inspection, an inquiry, discovered that years of.... how do you say? ... problems...."

Some of the group nodded.

"After years of problems both financial irregularities and also behaviour unbefitting of a monk pope Benedict closed the monastery down. Now shall we go in?" he said turning and climbing the steps quickly. He used his umbrella as a walking stick and its metal tip click - clacked as he set off at a fast pace. At the entrance to the church, he stopped for them.

Natalie and Dennis were the first to join him at the top of the steps.

"What behaviour?" Natalie asked.

"Excuse me?"

"What behaviour was unbefitting of a monk?" Dennis asked.

"There were reports of a nun who was pole dancing to entertain the monks."

"No!" Natalie was shocked.

"What was her name?" Dennis asked.

"I'm not going to say. I'm sorry," Alberto answered. He turned his attention to the others ascending the steps. Clearly not wanting to talk about it.

"Oh go on. What was her name?"

"Mr Dennis I am a deeply religious man. This is of immense embarrassment to the church, to the Roman catholic church. I do not wish to discuss it. If you are that interested and I suppose you journalists always like to get your story google the monastery and her name will be there along with the scandal."

Dennis was going to reach into his jeans pocket for his phone but decided to leave it until later.

"No. It's um! It's not that important. I hope I have not offended you."

"Not at all."

The others got to the top of the steps.

"I would ask you to all put your cell phones on silent or turn them off. It will be quiet inside. Despite the importance of the church, it gets very few visitors."

"Has it always received few visitors?"

"No doubt Mr Hutchinson that in history its visitor numbers were many more. Helena had this holy place built for pilgrims who were unable to travel to Jerusalem. It is important to remember that the church did not take the name 'Holy cross' until the Middle Ages. Now if we are all ready."

He turned and stepped inside.

The church was brightly lit and they all stood and marvelled at the nave in front of the altar at the far end of the church.

"The style of building over the altar is eighteenth century baroque. The eight granite columns supporting the roof are the original ones from the fourth century. The flooring and frescoes are twelfth century. Underneath the altar is an urn which contains the relics of the saints Anastasius and Caesarius."

Alberto gave them a minute to absorb the sights and sounds. Priests were going about their business in silence. One was lighting candles. Another was tidying a table containing leaflets and postcards. A few people were seated and praying. There were a few foreign tourists, English speaking, who were talking and giggling. One girl of the group was receiving text messages on her phone while two other girls crowded around her. Alberto frowned at them and was tempted to say something, but it was Hutchinson who went over to them and said.

"Show a little respect."

The girl quickly put her phone away and the three looked at each other and giggled again. Hutchinson re-joined his group.

"Bloody kids."

"If we make our way downstairs to the right of the high altar," Alberto said leading the way. At the bottom of the steps, he stopped once again to let them catch up.

"This is the chapel to St Helena. This and the two rooms off to the side are part of the original palace owned and used by Saint Helena herself. We are two metres below the current building. This Roman statue is of Saint Helena holding the true cross of Christ. This glass covering on the floor is protecting the soil brought from Jerusalem. The papers and envelopes that you can see underneath the glass are prayers from pilgrims. The mosaics on the ceiling were originally done in the fifth century during the reign of the Roman emperor Valentinian II. They were re-done in the fifteenth century. In the second room of the chapel there is a fourth century statue with the inscription to St Helena on it. The room opposite this one is the Gregorian chapel which was built between 1495 and 1520. It is an exact copy, a mirror image of the St Helena chapel."

Alberto led them through to it.

"In the silver frame there are over two hundred relics."

Knowing that they would want time to examine the artefacts Alberto continued.

"I will wait for you upstairs."

It wasn't long before they re-joined him.

"I must say," Hutchinson was very impressed, "You give one hell of a tour."

"We have saved the best for last," Alberto replied, "In a moment I'd like you to all follow me upstairs but before we do this shrine at the bottom of the stairs is for a young girl aged seven called Antonietta Meo, also known as Nennolina."

"What happened to her?" Natalie asked.

"She had bone cancer at the age of six which resulted in her having to be.... I don't know the English," Alberto mimed a cut across the top of his thigh.

"Amputated," Hutchinson said.

"Yes. She wrote letters to Jesus Christ telling him of her suffering. Since her death there has been one miracle which was attributed to her. She was buried in the graveyard and her remains were moved inside in 1999. She is currently on the Vatican's shortlist to become a saint."

"Why this church?" Dennis asked.

"She was baptised here as a baby. This was her church."

"That is such a sad story," Natalie said. She reached out and touched the shrine. Her lips moving in silent prayer for the child.

"I will now show you the chapel of the holy relics."

Alberto led the way upstairs and into a small room. The others filed in silently and spread themselves out. There were two other tourists in this room and they were hastily trying to hide a small Nikon camera, caught in the act of taking photographs. Alberto frowned at them and they quickly left.

"I thought that was kept in Turin," Hutchinson said.

"Oh, it is Mr Hutchinson. This is an exact copy."

"What is it?" Dennis asked, looking at the large piece of stained cloth through the protective glass.

"It is an exact replica of the shroud of Turin."

"What?"

"The shroud of Turin," Hutchinson said, "It is said to be the very linen that Christ's body was wrapped in. Scholars have argued for centuries about its authenticity."

"It looks medieval," Dennis said.

"It is a work of art," Hutchinson defended the piece.

"Art? I think it's disgusting," Dennis said, "and probably a fake. Just my opinion," he said when he saw Alberto's expression.

"But of course," the guide replied.

Alberto led them into the final room. This room was brightly lit, the floor and walls white marble. At the far end were four black marble, square columns supporting a large roof, atop of which was a simple gold cross. Behind this, at the far end of the room was a glass case surrounded by brown marble.

"It's beautiful," Natalie said.

"This is the chapel of the holy relics," Alberto said, leading them up to the glass.

"If you look to the left you can see a fragment of the good thief's cross, the largest in the world. Now to the glass case."

The shelves were filled with a variety of gold and silver ornaments, intricately decorated with adorning crosses.

"On the top shelf is the bone of an index finger said to belong to St Thomas. This reliquary with the cross on top of it contains very small pieces of Christ's crib and pieces of his sepulchre, his tomb and also pieces of the scourging pillar where he was whipped by the Romans."

At these words Hutchinson felt goose pimples rise on his forearms. He rubbed at them.

"My God," was all he said.

"Also, on this shelf you can see two thorns from the crown that was placed on Christ's head. On the next shelf down you can see, once again the reliquary with the cross on top, this contains the three pieces of the true cross once found by St Helena. On the bottom shelf is a nail used in the crucifixion. However, and I must warn you now, that only three nails were used in a crucifixion and around the world there are far more than three nails claimed to be original. It doesn't help of course that some Popes throughout history made copies of these nails and distributed them around Christendom. Finally on the bottom shelf you can see what is known as the Titulus Crucis or title of the cross. This was discovered here in the church in 1492. The same year as

Columbus. This is a piece of wood written in Hebrew, Greek and Latin. Legend has it that this piece was personally written by Pontius Pilate the Roman governor of Judaea at the time of Christ's crucifixion. For many years it has been thought to be a forgery from the medieval period. However new evidence suggests that the inscriptions were written from right to left and not left to right as would be the case with a medieval translator. In the 19th century this relic was further proved by the discovery of a travel journal belonging to the Spanish pilgrim Egeria, a lady who had visited the holy land in the 4th century and recorded that she'd seen this relic in Jerusalem."

"Wow! That is amazing," Hutchinson said, "So much history," he could feel his goosebumps returning.

"Yes history is my passion," Alberto said, "I am in love with history. I am extremely fortunate to have been born in such a city where I tread in the footsteps of some of the most famous people who have ever lived."

"That you are," the American replied.

"And now lady and gentlemen that concludes our tour of the Santa Croce en Gerusalemme in Rome. I will wait for you all outside to give you free time here in the church. On your way down the stairs look for the brick in the wall with the inscription 'Titulus Crucis' which I noticed none of you saw on the way up."

They weren't very long in meeting Alberto outside.

"That was a wonderful tour," Natalie said.

Hutchinson came forward and shook Alberto's hand.

"Truly fantastic," the American said, "If it's not too personal a question may I ask how you are paid."

"I do a lot of work for Citalia holidays. This particular tour was, I believe, paid for by the Vatican."

"Oh, I see. Are you allowed to accept tips?"

Alberto gave his best smile. Jim pressed a twenty euro note into the Italian's hand.

"And did the Vatican tell you why we needed a guided tour?" Bauer asked. It was the first thing he'd said since arriving at the church.

"No. Just that I was to give a private tour."

"Do you also give personal tours?" Hutchinson asked.

"Yes of course. Though my fees are expensive."

"Would you be able to give us a tour tomorrow. Myself, Miss Feltham, Mr Dennis…." Jim waited for their re-action.

"Yeah I wouldn't mind Jim," Dennis answered. Natalie nodded. "Sounds good."

"Inspector Bauer?"

"No thank you. I have reports to make tomorrow."

"Just the three of us then. That's if you can manage tomorrow?"

"What do you want to see?"

"Oh uh! I don't know. Ancient Rome, the Vatican."

"My fees are three hundred euros per day."

"That's only a hundred each," Dennis said quietly and sarcastically.

"Ignore him."

"That is my fee."

"That sounds most satisfactory. I could pay you up front."

Alberto's beaming smile returned.

"Pay me tomorrow. I would be delighted to show you around my beautiful city."

"Thank you so much. Would you like us to come to you?"

Alberto reached into his jacket pocket, took out a map of Rome and placed a cross on it with his pen.

"This is the arch of Titus in ancient Rome. I will be there at 9 o'clock tomorrow morning. I'll look forward to seeing you all then."

Alberto shook hands with them all again and then went to a Fiat 500 and drove away.

"What a thoroughly interesting man," Hutchinson said.

De Luca signalled to his men by the minibus. They jumped into action and soon brought the minibus over.

"Now lady and gentlemen if you are ready, it's time to show you to your hotel."

CHAPTER SEVEN

Carlo Bonomi was good at his job. No not good but excellent. He had been a property agent for four years. He felt that he, at only age twenty-eight, was probably the best in Rome. He certainly worked for the best agency in Rome. The 'Centauro' letting agency.

"That's me," Bonomi said to himself, "Half man half horse."

He had shoulder length black hair which he always gelled back so that it was tight to his scalp. He also liked to dress well, always in Italian designer suits and shirts and he always wore a pair of mirrored sunglasses. He believed himself to resemble Tom Cruise in the movie 'Top Gun'.

He glanced at himself in the rear-view mirror of his metallic red sporty Alfa Romeo Giuletta. He liked what he saw. He had a swarthy complexion, his skin olive and easily tanned. He also had a string of girlfriends, loved partying, champagne and fine food. He was also, when the need arose to impress a young lady, a lover of horses, the arts, fine art, in fact anything that would help him achieve his gains.

He also loved God and wore a large gold crucifix on a chain under his shirt. Carlo, once upon a time, had intended to become a priest and had started training at the age of eighteen. He had soon found however that he loved girls more than his deity and after numerous jobs and narrowly missing Italian national military service which was abolished in 2004 he had settled on his current occupation, real estate.

This morning he was en-route to a potential buyer for an old, abandoned airfield forty-five miles north of Rome. The folder containing the details of the purchase was on the passenger seat next to him. Whoever it was they had left no name. Bonomi just had a date and time to be at the airfield. He was hoping it would be a cash sale. With cash there was always scope for a little, personal, profit.

He turned up the music on the CD player and put his foot down as he left the outskirts of Rome, and his little Alfa began climbing inland.

The roads were not busy. The rush hour traffic long since abated. It was a warm Wednesday morning but as the Alfa got up to the national speed limit, he found himself pushing the buttons for the electric windows to go up against the chill of the wind. Carlo drove everywhere he could, weather permitting, with the top on his car down.

He glanced across at the display panel as the CD he was playing stopped and the panel lit up as the Bluetooth indicated an incoming call. The display showed the caller's name. It was Claudia. A regular girlfriend. He smiled as he heard her voice and he shifted down a gear to take a tight turn.

Forty minutes later and Bonomi was still smiling as he said goodbye to her and pulled up at the small layby at the gates to the abandoned airfield. First inspection told him that he was alone. There was no sign of another vehicle. He glanced at his Gucci watch. He was fifteen minutes early. His favourite track on the CD he had been playing came on and he turned the engine off and the volume up, put his head back against the head rest, closed his eyes and began drumming his fingers on the steering wheel to the beat. The track ended and he opened his eyes and reached for the off button. He looked around. Still no-one. Still ten minutes. He yawned, stretched, then slowly got out of the car.

'May as well open the gate ready' he said to himself.

There was a large heavy chain looped through the tall chain-link gates held together by a large rusty padlock but to his surprise it clicked open easily as soon as the key entered. He closed the padlock and let it dangle from the chain and without clicking it shut he let the chain drop and pushed the gate inward as far as it would go. He did the same with the other gate and then returned to his car, started it and drove inside.

The runway was all grass and surprisingly short considering it hadn't been cut in a generation. There was a small strip of tarmac which led up to the few buildings and he turned and drove towards them. The largest building which was two storeys had at one time been painted white. Now it was a mix of shades including algae green in places and peeling in others. There were some windows from which he could see only one was broken. At the corner of an outbuilding, he could see that a large tree had grown. Infusing itself with the building it had caused large cracks in the masonry.

Bonomi stopped his car and got out. He reached for the folder on the passenger seat and opened it.

"No water. No electricity supply," he read out loud.

He closed the folder and had a quick walk around the outside of all the buildings. Some of the doors were rusted off their hinges. In many cases the wood was rotten. He found a small outside toilet of the old type with the cast iron cistern high on the wall. He pulled the chain, but he already knew there would be no water to flush. The toilet bowl itself was layered in decades of dirt and dust. In a small storage room next door, the branches of the tree had grown through the window and were pressing against the ceiling. To the main building there were steps that led up and Bonomi ascended them slowly. They led to a room with a large double window that looked out over the entire site.

Bonomi looked towards the gates he had opened. He could see that the chain-link fence ran around the entire complex. It was intact apart from one concrete post which had at some point in history snapped and was hanging while pulling the fence either side of it down.

There was no sign of the prospective client yet. He looked at his watch. Five more minutes to go.

Bonomi turned away from the window and surveyed the room. Black, dirty cobwebs littered the ceiling and walls. Their hosts long since dead. On the floor were small pellets scattered about. He was sure they were rat droppings.

There was an old wooden desk by the large window and a very old wooden chair. Both were covered in layers of dust. On the table was a very old radio transmitter with an old-style microphone on a stand placed on top of it. Both were extremely dusty. There were some dusty papers strewn across the desk. Bonomi picked a sheet up and blew dust from it. It was about a change of procedures and was signed and dated July 1981.

"Thirty years ago," Bonomi said out loud.

The airfield had been in use during World War II.

Bonomi put the paper down. Then noticing the radio transmitter was still plugged in to a wall socket he began flicking switches at random. The transmitter was dead. He went over to the light switch and flicked it on. Nothing.

There was no electricity to the building. It had been disconnected years before.

Not wanting to sit on the filthy seat in his suit Bonomi went back to his car to read about the purchase. The site had potential and was worth the three hundred thousand euro asking price for the land alone.

Bonomi sat back in his car and began to read the file again. Then he put it aside and turned the CD player on and turned the volume down low. He closed his eyes and thought of Claudia. A few minutes later the track ended and before the next one started his ears heard the distant drone of an airplane engine. He looked around for it. He couldn't see anything, but it was coming closer. The sun was bright and he put his hand up to shield his eyes. Then he saw it. A small aircraft approaching the airfield. He got out of his car and for effect he put his mirrored sunglasses on again. He smoothed down an already impeccable suit and reached up a foot and rubbed a smear from his shiny shoe.

The plane swooped in low, coming out of the sun. It bumped the grass runway then all wheels were down and the plane slowed and Bonomi could now see that it was a Lear jet. The letter 'D' preceding the numbers told him it was registered in Germany. Up until now that was the only information he had on the prospective client. The Lear jet came to a complete stop.

Bonomi waited and watched for a few moments and was about to move forward when he heard approaching vehicles. He turned to look towards the gates. Three black Hummer H3's had entered the airfield and drove towards him in single file. They pulled up quickly and as Bonomi watched their occupants get out and spread themselves out. Bonomi sprang forward but stopped as the aircraft door opened, and the steps began to descend. He remained where he was. One man from the lead Hummer came towards him. Bonomi grabbed the folder from the Alfa's front passenger seat and moved forward putting on his warmest smile. He extended his hand in a friendly gesture.

The man approaching him had very short dark hair and was wearing dark sunglasses. He and all his men were wearing black combat shirts and trousers. Bonomi had expected men in suits. This was like something out of the movies.

His outstretched hand was ignored as the man facing him held out his hand for the folder. Bonomi handed it over in silence. He suddenly felt nervous and glanced at the Lear jet. The open door and steps seemed like an invitation. Bonomi puffed out his chest and put his hands together in front of his waist. Bonomi glanced nervously over his shoulders at the men searching around. One even had a quick glance in Bonomi's car. They moved away to begin searching the outbuildings. Finally, the cold features of Anatoly Petrov looked up from the file and stared at Bonomi. There was no emotion in the black eyes.

"Nice day," Bonomi said, trying to break the stalemate.

The cold eyes remained fixed on him. Then they moved past the estate agent as one of Petrov's men gave the thumbs up. Petrov nodded. He held the folder up.

"Is this everything?"

"Yes sir. My name is Carlo Bonomi of the Centauro property services. Yes, all the details are there."

Petrov ran his eyes over the contents of the file again. Bonomi studied the man, very afraid of him. Then he caught movement out of the corner of his eye and saw a face at a window on the Learjet before the shutter came down. Bonomi couldn't be sure, but he thought the face was disfigured somehow, possibly scarred.

"Were you followed?" Petrov asked.

"Followed?" Bonomi glanced about nervously. This whole situation was getting weirder by the minute.

"Followed by who?"

Petrov snapped the folder shut.

"No matter."

He beckoned another man forward. One who had been hovering near the lead Hummer. This man was carrying a black briefcase. He popped the locks open and raised the lid. The case was presented to Bonomi at chest height, and he looked down at used Euro notes.

"You'll want to check it," Petrov said.

Bonomi shook his head.

"I'm sure it's all there."

The case was closed, and Bonomi took it. Petrov handed the folder to his aide who took it to the aircraft. The man returned shortly and gave the folder to Petrov. The Russian opened it to show Bonomi the signed document. The estate agent nodded. Petrov snapped the folder shut again and handed it to the Italian.

"I guess that concludes our business." Bonomi said.

"Not quite," Petrov said. He reached down into the side pocket of his combat trousers and produced a large, padded jiffy bag. He tossed it to Bonomi who had to catch it to stop it from hitting him in the chest.

"Open it," the Russian ordered.

Bonomi did as he was told.

"There are two thousand Euro's there," Petrov said, "No questions. No answers. Understood."

The Italian nodded nervously. Petrov merely smirked then beckoned to his men. They moved towards him as the Learjet's engines started. The steps were retracted, and the small jet began to move across the grass. They all watched until it disappeared into the sun. Then Petrov looked at Bonomi once more and got into the lead Hummer, his men following. The Hummer's moved off towards the hangar. Bonomi put the case into his car, started it up and left the airfield as quickly as he could. He didn't even stop to close the gates.

CHAPTER EIGHT

Officer Gianni Balotelli of the Carabinieri glanced at his watch. It would soon be time for his break. He patrolled a section of the A12, a major road in the Lazio region of Italy. Speeding tickets were his thing and there was a particular section of the highway which had a long hill that articulated lorries struggled up. There were solid white lines in the middle of the road, but motorists could see for quite a distance ahead and impatient drivers would often overtake the lorries thus crossing the white lines and that's where Balotelli came in. He enjoyed sitting in his police car at the brow of the hill where there was a large pull off area and catching the offending motorists. On the spot fines were his speciality and he always gave chase. He liked to listen to offender's excuses and would occasionally nod or agree with them while writing out tickets.

This morning had been quiet though. He'd only issued two tickets and so far it had been an uneventful day. The only highlight so far that had caught his attention was witnessing three black Hummers that had passed about an hour before. They had been moving swiftly in a convoy. With their blacked-out windows and German number plates Balotelli had assumed that they were diplomatic vehicles. They certainly looked it.

Balotelli watched more lorries coming up the hill. No-one attempted to overtake and he sighed. The road was clear for a long way and he looked at his watch again. It was 11.45am and he decided to go for his lunch break.

He started his police car and moved into the road, deliberately slowing other road users down until someone stopped for him to pull out. There was an old, abandoned airfield nearby with a small lay-by at the metal gates and he liked to stop there and doze in his car every day.

When he got there, he was surprised to see the gates were open. He was even more surprised when he had to stop suddenly as an Alfa Romeo convertible sped out of the gates narrowly missing him. He looked over his shoulder through the back window of his police car with one hand still on the gear stick. He was very tempted to give chase. The convertible was soon lost from sight. It had happened so quickly Balotelli hadn't even caught a glimpse of the number plate. He turned his attention back to the open gates, put his police car into first gear and moved slowly through them.

Petrov's men had almost finished unloading the Hummer's. The last crate was being carried upstairs by two men and they bumped into the man who was drilling new locks into the door and he cursed them when his drill slipped. Mocking him in return they bumped the heavy crate down. One of them stood up straight and pressed his hands into the small of his back to ease his aching muscles. He glanced out of the window and his eyes widened. He was reaching for his radio as his colleague turned to look outside.

Petrov was outside with a laptop and a small satellite antenna. He had the equipment on a pile of old, rusty, oil drums and he was placing a memory stick into the computer's USB socket when his radio crackled and he heard his name being called. He took his own radio and pressed the talk button.

At this moment the small satellite dish connected to the internet, and he put the radio down to concentrate on the laptop. He stopped to look at the radio when he heard the word 'police.'

Petrov moved away from the oil drums slowly and went to the corner and peered round. He saw the Carabinieri police car come to a slow stop. He watched as the policeman got out and glanced around slowly. Then the man reached back into the car and took out his hat and put it on. The car door was closed slowly and quietly. Petrov shrank back away from the corner. He held his radio to his lips and pressed talk.

"Radio silence," was all he said.

He returned to the laptop. The download on the screen was at 86% and he cursed under his breath and clicked cancel download and closed the laptop. He quickly put it back in its case, folded up the satellite dish and placed both on the ground in amongst the oil drums. He then returned to the corner and unclipped his handgun from its holster in front of his chest.

Balotelli was poking around the outbuildings. He'd noticed some fresh tyre marks on the grass and in some mud and assumed they belonged to the speeding Alfa Romeo he'd seen earlier.

He pushed the door open to the outside toilet and turned his nose up at the filth. Then he decided to use the toilet and he aimed his stream making patterns in the dirt and dust to amuse himself. He shook himself off and pulled the chain. There was no water and he shrugged and pushed the door to when he left. He poked around the other buildings for another minute then looked across at an old building which must have served as a hangar years before.

Balotelli found himself at the foot of a flight of steps and he glanced up them. He thought for a moment about climbing them and decided against it. Whatever that Alfa Romeo was doing here it didn't appear to be much. Probably a drug deal Balotelli decided, and the participants long gone. The policeman hovered around for a few more moments then turned to leave.

Behind the door at the top of the stairs the man who had been replacing the locks stood silently with a Glock pistol in his hand. He watched through a crack in the door as the policeman turned to leave. His radio suddenly screeched at his hip. At the foot of the stairs Balotelli spun around and drew his gun from its holster. He moved up the stairs hugging the wall with his gun raised. At the top the man watching put the Glock in his pocket and picked up his cordless drill.

Halfway up the stairs Balotelli tensed as he saw the door move. He readied himself to rush up the remaining steps and burst through the door when he heard the sound of a drill. Relaxing slightly, he lowered the gun though still holding it in both hands at his waist.

"Policia," he called.

He heard the drill stop and Balotelli pushed the door open to be greeted by a man holding a drill while holding a large screw between his teeth. The man looked genuinely surprised. Balotelli rolled his eyes and holstered his Beretta.

"I nearly shot you!" he said, "I thought you were an intruder. What are you doing here Signori?"

The man with the drill took the screw out of his mouth.

"I'm fixing the lock," he said in English.

"The lock?" Balotelli looked around at the state of the room.

"My boss has just bought this airfield and he wanted the lock repaired. This is the control room."

"Yes. It needs a lot more than just the lock replaced. It's not been used in years. Any of it."

Balotelli watched the man for another minute as the lock was fiddled with.

"Who is your boss?" he asked.

The man stopped what he was doing.

"Pardon?"

"I asked you who your boss was."

The other man looked at him for a moment.

"No one you would know."

"Oh really? Try me."

"He is a successful German businessman. No one famous."

"German!" Balotelli nodded, "I like Germany. I've been there many times."

Now it was the man with the drill who nodded.

Balotelli wandered closer to one of the crates.

"What's in these?"

The man shrugged at the ammunition crates.

"Just equipment."

He glanced towards the door to the other room where his two colleagues were hiding, no doubt with guns drawn. The man with the drill moved his hand closer to his pocket with his gun in it as Balotelli got dangerously close to the other door. Then he relaxed as Balotelli turned and smiled at him.

"Oh I almost forgot. Do you know anything about a speeding Alfa Romeo?"

"No. Sorry!" the man shrugged.

Balotelli smiled again.

"Well good luck! I must go," he said cheerfully, "Ciao."

The man with the drill just nodded. The drill poised. Balotelli put his hand up in a friendly gesture then left. The man with the drill rested his head against the door and blew out his breath in relief. The two that had carried the crate came back into the room.

"That was close," one of them said. He had an MP5 machine gun across his chest. Balotelli suddenly burst back through the door.

"Hey I almost forgot. There's no water in the downstairs...."

His voice trailed off as he saw the gun. Instantly his hand went for his gun as he reached for the radio at his left shoulder. The man with the MP5 was lightning quick and he swung the muzzle of his gun and sent a burst of machine gun bullets into the policeman's chest throwing him backwards. Blood dribbled from Balotelli's mouth as he slid down the wall.

Petrov bounded up the stairs two at a time with his Glock handgun drawn. He peered around the door then put his gun back in its holster when he saw the inert form on the floor. Two of his men were arguing but they both stood to attention when they saw Petrov.

"What happened?"

"He went for his gun sir."

"Did he make a radio call?"

"No."

"Let us hope he didn't radio his whereabouts before he came here. You two! Get rid of the body. You," Petrov said to the man with the drill, "Get rid of that police car."

"Yes Anatoly. What should I do with it?"

"For now put it in the hangar with the Hummers. You've killed a policeman," Petrov said, looking out of the window, "They will come looking for him."

CHAPTER NINE

De Luca entered his office at 8.30am to a telephone ringing on his desk. He picked it up.

"Sir it's Mario," the person on the other end said.

"Ferrara! What are you calling the office number for?" De Luca asked his assistant.

"I've tried your home number and mobile sir, but you weren't answering."

De Luca took his mobile out of his pocket. It was still on silent from the night before.

"My parents-in-law were round for dinner last night, so I put it on silent. Must have forgot to put the sound back on this morning. What's up?"

"We've had a report that an officer has gone missing."

"Gone missing?"

"Yes sir. A Gianni Balotelli. He's with the traffic division."

"What do you mean gone missing?"

"Well sir his wife has telephoned the station to say that he didn't come home last night. He's also failed to report for duty this morning. He hasn't returned his car to the pool either."

"Is he known for not turning up?"

"No sir. First time in eight years."

De Luca thought about the possibilities.

"I expect he's got a mistress somewhere and has overslept."

"Possibly sir. I suggested that to his wife sir and she uh…. Well, she wasn't very happy with that response. I won't tell you exactly what she said to me sir, but I was surprised at the language."

"I see," De Luca said, "Well give him more time. He may show up yet. Twenty-four hours remember before someone is missing."

"That's what I told division sir, but they asked us to look into it."

"Can't they get uniformed officers to investigate it. After all he is one of theirs."

"I did ask sir, but they said they didn't have any leads."

"Well look I don't know that there is much we can do. If we just look into it, will that be enough?"

"I assume so sir."

"Very well," De Luca said, "Get me his home telephone number. I'll speak to the wife. What's her name?"

"Maria."

"I'll speak to Maria. In the meantime, you find out what area he patrols and find out his last reported position. If known. Meet me out front in.... say...." De Luca looked at his watch, "Fifteen minutes."

De Luca put the receiver back and set his telephone to answer phone. A message came through on his mobile. It was Balotelli's home number and he selected options, extracted the numbers and dialled them. The telephone at the other end answered almost immediately.

"Maria?"

"Si."

"Maria. My name is Cesare De Luca. I am a detective inspector with the Vatican police. I understand you wish to report your husband, a policeman of the Carabinieri, missing."

"Yes," she replied. De Luca thought she sounded close to tears.

"Has your husband ever done anything like this before?"

"No, he hasn't. He's a good man. A good husband and father."

"Maria please try to remain calm. Can you tell me when you last saw him."

"Yesterday morning. He left for work at 8 o'clock. He kissed the children goodbye and then me. He always does," she continued whilst choking back the sobs. "I just want him home."

"Yes, I understand Mrs Balotelli. Please try not to get upset. I would like to assure you that we are doing everything we can to locate him. I know this is probably the wrong thing to say to you right now, but we would not treat a person as missing until 24 hours has passed. Not even one of our own."

De Luca heard her sobbing again.

"I truly understand how you feel Maria. I'm sure there is a perfectly logical reason to your husband's whereabouts. Is there any family or friends he may have stayed with overnight?"

"No. I've tried them all. Everyone I can think of. He's never done this before in six years of marriage."

"Is there anything else you can think of to help us Mrs Balotelli."

"I can think of nothing."

"I understand. As I said I'm sure there is a perfectly good reason as to why he didn't come home last night.... Probably a mistress," De Luca was thinking. He decided not to tell her about the missing police car, "I will personally get back to you as soon as there is any news. In the meantime, Maria the number I'm ringing you from is my own mobile number. If you can think of anything else, please don't hesitate to call. Don't worry Maria. We will find him as soon as we can."

She thanked him and he waited until the line went dead. De Luca reached into his trouser pocket and took out his keys. He selected one and opened the drawer in his desk, reached in and took out a 9mm Beretta, checked it and put it in its holster on the belt around his waist.

Thirty minutes since he'd spoken to Ferrara and De Luca left the police station and got into the black Lancia that was waiting for him.

"Have you got details of Balotelli's patrol patterns?"

"Yes sir. Did you speak to the wife?"

De Luca nodded.

"She wasn't much help. Just kept bleating on about how he'd never done this sort of thing before. He's probably been shagging some bit on the side all night. When I catch up with him, I'll have his balls for not returning his car. The taxpayers own that car not him!"

"Yes sir. Did you tell his wife all this?"

De Luca turned his head.

"Of course, I didn't. I told her we were doing everything we could and that there must be a perfectly good reason. But I'll tell you this. If he's used that car for anything other than police work, we won't have to worry about the wife killing him. I'll do it myself."

"Yes sir."

"Now. Where does this Balotelli patrol?"

"I quickly checked with records and he…." Ferrara pulled out a map and pointed to the A12 road, "He issues most of his tickets here. He books motorists for overtaking on the white lines."

De Luca was reading the map.

"I know it well. We'll start there."

De Luca got out of the black Lancia and stretched his legs. Ferrara had stopped the car at the large run off area that was triangular in shape. Armco barriers stopped anything from tumbling off the cliffs. De Luca looked down the road at the approaching traffic. A Porsche sped past a lorry, overtaking on the white lines. The two detectives stared at the driver who slowed down and looked guiltily at them as he drove past.

"I can see why he likes to sit here and catch offenders," De Luca said, "There's another one."

This time it was a speeding BMW. De Luca watched another two cars break the law before turning his back on the traffic. He looked at tyre marks left in the dirt. Some were clearly HGV'S or coaches. No doubt providing tourists with photographic opportunities. Many were car tracks. One of which caught his eye.

"Hey Mario. You've got one of those I-phones haven't you. Get over here with it."

Ferrara offered his phone.

"These have a really good camera on them, don't they?"

"Very good."

"Take some pictures of all these tyre marks. Especially this one." Ferrara began flicking the touch screen on his I-phone until he got the camera symbol.

"Just stills or video?"

"Do both."

"Yes sir. Why am I photographing tyre marks?"

"Why?"

"Yes why?"

De Luca smiled at his apprentice. He had much to teach the young detective.

"The Carabinieri had new vehicles earlier this year, didn't they?" Ferrara nodded while clicking away.

"To my knowledge, apart from the vans the cars were all Alfa Romeo's."

"Yes."

"Then they would have all been supplied with the same brand of tyres if straight from the factory."

"So, if the cars are all new, they would still be on their first set of tyres."

"Correct and one of these tracks may match the tyres on Balotelli's Alfa and if I'm right I think it's this one."

Ferrara took photographs of the tracks in as many angles as he could.

"Get those sent to Ezio in forensics straight away."

"Yes sir," Ferrara began sending the MMS data.

"And tell him I want analysis immediately. The moment he can pinpoint make and brand."

Midway through the messages being sent Ferrara's phone rang in his hand.

"It's Ezio," Ferrara said answering.

The conversation was very brief.

"They've got a location for Balotelli's last known position."

De Luca reached into the Lancia for the map. Ferrara drew his finger on the map until he found the coordinates he was searching for.

"Balotelli's car's tracker last reported from this area here. It's an old, abandoned airfield."

De Luca folded the map.

"I'll drive," he said as Ferrara raced round to the passenger side. De Luca reached out of the driver's side window and placed a single blue light on the roof. Traffic instantly slowed on the busy road to allow him to pull out.

De Luca turned off the blue light and reached out and removed it from the Lancia's roof as they approached the mesh gates to the airfield. The gates were locked as De Luca had expected them to be. He stopped the Lancia on the small, dirt, pull off area and looked around.

"There's nothing here," Ferrara said.

De Luca shook his head.

"It's been derelict and up for sale for years," De Luca noticed the heavy chain and padlock on the gate, "That's new though," he said pointing out of the windscreen. He opened the driver's door and got out of the car slowly. He examined the heavy, brass padlock attached to the chain.

"Definitely new," he said. He looked through the gates, "There are tyre marks on the grass. More than one vehicle and recent."

De Luca bent forward with his knees far apart and cupped his hands between his legs.

"Come on."

"What sir?"

"You're going over the fence. I'll give you a boost."

Ferrara scrabbled over the gate and dropped down onto the soft grass on the other side. De Luca reached into his pocket and withdrew a Leatherman tool and tossed it over the fence. Ferrara caught it.

"You'll find pliers on that. Cut some of those clips and let me in."

Ferrara cut through the clips holding the mesh panels taut. When he had done four, he took handfuls of the mesh and lifted up the fence with all his might. De Luca was now able to scramble under the fence. He stood upright and brushed dirt from his palms.

"Good work," he said patting Ferrara on the back, "Now let's have a look around."

They searched around the buildings. De Luca spotted another tyre track in some mud which appeared to match those Ferrara had already photographed.

"Photograph this," the inspector said, "See if it's a match."

Ferrara took a shot from every angle.

"Send that through to Ezio as well. Tell him to get back to us ASAP and find out who is the agent for this site. I want to know who has been in and out of here recently. Someone bought a new padlock for that gate."

De Luca left Ferrara to make his phone call while he explored the upstairs of the main building. He found the door to the main building heavily fortified. He went back downstairs. His assistant had just finished on the phone.

"The door upstairs has a new lock as well."

"The Centauro letting agency is dealing with this site."

"Do we have their details?"

"Ezio is looking into them as we speak."

"Very well. We may need to pay them a visit. Now let's check out that hangar."

The main hangar was empty. In the corner against the wall was a large dustbin and a brush. De Luca tipped the dustbin up and emptied its contents onto the floor. He bent down and sifted through the rubbish with his pen, then stood up.

"Nothing."

He glanced around the hangar. Then conceded that there were no more clues. They were just crawling back under the fence when De Luca's mobile began ringing in his pocket. He looked at the caller display. It was Sonnenburg.

"Commandant," De Luca said answering the phone.

"Cesare that police car you're looking for has turned up."

De Luca turned to look at Ferrara.

"Where?"

"Here.   At   the   Vatican."

CHAPTER TEN

Natalie, Dennis, Hutchinson and their guide Luigi Alberto all squeezed through the airport style scanners and into St Peter's square to join the hundreds of tourists already there. They had spent the morning exploring ancient Rome and had left, in what was Alberto's opinion, the best for last. Natalie smiled and pointed. They all turned to see the basilica of St Peter's church towering above the square.

"Now that is a sight," Hutchinson said, "I've always wanted to see it."

"Vatican City is an independent state created by the Lateran treaty of 11th Feb 1929 which was signed by Pope Pius XI, the holy see and the Italian government. It covers an area of 108 acres on the hill west of the Tiber River. It is separated from the rest of Rome by high walls on all sides except at the Piazza of St Peter. Over one thousand people live within these walls. The Vatican issues its own coins, postage stamps and has its own postal service. The head of state is his holiness, Pope Benedict XVI. He is the 265th Pope of the Roman catholic church. He has full legislative and judicial powers with freedom under the Lateran treaty to organize his armed forces. He is also free to move or live through Italy as he should so desire. The Pope reigns over one billion Catholics throughout the world and is assisted by the college of Cardinals and synods of bishops, synods being church councils.

The building you are looking at now, St Peter's church, is the largest church in the world. The Vatican palace has been the official residence of the Popes since 1377. The original building was built in AD 319 by the Roman emperor Constantine who built a basilica over the tomb of St Peter himself, the first bishop of Rome. In the fifteenth century the building looked as if it would collapse and in 1452 the reconstruction was begun. The whole project soon ran out of money though and it was abandoned for over 50 years until 1506 when Pope Julius II gave instructions for the entire area of buildings to be demolished and the new St Peter's to be built. Pope Julius II commissioned an architect by the name of Donato Bramante to do the work. Though it wouldn't be until 1626, another 120 years before the work would be completed. Bramante died in 1514 and four other architects would work on the buildings. Namely Baldassare Peruzzi, Antonio Sangallo, Raphael and of course the most famous of them all, Michaelangelo.

A year before Bramante's death, in 1513, Pope Julius II commissioned Raphael to decorate the Vatican apartments and Michaelangelo to paint the Sistine chapel.

In 1527 Rome was sacked by the army of the holy Roman empire led by the Holy Roman Emperor Charles V and the work once again ground to a halt. Over the next twenty years very little was done and then in 1546 Pope Paul II persuaded an elderly Michaelangelo to complete the building. Michaelangelo reverted to the original plan of Bramante's to create a church of Greek style cross plan. Do any of you know what that is?"

Natalie nodded.

"It means that the arms of the church are all the same length."

"That's good Miss Feltham. Have you excavated churches in Greece?"

"No. During the summer months the institute runs diving tours for extra funding from the island of Zakynthos. It's just something I learned somewhere. The sort of thing one picks up."

"What do you dive for?"

"Oh, there are a few ancient shipwrecks off the coast, Roman mainly, though there's virtually nothing of the ships left themselves. There is an amazing display of hundreds of amphorae all standing upright in the sand."

"It sounds very interesting. You must surely love your work as I love mine."

"You have a fascinating job," Hutchinson added, "This tour is fantastic."

"I live in one of the oldest and greatest cities in the world. I knew when I was just a small boy that I would dedicate my life to her. To me, she is the most beautiful city in the world."

"I'd say," Hutchinson concluded.

"Now," Alberto said, bringing them back to his tour, "The best of Michaelangelo's work on St Peter's church would have been the dome itself but it was never completed during his lifetime and his plans were modified after his death by the architect Giacomo Della Porta. Later when we go inside, I will tell you more about the church itself. Now in front of the church is the most beautiful, I think, architecture in the world, St Peter's square. The Piazza Di San Pietro designed by Gianlorenzo Bernini. It was started in 1656 and completed in 1667. Now it's called St Peter's square, but this is in fact wrong. Its shape is not square but elliptical. You can see there are four rows of giant columns', creating two colonnades. Miss Feltham, Mr Dennis, if you would like to stand on either of the stone discs on the ground here and here," he waited until they were in position, "We are lucky that the crowds aren't too big. You'll note that the colonnades now appear to be single rows only."

Alberto paused long enough for Hutchinson to have tried it also.

"That is amazing," the American said.

"The Egyptian obelisk," the Italian guide continued, "Is 25.9 metres in height or 85ft if you don't measure in metric."

"Never did understand metres," Hutchinson said, "Pounds and inches are what I know best."

"The obelisk was brought to Rome from Heliopolis in Egypt in 35AD by the Roman emperor Caligula. It was originally used in the circus and was moved to here in 1586 by Pope Sixtus V. The star at the top of the obelisk is the Chigi star named after Fabio Chigi who became Pope Alexander VII and under whose reign the Piazza was built. During the moving of the obelisk there was almost disaster when the ropes holding it began to break. A warning shout from a Genoese sailor saved the obelisk from falling and the palms used every Palm Sunday thereafter came from his home town of Bordighera. They still do to this day."

"Wow!" Hutchinson said, "So much history."

"Indeed, there is. Now shall we go inside the Vatican Museum?"

De Luca and Ferrara jumped out of the Lancia and ducked straight under the police cordon tape stretched across the street. They each flashed police I.D. at the uniformed Carabinieri officers who, due to the blue flashing light on the roof of the Lancia, would have let them through anyway. The officers stepped out of their way. The street ahead had been evacuated and they approached a larger group of police standing a couple of hundred metres ahead. As they got nearer Sonnenburg turned and strode towards them. He shook hands with them both then almost instantly began leading them towards another line of police tape. They passed under this cordon and now De Luca and Ferrara could see the Carabinieri Alfa Romeo parked amongst other cars at the side of the street.

"Balotelli's car was discovered by a parking ticket officer. She was doing a routine inspection of parked vehicles. That's her over there," Sonnenburg pointed towards a small woman in a police uniform giving a statement to a detective.

"She noticed that the back of the police car seemed to be considerably lower than the front. She called in its registration number unaware it was reported missing."

De Luca nodded.

"And the car's tracker?" he asked.

"Disabled. We are unable to trace its whereabouts even though we know it's parked right there."

"I see. And the reason for the suspension appearing low?"

"That's why we called you," Sonnenburg said, "Although the car is within Vatican City. It belongs to the Carabinieri and it's your jurisdiction. Your call."

They passed the last line of uniformed police and now the street was empty.

"We're keeping the public back for a block in each direction," Sonnenburg said.

"And the Vatican?"

"As normal for the moment. There's no need to cause unnecessary alarm."

"What do you think is in the trunk of Balotelli's car?"

"I'm guessing Balotelli himself."

"That's what I'm fearing."

They got to the police car and De Luca walked around it, slowly, looking for clues. There was clearly something heavy in the boot. De Luca called out twice. There was no answer.

"Do we have a spare set of keys?"

"No. Balotelli has, had, the only set."

"We're going to have to get it open," De Luca said tapping the black paintwork with his forefinger, "Get someone who can open it."

Sonnenburg turned to a group of police nearby.

"Get a crowbar."

Ferrara's phone started ringing. He moved away from the group to answer it. A policeman ran up with a crowbar. Sonnenburg and De Luca moved aside for him.

"Open that," Sonnenburg ordered pointing to the Alfa Romeo's boot.

"Si commandant."

The officer tried gently to enter the crowbar into the gap in the boot. The metal of the bar being too thick for it to enter. De Luca watched with impatience.

"Here let me try."

He snatched the crowbar and began attacking the boot with gusto. He was unconcerned as to the damage he was causing to both the bodywork and paint.

"You know if you were to smash one of the windows, particularly the driver's or front passenger's side you could reach in and pull the switch for the boot," the officer who'd brought the crowbar volunteered.

De Luca stopped what he was doing and looked at the policeman openmouthed.

"What?"

"This model has a switch which opens the boot from the front."

"Well why didn't you say," De Luca replied, irritated.

Sonnenburg turned at the sound of a siren approaching. The police tape was lowered, and an ambulance came slowly up the street. The siren was switched off, but the blue lights remained.

De Luca approached the driver's window of the Alfa, kept close to the car to avoid any flying glass and swung the crowbar with all his might. The first blow bounced off the toughened glass but the second shattered it in a shower of green cubes. De Luca reached into the car and found the small switch he was looking for. He heard the click as the boot opened and he quickly rushed round as Sonnenburg lifted the boot and stepped back. They both looked down at the dead police officer. The body was starting to smell. Early stages of decay and De Luca noted the congealed blood on the black uniform jacket.

Sonnenburg clicked his fingers at the paramedics who both rushed forward with their medi-packs. The first of them instantly reached for a pulse on the neck. Then he tried the wrist. He shook his head at the two policemen and closed his medical kit and stood up.

"Thank you," Sonnenburg said, dismissing the paramedics.

"Well, I guess we now have a murder case on our hands," De Luca said. He turned to look for his assistant just as Ferrara finished the phone call.

"Mario, we need forensics here as soon as possible. We now have a murdered cop on our hands."

"Sir I've just got off the phone to Ezio. Those tyre marks you told me to photograph, they've come back as a match. The one's at the roadside and the abandoned airfield are the same. They are identical to tyres supplied to the Carabinieri Alfa Romeo's. Sir this proves that Balotelli was at that airfield."

"But you and I investigated that airfield. There was nothing there."

"Who would want to murder a policeman at an abandoned airfield and dump his body here?" Sonnenburg asked.

They turned at the sound of approaching footsteps. Bauer had just flashed his I.D. and was now hurrying towards them.

"I've just heard from my office. German police have been monitoring Von Werner's bank accounts and guess what? You'll never believe this. Von Werner has purchased an old, abandoned airfield just North of Rome."

De Luca met Sonnenburg's gaze.

"I think we just found our suspect."

"I should say," Bauer continued, "And that's not all. Interpol have upgraded the notice on Von Werner to red."

De Luca was confused.

"What does that mean?"

"It means," Sonnenburg answered, "That they've issued an international arrest warrant for him. Red is the highest notice that they can issue to all member forces. It also includes the power to extradite persons or individuals to the warrant issuing authority."

"So, this means that the German's want him."

"As well as the Americans and Austrians," Sonnenburg added.

"Actually, you're both wrong. It is Tunisia who have requested his extradition."

"Not a chance," De Luca shook his head, "If he's killed or is responsible for the death of one of my officers then I want him."

"Yes," Sonnenburg agreed, "If he's still in Italy."

"And if he is. I intend to catch him."

Dennis, Natalie, Hutchinson and Alberto, their guide, all stepped back out into the late afternoon sunshine. They thanked their guide for a wonderful tour which had culminated in the viewing of the Sistine chapel.

Despite signs everywhere telling visitors to switch off mobile phones Dennis had kept the one Sonnenburg had given him on. It now began to ring incessantly.

"Excuse me," he said reaching into his jeans pocket for it.

Hutchinson was busy passing a large tip to Alberto. Natalie took her eyes off the transaction to look at her boyfriend. He cupped his hand over the mouthpiece to speak to her.

"It's Bauer."

He turned his attention back to the phone call. He couldn't hear over the large crowds of visitors, and he apologised and asked the Austrian to speak up. He tried putting a finger in his other ear to drown out surrounding noise but it was still no use.

"I'm sorry Thomas, I still can't hear you."

He heard the voice reply but still didn't catch any of it."

"Hold on Thomas. I will try to get somewhere quieter. Just bear with me…."

Dennis moved through the crowd looking for a vantage point. Then he saw a large gap in the crowd and he pushed his way to it.

"Right Thomas. I might be able to hear you now. Sorry, what were you saying."

"Peter, I need the three of you outside St Peter's now. I'm at the square of Pope Pius XII in a black Lancia. Meet me there…."

Some tourists waving Brazilian flags suddenly appeared next to Dennis. They were shouting excitedly whilst having their photographs taken against the backdrop of the papal palace. Dennis couldn't hear what Bauer was saying again and he looked at them with irritation. Then his eyes grew wide as he caught the single word.

"Bomb!"

CHAPTER ELEVEN

Natalie and Dennis ran out of St Peter's square and onto the via Della Conciliazone Road. The black Lancia was parked just in front of the square of Pope Pius XII. Bauer had the driver's door open and was standing and leaning on it. In his hand was a police radio. Beyond the Lancia Natalie and Dennis could see a Carabinieri minibus blocking the road and a dozen uniformed officers setting up a cordon with police tape. Visitors to the square were being moved back away from the Vatican.

Natalie and Dennis rushed up to Bauer who looked past them to Hutchinson who, at fifty-eight, couldn't keep up with his companions. He slowed down to a fast walk.

"Just a second!" he shouted between great gulps of air.

"What's going on?" Dennis asked when they were still a dozen paces away. Concerned looking Romans and tourists were gathering in crowds to watch at the cordon tape.

"We've had an officer murdered and his body dumped in the boot of his police car which was then parked on the via Di Porta Angelica Road just a couple of blocks from here. We now know that his last known position was here. An old, abandoned World War II airfield 45 miles north of Rome called Tarquinia. An airfield which has been purchased by Count Otto Brest von Werner…."

"Von Werner is here?" Dennis blurted out.

"We don't know that for sure, but we've had an officer gunned down. Presumably taken by surprise because he didn't radio in that he was in trouble. No known associates of Von Werner's or Von Werner himself have entered Italy with their passports but there was a private flight that used the airfield sometime between eleven and eleven thirty this morning. We are waiting for details of that flight and its origin."

"You said something on the phone to me about a bomb," Dennis said.

"When the crime scene investigators attempted to move Balotelli's body to look for clues, they discovered the boot of the car is packed with explosives. We are now waiting for an army bomb disposal unit to arrive. As you can see," Bauer gestured at the uniformed police, "We are sealing off an area four blocks square."

The uniformed officers now walked towards them and spaced themselves around Bauer and the Lancia.

"What do you want us to do?" Dennis asked.

"Miss Feltham, Mr Hutchinson, this is detective Mario Ferrara…."

Ferrara nodded at them.

"…. I would like you to both go back into St Peter's square with him and these officers and mingle in the crowds. If you recognise anyone or see anything suspicious these officers will make arrests. Can you do this for me?"

They both nodded.

"Isn't that a little dangerous for them?" Dennis asked, "I mean they've already killed one policeman."

Bauer turned as the sound of a helicopter got nearer. It swooped in low over rooftops, flew directly over them and hovered over the Vatican.

"Sonnenburg is putting snipers on rooftops," Bauer said, "And as we can see we now have support from the air."

Dennis looked at Natalie.

'Will you be all right?' he mouthed silently.

She smiled and nodded.

"Aren't you evacuating St Peter's?" Hutchinson asked, having only just got his breath back.

"Not as yet," Bauer replied, "The car bomb is a few blocks away and as you can see the Vatican is protected by high walls. The papal office has been alerted and his holiness' speech for this afternoon has been postponed. We are still not sure if this is a diversionary tactic or a direct attack on Vatican City itself. We may, of course, have been wrong about the intended target."

"And what do you want me to do?" Dennis asked.

"Mr Dennis, I need you to come with me to the church of Santa Croce," Bauer looked at his watch, "It is almost three thirty now. The church closes at four. You and I will watch it this evening. If they're planning an attack, it will come tonight. Now everyone," Bauer continued, "You all know what to do."

He got into the driver's seat of the Lancia and slammed the door. Dennis held Natalie's face in his hands.

"Are you alright?"

She nodded and smiled.

"If you think that you're in any danger you get out of there," he said, "Just get out. You promise me that."

She nodded again.

"I will."

"Don't worry Pete. She's safe with me," Hutchinson added.

Dennis kissed her on the mouth.

"I love you," he said.

She repeated it and watched as he got into the Lancia and Bauer put the car into reverse, spun the steering wheel rapidly and with tyres squealing the Lancia sped off down the now closed one way street the wrong way.

Natalie and Ferrara moved through the crowds in St Peter's square. The hustle and bustle of the day's tourists had begun to thin and unwind as the afternoon stretched on and the light began to fail. Late arriving tourists and those that stayed settled into tones of hushed conversation or even silence. Many formed groups that lit candles in vigil and prayer. Here and there were single people all doing their own personal thing. One tourist seeing Natalie and Ferrara, who in his suit, the man mistook for a bodyguard and the four uniformed policemen took her photograph, clearly thinking she was a celebrity. Ferrara stopped to give the man a severe talking to.

"He thought you were the prime minister's daughter or wife or something," Ferrara apologised to her, "I told him he was lucky I didn't confiscate his camera."

Natalie wasn't bothered by the incident. She had other things on her mind. She was concerned about Dennis.

"Do you think they'll be all right?" she asked the detective.

"Who?"

"Bauer and Peter."

"Yes of course. From what I can make of it Bauer is a very experienced police officer. We have Carabinieri swarming all over the church. I'm sure they'll be fine. Remember it's just a precaution. We don't know what their true intentions are. For all we know we may have got it wrong."

Ferrara looked up at the light coming from the windows of the papal offices.

'Blessed father please watch over his holiness,' he said in silent prayer.

"I don't know what I'm supposed to be looking for," Natalie said, "I can't imagine Von Werner's mercenaries will be out here wandering around armed to the teeth."

"We just need to have our presence felt. I want any would be suspects to see uniforms at every turn."

The last rays of October sun had now left the square and were now a dark yellow on St Peter's church.

"It's getting dark," Natalie said, "What time is it?"

Ferrara brought his wrist up to check his watch.

"It is almost a quarter to seven."

"What time does the square usually close?"

"From April until September the opening times are until seven o'clock. From October until March six o'clock. We are not closing this evening because of the bomb. The last thing Commandant Sonnenburg wants is thousands of people leaving the square and taking routes that will take them close to Balotelli's police car. We do not need a panic on our hands."

"So how long will it stay open to visitors?"

"All night if we have to."

Ferrara looked at faces around him.

"Everyone seems content at the extended opening. "Let us hope it stays that way."

No more than a hundred metres from them a man glanced impatiently at his watch again. It was now six forty-five. He glanced around. The crowds should have been leaving at six o'clock. Filing through Pope Pius XII's square the crowds would continue down the via Della Conciliazone or they would take the roads to the left or right. The bomb would cause absolute chaos and mass hysteria, distraction for the police.

Twice uniformed officers had passed by very close. One group had a very attractive blonde with them. Each time he'd averted them. He held an Apple I-pad in his hands, the code for the car bomb already programmed in. He had only to hit the enter button now.

He was still wearing his dark sunglasses. Suddenly a tourist stepping back to take a photograph bumped into him. The girl apologised and the man with the I-pad replied in Russian. The American tourist didn't understand a word of what was said and she shrank away at the cruelty in the voice. A large, heavily muscled, heavily tattooed American man rounded on the Russian.

"Hey, she said she was sorry."

The Russian stared back through his sunglasses as the American glared on. The Russian had already decided that his training gave him the tools to cut the American down in a dozen different ways. He didn't move though, unwilling to draw attention to himself from the police. Finally, the Americans, realising there wouldn't be an argument forthcoming moved further away. Now the Russian had a clear line of sight to the attractive blonde. That she was with a policeman, no doubt a detective, was obvious. Then the detective was holding a finger to his ear and was talking quickly into his collar. Now the blonde was looking straight at him.

Natalie stared straight at the dark sunglasses. A chill went through her. She frantically tugged Ferrara's arm, the one up to his ear. He stopped talking into his collar to look at her open mouthed.

"Him," Natalie said, not taking her eyes off the man with the I-pad.

Ferrara spun round and met the cold stare. He undid his jacket and reached for his gun. The man with the I-pad turned and began to walk away.

"Stop!" Ferrara shouted.

He took his Beretta out and held it up into the air.

The man in the sunglasses was charging through people barging them out of the way. The four uniformed officers began to give chase, but Ferrara stopped them. He fired a warning shot into the air causing people to scream and panic.

"Everybody down on the ground now!" Ferrara shouted, firing another warning shot into the air. People dived for the ground; many covered their heads with their hands. The man with the I-pad still in his hand turned on the run and pulling a handgun out of his pocket he fired at Ferrara. The bullets whizzed past the detective as he returned fire hitting the man twice in the chest. The gun man cried out as the impact of the bullets sent him sprawling. He looked over his shoulder, his eyes wide with pain and terror as he crawled towards the I-pad. Ferrara advanced on him quickly, the gun held in both hands never wavering from the target. Ferrara realising the man's intent shouted.

"STOP!"

Too late.

The Russian reached the I-pad which had skittered out of reach and brought his hand down onto the touch screen as Ferrara shot him dead. A last groan escaped from his lips as he collapsed to the ground.

Ferrara, Natalie and the uniformed police all spun around as a huge explosion rocked the very walls of the Vatican and a large ball of fire rose into the darkening sky.

Sonnenburg and De Luca watched the scene from behind a jersey barricade which had been put in place four hundred yards from Balotelli's police car.

Thirty minutes earlier a black army car along with the bomb disposal truck had arrived. An elegant officer had jumped out of the car and had introduced himself to the two senior police officers as Colonel Antonio Farina, an army bomb disposal expert who had done two tours of Afghanistan and three in Iraq with the United Nations. He had instantly taken control of the situation and launched a rubber wheeled robot to investigate the car.

Sonnenburg and De Luca had been invited into the back of the bomb disposal truck which was also the incident unit and had watched on a bank of computer screens as the robot had set to work. Six rubber wheels and two mechanical arms had approached the Alfa Romeo. The two policemen had watched with keen interest as the robot had investigated the boot. The live video images streaming to the computers had shown the dead body being moved to examine the incendiary device. The robot had then moved around to the front of the door and peered inside the window De Luca had smashed.

Farina had noticed wires taped to the console which housed both the parking brake and the gear stick and then disappeared beneath the accelerator pedal. The robot had cleverly reached inside and pulled the door handle, reversed back and opened the door to Sonnenburg and De Luca's total amazement. Next the robot had beamed back images of the car's interior.

Finally, Farina had moved away from the bank of computers to address the two policemen.

"It's a simple device which is activated by someone depressing the accelerator pedal," Farina explained, "This is why the bomb didn't explode when you broke the window and opened the door."

"Can you defuse it?"

"Absolutely. This will be a fairly routine disarmament. Has anyone taken responsibility for it yet? Any demands made?"

"Not as of yet. Would it make a difference if anyone had?"

Farina got up and approached one of the heavy blast suits as aides rushed to help him.

"It would of course help to know who we're dealing with. Certain groups prefer certain methods. With no-one coming forward to claim responsibility this could be just a political statement, someone who is angry with or at the Vatican or it could be a diversionary tactic."

"What do you mean a diversionary tactic?" Sonnenburg asked.

"It could be to divert the police's attention away from another target, possibly a political one. There is a football match tonight isn't there? Between Roma and Lazio."

"There is," De Luca replied, "But we don't think that is the target."

"Then it must be just someone making a name for themselves."

De Luca looked at Sonnenburg who read the other's mind and nodded.

"It seems a bit ridiculous, but we believe there is someone, possibly a group, in Rome who is or are intending to steal relics from the church of the holy cross of Jerusalem."

"A terrorist group?"

"No. A previously unknown group not linked to any organisations. We haven't got all the details yet and what we do have is sketchy. We're not even sure of their intentions as yet," De Luca said, not sure as to how much information he should divulge to the army officer.

"Well, I'll say one thing," Farina said as layers of Kevlar were folded over each other in front of his throat, "They've gone to a lot of effort just for a few relics."

Now Sonnenburg and De Luca watched as Farina and his Lieutenant both suited up, left the truck and began a slow, heavy

117

walk towards the police car. They passed the robot going in the other direction.

"Why is the other one carrying pipes and a jerry can?" Sonnenburg asked.

"They'll attempt to drain the fuel tank," De Luca answered.

"The fuel tank?"

"Yes. The petrol in the car's fuel tank will create a worse situation if the bomb does blow causing fire to spread."

"Well, they'd better hope there's no more than twenty-five litres because that's all that can will hold."

Farina and his lieutenant Gianni Sforza reached the Alfa Romeo. Farina went straight to the open driver's door and awkwardly, because of the heavy bomb suit, knelt to examine the accelerator pedal. He flicked on a small but very intense light on his helmet to see into the dark footwell. The red and green wires were attached to a small box on the underside of the pedal, reached up to the bulkhead and disappeared under the vehicle's carpeting, reappeared by the parking brake, ran under the driver's seat through the back seats and disappeared again into the boot.

Sforza pushed the fuel filler flap inwards, and it popped open. A modern filler flap that didn't have a lock. He fed a dipstick into the neck of the fuel tank and pushed down gently until he felt it touch the bottom of the fuel tank. Then he withdrew it quickly and was relieved to see that the fuel tank was only a quarter full.

They hadn't filled it to cause the maximum explosion or fire.

Farina joined him at the back of the Alfa Romeo.

"A quarter full," Sforza shouted.

Farina heard the muted message.

"Let's get this body out," he said back, moving into position to take hold of Balotelli's legs.

Restricted by their equipment they struggled to lift the body out. They settled it onto the pavement. Now Farina could see the boot of the Alfa Romeo was lined with C4 plastic explosives.

"What in the name of God," he said out loud.

He got Sforza's attention and pointed into the boot of the car. Farina clicked on the microphone in his blast suit and reported back to the incident unit. The monitor operator listened carefully then turned to Sonnenburg and De Luca.

"The boot of the car is rigged with C4 plastic explosives. You can't buy this stuff. It's for military use mainly and is impossible to get, even on the black market, especially in the EU."

"What is C4 exactly?" Sonnenburg asked.

"C4 is a composition of explosives, odorizing taggant, Dimethyl Dinitrobutane, plasticizer and plastic binder…."

The man speaking could see that he'd already lost the two policemen. He had intended to include that the explosive was Cyclotrimethylene Trinitramine which is approximately ninety percent of the C4 mass. The plastic binder is Polyisobutylene, and the plasticizer is Diethylexyl. Instead, he said.

"You take these three items and mix with a small amount of non-detergent engine motor oil and you dissolve all these in a solvent, such as a thinner for example. The solvent then needs to be evaporated, filtered and dried and then you're left with a white substance like clay. The type of clay a potter or modeller would use."

"And then it's a deadly explosive?" Sonnenburg asked.

"Oh no. It's very stable and can take a lot of shock. Which is why it didn't go off on its journey in the car to its current location. You can drop it, throw it into a fire. You could even empty your 9mm into it and it won't go off. It needs a detonator, extreme shockwaves or heat. The advantages of it are that it can be moulded into any shape. Ideal for inserting it into gaps or cracks for whatever you want to blow up, bridges, buildings, etc. Mostly it is in the form or shape of bricks. Colonel Farina just has the job of removing the detonators. He will start by disabling the device on the accelerator pedal."

"Well, he'd better get a move on," De Luca said noting that the shadows had got long.

The explosives man didn't answer. He was listening into his headset. He turned to the two policemen.

"The C4 is Russian."

The two policemen looked at each other.

"Russian Mafia?" Sonnenburg said.

De Luca shrugged.

The explosives man spoke into his headset. Then he turned.

"The wires connected to the accelerator pedal are dummies. The bomb is set for remote detonation."

De Luca's radio suddenly burst into life. Ferrara was shouting into his.

"Sir it's going to blow!"

De Luca turned to shout up the road as the Alfa Romeo exploded. The detonation sent the car fifteen feet into the air, blowing the fuel tank, sending burning petrol into a rain that fell onto the road as the car crashed back down onto its roof destroyed. In moments the Alfa was a burned-out shell.

Farina and Sforza were thrown over a hundred metres like rag dolls and they crashed heavily. Farina's bomb suit was on fire. Police and firefighters began rushing towards the scene. De Luca ran to Farina first. The inside of his helmet mask was completely red. Nothing could be seen within. Firefighters called out to him but there was no response. Gently they removed the helmet. Farina was dead. His entire face soaked in his own blood. Sforza's helmet had been ripped off by the blast. His neck had snapped, and the back of his head was caved in.

De Luca pressed the talk button on his radio.

"Bauer! Come in Bauer!"

CHAPTER TWELVE

The black Lancia sped through Rome's crowded streets. Dennis was calling out what he saw on the satellite navigation's screen. The voice was naturally in Italian and neither he nor Bauer spoke it. Dennis had tried to change the language to English but couldn't work it out. Instead, he shouted instructions to Bauer as quickly as he could.

They blasted over the Ponte Victor Emmanuel, the bridge dedicated to the first king of a united Italy and raced down the Victor Emmanuel Road. The traffic they encountered was heavy and the blue light and siren bought them some time. On and on they sped through red lights. Dennis found a map in the glove compartment.

"Ah this will help," he said reaching up for the lights in the roof of the Lancia, "Can you cope with a light on?"

"Yes."

The traffic was thick and Bauer commented on it as he wove the Lancia in and out of motorists trying to avoid him.

"It might be better if we get off these main roads and onto quieter ones," Dennis said looking from left to right down side streets, "What do you think?"

Bauer didn't know Rome. It was the first time he'd been. The main streets seemed to be the better option, but the traffic was getting heavier.

"There seems to be a lot of heavy traffic heading into Rome. I wonder if that's usual for a Wednesday evening?"

"I don't know," Dennis replied. Then a thought struck him.

"There's a champion's league football match on tonight. Between Lazio and Roma. It's a local derby. I saw it advertised this morning on television. It's being played at the Olympic stadium which is home ground for both teams. It's on the other side of Rome from the church. That'll explain why there is so much traffic heading in from the south and east. The game doesn't start for a while, but I guess like most cities the traffic starts early."

"I think we should take the side streets," Bauer said weaving in and out of slower moving vehicles.

"It's your call," Dennis said.

Bauer could see the traffic ahead was slowing. The road a mass of brake lights.

"Well, you have the map."

"Okay. Okay. Let me just think. We are somewhere here. I can't see any of the names of the side roads…."

Dennis kept glancing at the sat nav looking for road names to appear on the little five-inch screen. Then he spotted one to the left.

"Via De Gesu. That means we are here. On the via Dellia Plebiscito. These roads here," Dennis said talking more to himself, "Are no good and some will double back on us."

Bauer raced down this road frantically sounding the Lancia's horn as he dodged in and out of traffic. A bus pulled out of a bus stop in front of him and he sounded the horn cursing. The bus driver saw the blue light and stopped.

"Turn right here," Dennis ordered.

Bauer swung the steering wheel and with a squeal of tyres the Lancia changed direction and careered off down the via Dei Fori Imperiali.

"Hey there's Trajan's column," Dennis shouted excitedly. Then he looked ahead. "Oh, shit there's the Colosseum!"

Bauer looked ahead at the massive building dominating the Roman skyline.

"So what?"

"The colosseum is one big roundabout."

"Then get us off."

"There's nowhere to go. These roads to the right double back on us. This is ancient Rome. Over there is the Palatine hill."

"What's to the left?"

"There's one more road and then nothing until we get to the Colosseum."

"Where does it lead?"

"Hang on," Dennis said turning the map this way and that.

"Too late," Bauer said turning at speed down the road to the left. Dennis fought the g-forces to hold onto the map.

"Which way?" Bauer asked.

"I don't know. Hang on."

Bauer looked across at the map as Dennis turned it and held it closer to his face to read it. Bauer spent a second too long looking at the map. Movement ahead caught his attention. A refuse lorry had pulled out into the street they were now on regardless of the other traffic it forced to stop. Bauer was a hundred metres from it and gaining fast. He sounded the horn as he caught up to the tail end of the jam. The driver of the refuse truck heard the horn being sounded and ignored it. He looked into his mirror and saw the blue flashing light and heard the siren. He shrugged and continued to watch in his mirror for a bit longer. Other road users were doing their best to move out of the way. Bauer nosed through stationary vehicles until he was close to the refuse lorry. The truck driver leaned out of his window and shouted his innocence at the situation. Bauer pulled the parking brake on and threw the driver's door open and flashed his police I.D. The refuse lorry driver continued to protest his innocence and begrudgingly moved out of the Lancia's way. Dennis was listening to the police radio as Bauer squeezed through the gap now provided by the lorry. He pointed his finger at the driver who was still unconcerned. Dennis now pointed at the radio.

"That was De Luca," he said, "They've lost contact with the unit stationed at Santa Croce."

"Are we still heading the same way?"

"Yes. Take the next right. Follow ahead," Dennis said as parked cars whipped by in a blur, "Take the next right...."

Bauer was encouraged by the time they were now gaining. The streets Dennis was taking them down were much quieter. Then suddenly Bauer had to slam the brakes on as a large group of football fans in red shirts, Roma followers, were crossing the road for the metro station. By the look of them they had been drinking and the last few raised red and yellow scarves and chanted a football song at Bauer as he raced away.

"Football is a passion in Italy," Dennis said helpfully.

"The next person who gets in my way will get run down. You would think that a siren and flashing blue light would be enough."

"This is Rome. Everything here happens at a fast pace."

"I suppose."

A carabinieri police car with flashing blue lights and siren sounding went racing past in the other direction.

"Get on the radio," Bauer said, "See if they're sending back up."

Dennis got through to Sonnenburg.

"As soon as we can," was the reply.

Dennis went back to the map. To their right were the Terme de Traiano, the baths of Trajan. Next Dennis saw a large sign for the national museum of oriental art.

"Turn right here!" he shouted as Bauer spun the wheel.

They were now on the Via Merulana.

"Follow this road, straight, for about one kilometre."

The traffic was heavy on this road, but Bauer was able to weave in and out without much difficulty. Three public buses in convoy stopped for him as they fast approached the end of the road.

"Left at the end!" Dennis shouted.

They raced past the Lateran palace. Once the home of the popes until their residence was moved to Avignon in France in the fourteenth century.

Now the Lancia was on the Viale Carlo Felice Road.

"The church is at the end of this road," Dennis said, "It's just over a quarter of a mile."

Bauer turned off the siren and reached out and plucked the flashing blue light off the roof and switched that off also. He looked into the rear-view mirror. The sky behind was still bright but ahead it was getting dark. Bauer slowed the Lancia to a more appropriate speed as they completed the last few hundred metres. He brought the Lancia onto the piazza in front of the church and pulled up under a tree. A carabinieri Alfa Romeo was parked ahead also under the trees. Dennis and Bauer got out of the Lancia and headed towards them.

"Stay behind me," Bauer said unclipping his gun holster on his belt and resting his hand on his gun.

Dennis could see the officers moving about inside the car. One of them suddenly glanced in the door mirror and saw the Austrian and the journalist approaching. Both doors on the police car opened and two uniformed officers stepped out.

"Can we help you?"

Bauer released his grip on his gun and showed them his I.D.

"They've been trying to radio you from the Vatican," he said, "they said they'd lost contact with you. Do you have a problem with your radios?"

The two officers looked guiltily at each other. Dennis peered into the police car. There was a small portable television on the seat.

On the nine-inch screen were three men in suits in front of an empty stadium talking. Dennis reached in and took the television out and showed it to Bauer.

"Tonight's game?" Dennis asked.

Bauer frowned at them.

"We turned the car radio down to hear the commentary," one of the officers said.

"And your lapel radios?"

"Switched off," the other officer replied.

"What are your names?"

"Officer's Bossano and Angelo sir. Will you be reporting this matter?"

"Probably."

For the first time since arriving Bauer now looked at the church. He noted the large double doors were closed.

"Is the church closed?" he asked the carabinieri officers.

"Yes inspector," Bossano replied.

"When was this?"

"Possibly half an hour ago Inspector."

"You saw it close. The doors were open before then?"

"Oh yes. Like I said it was about thirty minutes ago."

Bossano looked at his colleague for approval. Angelo nodded.

"The priests closed the doors when, presumably, the last visitors left."

Bauer looked at his watch. It was just after seven o'clock.

"What time does it usually close?"

"Usually at seven thirty."

Bauer showed him his watch.

"Yes, sir but sometimes the church does and has closed suddenly and without warning before. All churches in Rome have been known to do this."

Bauer was concentrating on the church still.

"And you definitely saw the priests close the doors?"

"Yes sir."

Bauer continued watching the church for another minute.

"Well, it does appear to be quiet."

"Yes Inspector."

"Have you noticed anything else unusual?"

"No."

"How long has that Hummer been parked there?" Dennis asked.

"I beg your pardon signori."

They all turned to look in the direction Dennis was pointing.

"At the far end of the church near the wall there is a black Hummer. How long has it been there?"

"I don't know signori."

"You didn't notice it arrive?" Bauer intervened.

"No."

"It's definitely not a car a priest would drive," Dennis said.

"You. What was your name again?" Bauer pointed at the quieter of the two policemen.

"Antonio Angelo Inspector."

"Angelo, you stay here. Bossano you come with us. Mr Dennis stay at the back please. We'll check that Hummer out and have a quick look around the church before we disturb the priests."

They'd only gone a few paces when Bauer turned back.

"And Angelo...."

"Yes sir?"

"Turn that television off."

It took them less than a minute to reach the Hummer. Reluctant to set off any alarms Dennis peered into the blacked-out windows. They were too dark to see anything inside. Dennis saw a small torch on Bossano's belt.

"Can I use that?"

Bossano clicked it on and handed it over. Dennis shone the torch in the windows, but the beam of light only reflected back. Dennis put the slender torch between his teeth, pressed one hand against the driver's side door and pulled gently on the door handle. It was locked.

"Excuse me," Bossano said making Dennis look around.

"This vehicle has a proximity locking device that is not activated by a normal key. The owner will have a smart key with a transducer that unlocks the vehicle when the device is anywhere within two metres of the car. As you can see there is no door lock on this vehicle."

"Dennis shone the torch again just to convince himself. He circled the vehicle slowly while the other two watched. The radio on Bossano's lapel suddenly crackled into life. A split second later they heard the distant sound of an explosion. They all turned their attention towards the Vatican two and a half miles across Rome. A ball of orange fire was ascending into the darkening sky. It slowly changed into a black cloud.

"Inspector they're saying it was a car bomb somewhere near the Vatican."

Bauer nodded.

They all looked towards the church as the sound of muffled machine gun chatter came from within.

"Mr Dennis get back to that police car. Get Angelo to call for back up. Bossano you're with me."

"I think I should stay with you."

"Mr Dennis this is no time for heroics. Allow us, the police, to do our job," Bauer said breaking into a run. Bossano following closely behind. Dennis watched them until they got to the church wall and began to move along it using the wall as cover, Bauer remembering there was a small wooden door near the rear, then he sprinted back to Angelo.

"We've just heard gunshots from inside the church," Dennis said to the startled Italian policeman, "Bauer's orders are for you to stay here, call for back up and to give me your gun."

"Give you my gun? Bauer said this?"

"Yes," Dennis said holding his hand out for the weapon.

Angelo stared into the Englishman's eyes.

"You are sure of this. Are you a policeman?"

"Sort of," Dennis lied, "In London," he added.

Angelo pondered over this for a moment. Then not taking his eyes of Dennis he reached down to his belt, unclipped his holster and offered his gun.

"Are you familiar with this weapon?"

"Kind of," Dennis said taking the Beretta.

"Look. You push this, point and shoot. Understood?"

"Sure. Point and shoot," Dennis said. He began trotting backwards, "Call for back up." then he turned and sprinted for the church. He moved silently to the small wooden door that Bauer and Bossano had disappeared through, pressed down gently on the latch and moved inside the church with the Beretta held ready in front of him. He closed the door as quietly as he could but as the metal latch connected with its counterpart it gave a small click which sounded deafening to him inside the empty church. At the foot of the stairs Bauer spun around and pointed his gun straight at Dennis who froze. Then Bauer raised his eyebrows and lowered his gun. Dennis moved silently across the rows of pews then stopped and tiptoed to the high altar. The bodies of three priests, blood staining their white robes, lay flat on their backs in front of the altar. Shot dead without mercy as they prayed to their God. Blood had splattered the altar, defiling it. Apalled Dennis made his way across the church. At the main doors was another dead priest. Bauer and Bossano waited at the foot of the stairs that led up, they waited for Dennis. Bauer saw the Beretta in the journalist's hand.

"What are you doing here?" he mouthed silently.

"You need me," Dennis whispered back.

The sound of smashing glass came down to them from the rooms above.

Bauer put his finger to his lips and then pointed up the stairs. They moved silently up, the Inspector taking the lead. At the top they stepped over the body of a monk, blood trickling from his mouth. Bauer bent down and placed two fingers to the man's jugular. He waited for a few moments and then moved on, hugging the wall. Now they could hear movement and the sound of more glass smashing coming from the holy relics chapel on the left. Suddenly a man in black military fatigues came out of the chapel carrying a black holdall.

"Stop Police!" Bauer shouted.

The man dropped the holdall and went for the machine gun across his chest. Wasting no time Bauer dropped him with two shots to the chest. He kicked the man's hands away from the machine gun. A burst of bullets from the relic's rooms splattered off the far wall sending Bauer diving for cover. He, Dennis and Bossano crashed into the shroud room. More bullets sprayed the far wall accompanied with shouting. Dennis couldn't hear what was being said but thought it sounded eastern European, maybe Russian. Bauer pointed his gun around the corner and fired back. Then amidst another burst of machine gun fire he realised the intruders were on the move. The muzzle of a machine gun appeared at the door and another burst of bullets sprayed the shroud room. The three of them dived for the floor. Dennis put his hands over his head as glass splintered around him, and plaster rained down from the walls. The person firing the gun was retreating. They could hear them moving along the corridor and down the stairs.

Bauer and Bossano got to their feet and followed once again hugging the walls. Dennis stuck his head into the relics chapel. All cabinets holding relics had been smashed, the treasures within looted. He gave pursuit quickly catching the other two. They got to the bottom of the stairs and threw themselves into cover behind benches. The gunmen were retreating backwards towards the main doors. Dennis motioned to Bossano and together they pushed the bench they were crouching behind over to give them better cover, the wood being thicker on the seat. This was met with more gunfire. As the gunmen reloaded Bauer ran, bent over double, and took cover behind a thick stone pillar. A burst of fire followed him. Dennis got himself into position so he could see towards the main doors. There were three of them moving backwards. One fired a burst at Bauer who dodged forward two rows of seats and took cover. Two of the gunmen kept up the gunfire as the third lifted the heavy bar that locked the front doors of the church. He swung the massive double doors open with tremendous strength. They were going out the front way. Bauer gave Dennis a signal to stay put and he gestured for Bossano to follow. They got up to move forward when three hand sized orbs came arcing into the church. One landed spinning next to Bossano. Bauer threw himself down flat on his face. Bossano, not so quick was staring at the object when it exploded, throwing him into the air in a spray of his own blood. His body landed with a soggy thud and Dennis looked into lifeless eyes as the other two M67 grenades exploded deafeningly inside the church.

"Fuck," Dennis said, "Grenades now! They've stepped up their game."

Bauer got up from the floor. A quick glance at Bossano told him the policeman was dead. Then he pressed forward, moved into cover at the door, peered around as he heard more machine gun fire, saw Angelo's body fall to the ground, saw two of the gunmen shoot the tyres on the police car as the black Hummer raced up to them and they got in. Bauer rushed out into the open air.

"Bauer, wait!" Dennis shouted rushing to the doors.

He watched in horror as the back window of the Hummer was lowered and the barrel of an MP5 poked out and sprayed Bauer with bullets. He crashed heavily to the ground as the Hummer sped away. Dennis ran out onto the piazza in front of the church. Bauer was face down and Dennis turned him over. He was still alive, his shirt soaked in blood. He tried to speak to Dennis but only blood bubbled from his lips.

"Don't talk," Dennis said reaching into his pocket for his mobile phone. He dialled the emergency number and asked for an ambulance. Bauer was struggling to try and move.

"Bauer stay still. Help is on its way."

Bauer tried to speak again. Suddenly his body went into spasms then went still. Dennis watched as the eyes glazed over. The sound of the Hummer bouncing off the pavement and striking a parked car got his attention. It zigzagged across the road as it sped away. Dennis fished around in Bauer's pockets until he found the keys to the Lancia. He let Bauer's head down gently onto the road and stood up.

"Goodbye Thomas," he said.

He rushed over to the Lancia. The engine roared into life as Dennis stomped on the gas pedal and he had to swerve around Angelo's body as he roared away back the way he and Bauer had come. The Hummer's tail lights easy to see in the growing dark.

Dennis got his phone out again and selected dial and rang Sonnenburg. The phone rang five times before it was answered.

"Sonnenburg," the voice said.

"It's Dennis. I'm in pursuit of a black Hummer which contains three armed men. They've attacked the church and killed the priests, two carabinieri and Bauer."

"Understood Peter. Are you able to follow long enough for us to get a helicopter to you?"

"I think so. I'm in the Lancia driving down the Viale carlo Felice. Hang on! They've just swung onto the Via Appia Nuova. Jesus they nearly just ran a group of girls over."

"Hold on Peter I'm just getting a lock on the Lancia. We've got our problems here."

"I take it that explosion was the car bomb."

"It was."

"Anyone hurt?"

"We lost the bomb disposal guys. The blast killed them."

Dennis swallowed hard. Not wanting to ask the next question.

"And Hutchinson and my girlfriend?"

"They're both fine Peter. They are right here beside me."

Dennis closed his eyes with relief for a moment.

"Keep me updated Peter. Where are you now?"

"I'm trying," Dennis said struggling to see the sat nav now he was driving, "I'm approaching a large, what must be a roundabout. They've just gone round it the wrong way. Now they've hit another car. It didn't even slow them down."

"Large roundabout," Sonnenburg was saying, "All right I think you're at the piazza De Re Di Roma."

"I don't know. I can't see any road signs."

"That's because they're up high on buildings Peter. I know exactly where you are. We've got a fix on the Lancia's tracker. You're heading for the Grande Raccordo Anulare...."

"The what?"

"It's the motorway that encircles greater Rome. Now we've got them."

Dennis didn't answer. He was busy swerving around cars that were frantically trying to avoid the Hummer and the Lancia. Then suddenly a car was hit broadside amid a burst of sparks and it rolled onto its roof and onto the pavement until it tumbled to a stop. Two more Hummer's burst onto the road to join the other one in front of Dennis.

"Holy crap," Dennis shouted into the phone whilst performing an emergency stop, "Two more Hummer's have joined the chase and by the looks of it these two are armour plated."

Dennis watched in his rear-view mirror as the crashed car stopped moving.

"Two more Hummer's," Sonnenburg replied, "Well they're not ours. Peter, I need you out of there now. We now have air support. Leave it to our ground forces."

"Understood."

Dennis put the phone down and ducked his head down to look out of the top of the windscreen as a police helicopter whooshed past overhead, its bright searchlight on the road. He watched in the rear-view mirror again as a group of bystanders rushed to the upturned car to help its occupants. Ahead, the helicopter banked and disappeared from view, blocked from his eyesight by tall buildings. Dennis reached down and picked up the blue light and put it on the roof of the car. He flicked it on then flicked the siren switch.

"Peter what the fuck are you doing?" he said out loud as he stomped on the accelerator and the Lancia roared away once again in pursuit.

It didn't take him long to catch up to the trail of destruction. There were smashed and dented cars and mopeds. He passed what was obviously an outdoor pavement café. The tables and chairs were smashed to pieces along with the barriers displaying the café's logo. Dennis saw a group of people crowded around something laying on the ground amongst the destroyed furniture. Then he saw faces turn towards him as the people responded to the siren and blue light. He saw some of them stand up from crouching and move back. Then he saw the pools of blood in his headlights.

"Bastards!" he said as he raced past.

The phone on the passenger seat began to ring. Dennis picked it up and pressed the green telephone symbol.

"Mr Dennis, I told you to stop your pursuit and yet I can see on the screen that you are still following…."

"They've just run down some innocents who were enjoying an evening out for fuck's sake," Dennis shouted down the phone at Sonnenburg, "I'm not going to let them get away with it."

Sonnenburg glanced at Natalie who along with Hutchinson was standing next to the police chief. He saw the look of concern on her face. Then he turned back to the monitors.

"All right Mr Dennis. You have just entered the A91 motorway. This road takes you to the Fumicino airport. It is also a toll road. They have made a mistake leading you onto this. We will be able to set up a roadblock at the tolling station."

"They must also know this. Why would they take a road you can block?"

"This is the motorway that leads onto Tarquinia. For them it is the quickest route if they're planning to escape this way."

"Well if you ask me it all sounds too easy."

"Relax Mr Dennis. We've got them now."

Sonnenburg ended the call and nodded at Natalie.

"Don't worry miss. Everything's under control."

Dennis had the Lancia at 140KPH as he sped in and out of traffic, changing lanes, overtaking and undertaking, always gaining on the three black Hummers. They were speeding and chopping and changing lanes also. Dennis turned the blue light and siren off, hoping to catch up to them without giving himself away. What he was going to do once he caught up to them, he had no idea. He eased off the accelerator and maintained a fairly large distance. He saw headlights in his rear-view mirror and heard the sirens at the last moment as two police motorcycles blew past him and closed on the Hummers and Dennis watched in horror as men holding machine guns leaned out of the windows and sprayed the motorcycles with bullets. The first rider was killed instantly and fell from his BMW which slid on its side for a short distance before stopping, motorists frantically swerving to avoid it. The other one exploded when the fuel tank was hit and the rider was thrown clear. Dennis turned his head and closed his eyes for a moment as the body of the policeman went under the wheels of an articulated lorry. He opened them in time to see the back axles of the vehicle bouncing as they crushed the man.

"Jesus," Dennis muttered.

He had to brake hard and swerve as motorway users performed emergency action to avoid the carnage and now the traffic was slowing ahead. Two police cars raced past headlights and blue lights ablaze. Dennis switched on his siren and blue light again and changed lanes until he was on the hard shoulder. He raced the Lancia's engine through the gears and hammered down the middle lane now the road in front clear as far as the Hummers. The two police cars were keeping a safe distance. Dennis could hear their conversation with control over the Lancia's radio.

The Hummer's were back in traffic now. They raced past the junctions for the Fumicino airport. The traffic here slowing into two lanes. The telephone on the passenger seat began ringing again.

"We've got you on the scanner," Sonnenburg began, "We're setting up a roadblock. As you pass each junction more police cars will join. The idea is to box them in and slow them down, eventually stopping them."

"You'd better tell them not to get too close," Dennis replied, "They've got machine guns and they've already killed two of your motorcyclists…."

Dennis read the road sign ahead.

"Civitavecchia," he said, "Is that the port where the big cruise ships dock?"

"It is. Tarquinia is just beyond it and if you maintain the speed you're doing you'll be there in fifteen minutes."

Sonnenburg was right Dennis was thinking as he and the police cars tailing the Hummers raced past the exit for the port. Above, the helicopter kept a distance from any potential gunfire. Dennis was at the back of the carabinieri cars which were keeping a formation to stop any vehicles from behind in overtaking. Then ahead in the distance in the fading light Dennis saw the unmistakeable bulk of a transporter plane flying low. The flashing lights on the aircraft drawing his attention. Even from this distance Dennis recognised it as a C130 Lockheed Hercules. Dennis was going to dismiss the aircraft, but it suddenly occurred to him that it might be heading for the airfield bought by Von Werner. What was it called? Tarquinia?

Then Dennis saw the sign for Tarquinia, and he knew that must be where the transporter was heading. He picked up the phone to ring Sonnenburg to warn him when the unthinkable happened. Almost as if in slow motion Dennis saw the Hummers pass a coach full of tourists. As the last Hummer passed a man leaned out of the back window, aimed his gun and fired a burst of bullets at the front wheel which exploded in large lumps of rubber. Dennis imagined the driver fighting for control and then suddenly it was swerving across the lanes without slowing. The twelve-ton coach ploughed into the central reservation, destroying a few metres of it before the vehicle mounted it. The front end of the coach rose into the air, the chassis clearly visible, before it came crashing back down on its side in a shower of sparks and broken glass. The coach slid along the carriageway for a short distance and then completely stopped. The first two police cars were unable to stop in time and they ploughed straight into the wreckage. The third lost control and slammed into the central reservation. Another police car slammed into the two already embedded into the coach. The last was able to stop. Dennis in the Lancia was also able to stop, the Lancia's tyres squealing black smoke. Then Dennis was throwing open the driver's door and he was out running to the scene.

He got halfway when one of the police cars exploded, picking him up and throwing him through the air. Dennis landed in the road, his ears ringing. Then slowly he was able to get up and he groped past the other police car that had stopped. The driver of this car also slowly getting to his feet. Dennis helped him then moved forward. Three police cars were burning and he shielded his face with his hand as he got closer. A sickening pall of black smoke rising. Then Dennis was running for the coach knowing it too would catch fire at any moment. The smell of burning flesh was nauseating and Dennis saw the burning policemen sitting upright in their car seats and he fought the urge to vomit. He swallowed the bitter tasting liquid that had found its way into his mouth.

A window on the coach exploded and he heard the screams of the passengers trapped inside. Dennis made his way round to the front. He could see the coach driver was dead. Then the vehicle began to burn and the screams intensified. Some of the passengers were scrabbling through the smashed window and they crawled along the side which was now the roof of the coach. One man was struggling and he fell back twice. Willing hands outside tried to pull him up and then suddenly the flames leapt and he was consumed. Those trying to help him scrambled to safety. Dennis ran around to the back of the coach knowing there would be an emergency exit, the back window. He could see there was no outside handle to open it. It required a special hammer to break it. The hammer was inside. The back window like all the other windows was tinted and he could see hands frantically thumping at it. Then he saw a child's face appear at the glass and he began kicking the toughened glass. He kicked it repeatedly, but it wouldn't break. A policeman suddenly appeared alongside him and together they tried to break it. Still to no avail. Other faces appeared at the glass now, panicking. Then Dennis grabbed the policeman's gun and he banged hard on the back window.

"Move back! I'm going to shoot the glass!" he shouted.

He knew he probably couldn't be heard so he banged the gun on the window a few times then moved back and pointed it. The faces disappeared and he fired. The first three bullets travelling so fast just punched holes in the tinted glass. The fourth one shattered it into millions of cubes. Dennis knocked as much of the glass in as he could. Desperate hands reached out and Dennis grabbed the child and pulled her to safety as the policeman began pulling people from the wreckage. He carried her to the Lancia and opened the back door and placed her inside. She was crying and he bent down and brushed her long hair away from her face.

"Shh. Shh. You're safe now," he said.

A woman came hysterically running to the car. Dennis moved out of her way and she reached in and scooped the little girl up. She kissed the child repeatedly on the side of her head, the hug so intense.

"Grazi! Grazi! Signori!" the woman said, then, realising Dennis may be English she said, "Thank you for saving my little Rosa. Thank you."

Dennis placed his hand gently on the woman's shoulder and they exchanged a smile. The sound of another small explosion came across to him and he was running back to the coach. The policeman was still plucking people from the back window and Dennis rushed in and was helping to pull them out. Then his T-shirt was getting wet and he tasted the sweet water on his lips and he couldn't understand how it could be raining when the sky had been clear all day. Then suddenly the firemen were there and kind hands grabbed Dennis and helped him back, to safety. He saw the hose that was held by two firefighters that was already dousing the flames that now hissed and he realised that this was his rain. The fireman who helped him was checking him over for injuries and Dennis shook his head.

"I'm all right."

The fireman nodded and rushed off to help others. Dennis looked at the woman still cradling the small child her eyes never having once left him. He half smiled again and then a dark thought crossed his mind and he walked across the carriageway to see past the coach, to look for the Hummers. The road ahead was completely clear. The Hummers were gone.

CHAPTER THIRTEEN

Peter Dennis sat on the steps of the ambulance while he had his scratches and small burns on his face and hands attended to. He watched in grim silence as firefighters removed bodies in black bags from the overturned coach. A paramedic was dabbing at his face and the cool cloth was soothing. The policeman whose gun he'd used to break the back window was nearby also receiving treatment for burns to his face and hands. The police cars that had crashed into the coach were burnt out shells, their occupants reduced to ash. The front half of the coach was completely destroyed. The stench from it overwhelming.

A black people carrier pulled up and Dennis smiled as Natalie and Hutchinson with De Luca climbed out. De Luca surveying the aftermath of the chase. Natalie resisted the urge to run to Dennis but the relief of seeing him was plainly clear on her face. He winced as antiseptic liquid was applied to a sponge and dabbed on scratches on his brow causing them to sting. He smiled up at Natalie again as she got to him.

"Hey," was all he said quietly.

"Are you all right?"

"Yeah. Just a few scratches."

"Is that a burn?"

"And a burn."

De Luca was talking to the police officer in charge of the scene. He gave some instructions and then came over to the ambulance.

"Are you all right?"

"Yes," Dennis replied, "Just superficial wounds."

"I understand you saved some of the tourists from the coach. For that I thank you. Do you know how many are dead?"

"Firefighters have brought fifteen out so far and that includes the driver."

Natalie put her hand up to her mouth.

"You've also lost seven of your men. Two of which were on motorcycles. You'll find them back down the motorway."

"Their bodies have already been recovered. Bauer's too."

Natalie took her hand away from her mouth.

"Bauer is dead?" she asked.

Dennis nodded.

"What happened at the church?" De Luca asked.

Dennis told him. When he finished De Luca said.

"They killed the priests?"

"Yes, every last one of them."

"May God have mercy on their souls."

Dennis didn't know if De Luca meant the gunmen or the priests. He didn't bother to ask.

"I will need you to make a statement if you would please for police records.

Dennis nodded again.

"How does it end? The police report I mean."

"They made it to Tarquinia airfield and made their escape by a Hercules transporter plane. By the time we managed to get the air force to scramble jets it was too late. They turned out to sea almost immediately and dropped to an altitude low enough for radar to be unable to detect them. We had police on the ground, but they were unable to stop them. The Hummers drove into the back of the plane and it took off."

"I hate to say it," Dennis said, "But I think we widely underestimated our enemy."

"Yes."

Then De Luca reached into his jacket pocket and took out his phone. He opened images and showed Dennis a grainy picture.

"What is it?" Dennis asked not able to make out the shapes. Natalie craned her neck to see.

"It's the tail of the Hercules. A news helicopter caught it on camera earlier today. It has a very interesting mark on it. I wondered if you would be able to identify it."

The image was blurred and was worse when Dennis used the touch screen to enlarge the pic.

"It looks like the SS death's head emblem," Natalie said.

"You think?" Dennis said turning the screen around for a better view.

"Yes. Look take the pic back to its original size. Now that looks like the same skull that was painted on the Wavecrest!"

"I think you're right."

"What's that?" De Luca asked.

"Three months ago, we encountered Von Werner for the first time. He had a ship called the WaveCrest and that skull was painted on the side of it. It's the death's head symbol from Nazi Germany. It's also his trademark."

"So, it was definitely him?"

"It would seem so."

"In that case I think you're right about our underestimating him," De Luca said studying the burnt-out coach again.

"Where does this leave us?" Dennis asked.

"What do you mean?"

"Well, we came here to help you catch Von Werner. Bauer, some of your men and innocent people have died. What do you want us…." Dennis gestured at Natalie and Hutchinson, "To do now?"

"There's nothing you can do. They've gone. We're trying to find out where that plane was headed. The flight number was false. We have no leads. The items stolen will most likely not turn up for sale. They will go into a private collection no doubt or be disposed of once their worth is finished with. I don't really think there is anything left for you to do. If you could give me that report as soon as possible and then I guess, you'll want to return to London."

"So that's it? Goodbye."

"Pete," Hutchinson said, "Come on. You're tired. We all are. We've had one hell of a day."

"A hell of a day? You're not wrong. A car bomb. I've been shot at, nearly killed many times. There must be something we can do."

De Luca shook his head.

"We continue to appreciate everything that you've done for us but there is no need to risk yourselves any further. Listen Mr Hutchinson is right. It's been a hell of a day as he put it. Why don't you get yourselves back to your hotel, get cleaned up and go out for dinner. The report can wait until tomorrow."

Dennis looked at Natalie.

"Why not," she said.

Dennis looked at Hutchinson.

"Jim?"

"No. You kids run along. Have a nice night out. I've got computer work to do. It'll be building up. I'd better telephone my wife too."

139

The paramedic finished her work and closed her medical bag. Dennis thanked her. De Luca clicked his fingers at a uniformed officer who rushed over to him. He quickly gave the policeman some instructions in Italian. Then he turned to the group.

"This officer will drive you back to your hotel. Enjoy your evening. I will see you tomorrow. Sonnenburg will also want to talk to you before you go back to your country."

Dennis was the last to get into the people carrier. At the door he stopped.

"Cesare?"

De Luca, realising whatever Dennis wanted to say was obviously private, leaned in close to the journalist. Dennis quietly closed the car door so those inside wouldn't overhear.

"If there was something more that could be done to catch these criminals!"

"The trail is cold. We have nothing more to go on. But surely you wouldn't risk your friends any further. This has become an extremely dangerous situation. You wouldn't want anything to happen to Mr Hutchinson or Natalie."

"No of course not. But then theoretically I was referring only to myself."

De Luca looked into Dennis' eyes. He read what was behind them.

"You're serious, aren't you?"

"Deadly."

"We would welcome any help you can give."

When Natalie came out of the bathroom of their hotel room, she had a long towel round her body and knotted at her chest. She saw Dennis in his black dinner suit and wolf whistled at him. He was standing by the window with a large whiskey in his hand.

"Where did you get that?" she nodded at the glass.

"I went down to the bar for it."

"Dressed like that?"

He looked down at himself and then back at her.

"Yes. Oh and I think the barmaid fancied me."

"Well I'm not surprised with you looking like that."

She went over to him and kissed him on the lips. She pulled away.

"You look very sexy darling."

Then, to tease him, she dropped the towel and naked, turned and walked back to the bathroom. He followed and while she was at the basin he pressed himself against her back and kissed her neck. He undid his bow tie and the top button of his shirt. She was watching him in the mirror.

"Um what are you doing?"

He kissed her on the neck again.

"Why don't we uh, head into the bedroom."

She pushed against him to move him away.

"We haven't got time for that. I'm hungry and you've got whiskey breath."

"We've got all evening to eat."

"I'm hungry now."

"No chance then?"

"No chance."

Then she burst out laughing.

"Your face. You look like a schoolboy who's had his football confiscated."

She came forward.

"Make yourself useful. Go and see if Jim's all right and if he wants anything while we're out. Be patient," she said kissing him gently on the lips again, "And you might get what you want when we get back."

Dennis smiled at her and left. He went to the next room and knocked the door.

"Just a second," he heard the American call.

Dennis heard the lock on the other side release. Then the door opened.

"Pete come in," Hutchinson said going back to his laptop, leaving Dennis to close the door.

"Nat is just getting ready and I thought I should check to see if you want anything."

"No, I'm fine thanks. I'm getting some sandwiches brought up to the room."

"Sandwiches. Are you sure you won't come to dinner?"

"What? Oh no! You guys run along. It'll be nice, just the two of you. Get some time together."

Hutchinson noted the tuxedo and bow tie.

"Where are you going?"

"She wants to find a posh restaurant. Thought I'd better look the part."

"Well, I've got nothing to compete with that here anyway. No really, you run along. Have a great time. I've got to call my wife."

"Ok. Well enjoy your evening."

"You too."

Hutchinson picked up his mobile phone.

"Oh Pete."

Dennis stopped at the door.

"Have you got that old journal here with you?"

"Von Brest's?"

"Yes."

"I have. Why?"

"Just thought we might take a look through it tomorrow. See if there are any more clues."

"Do you want it tonight? I can go and get it."

"No. Tomorrow will do. I've got enough here to keep me up 'til late."

Dennis put his hand on the door handle. He paused and looked over his shoulder.

"You know it hit me earlier, sitting on the steps of the ambulance, just how dangerous this has become. As much as I would love to help further, I wouldn't want to see you or Nat in any more danger."

"Nor would I."

"I knew she was safe with you. Thanks Jim."

"She is the closest thing I've ever had to a daughter. That's why I'm glad we're out of this now. Nothing would make me decide to stay in the fight after what's happened."

Dennis opened the door.

"Me neither. Goodnight Jim."

It was just after eleven o'clock when a very tired Natalie and Dennis arrived back at their hotel in Rome. Dennis had left their room key with reception and while he went to get it Natalie went over to the lifts to wait for him. The male receptionist was watching the highlights of the evening's champions league match on a small handheld television. He put the TV down onto its screen when he saw Dennis approaching.

"How was your evening sir?" he asked the journalist.

"Very nice thank you. How was the game?" Dennis gestured to the upturned TV. The receptionist gave an embarrassed smile.

"Forgive me sir. It is my beloved Roma. We won 3-2."

"That's good," Dennis said, "Room 408 please."

The receptionist turned for the key. There was a large brown envelope in the pigeonhole.

"There seems to be a package for you."

"A package. Who from?" Dennis asked, turning the envelope over.

"My colleague accepted it for you. Carla," he called.

A glamorous brunette came from the office.

"Good evening, sir. That package was delivered by an inspector De Luca of the Vatican police. He dropped it off a couple of hours ago."

"Oh, De Luca. Thank you."

Dennis made his way over to Natalie. The brunette was watching him. She saw Natalie looking at her and she pouted her lips as she concentrated on tidying up some papers behind reception.

"It's from De Luca," he said. He waited until they were in the elevator heading for the fourth floor before opening it. There was a police complimentary slip and he read it.

"Dear Mr Dennis," it said, "I thought you might find these interesting. If there is anything else that you can think of, please let me know. Cesare."

Underneath were some photographs. Dennis flicked through them briefly. There were four in total.

"What are they?" Natalie asked.

"Blown up copies of the tail of that Hercules I saw."

The death's head, though blurred at this size, was unmistakable.

"Would you say that is identical to the one painted on the side of the wave crest?"

"I would say so. It certainly looks to be the same."

"I'm sure it is."

There was nothing else in the envelope. Just four photos and the complimentary slip. The elevator stopped on their floor. As they got out there was a commotion at the end of the corridor. Whoever it was, they disappeared around the corner a moment later.

"What was that about?" Natalie asked.

"Don't know. Listen I'm just going to show these to Jim."

"Peter not tonight. It's late. He may be sleeping. Leave him until tomorrow."

He took her hand off his arm.

"I'm just going to show him these. I'll be very quick. I'll knock gently. If there's no answer, I'll leave it until the morning."

"Don't be long," Natalie said putting their key in the lock.

Dennis put his knuckles against Hutchinson's door and was surprised to find it move a fraction. He rapped on it and pushed it open an inch.

"Jim? Jim?" he called.

There was no answer, so Dennis pushed the door open and stepped in. He instantly smelt trouble.

"Jim? Jim?" he called again. Still no answer. Dennis checked the bathroom. Then he went back to the room. The bed was made. Dennis took his phone out of his pocket and was about to ring Hutchinson's when he noticed the tall lamp by the window had been knocked over. He rang Hutchinson's number and it went straight to answer phone. Puzzled, he was about to ring reception when he realised Hutchinson's laptop appeared to be missing. The power cable for it still plugged into the mains. Then he saw the spots of blood on the table and floor and he was rushing for the door. He barged into his room. Natalie was still in her black mini-dress and heels.

"Peter! What the....?"

"Something's happened to Jim. That commotion in the corridor! Ring De Luca!"

He rushed out of the room, ran to the elevators and pressed the lift call button. He looked up at the digital display telling him which floors they were on. One was at the lobby. The other on the first floor. He slammed the palm of his hand against the button panel with irritation, briefly looked at the displays once more and ran for the stairs. He burst through the door and looked down. He could see the ground four floors below and could hear heavy footsteps and shouting.

Was that Hutchinson's voice?

Dennis bolted down the stairs three at a time. He swung the corner and raced down the next steps, always gaining on his opponents.

The fact that they might have guns didn't even cross his mind.

At the ground floor a bruised and panting Hutchinson clung onto the handrail in desperation and groaned in pain as the butt of a handgun smashed down onto his already battered knuckles forcing him to release his grip.

Dennis could see more spots of blood on the white marble stairs and he jumped down the last flight of steps, landing heavily. He landed harder than he'd intended to and his muscles and tendons screamed at him. His feet were stinging. He gritted his teeth and carried on, slow at first until the numbness wore off. He rounded the last corner and descended the last flight of stairs. Ahead was the already open door that led to the alley outside. It could only be opened from inside and Dennis charged through it. There were some wheelie bins here and a large dumpster. Ahead where the alley ended, he could see the men half dragging, half carrying Hutchinson. A dark 4x4 was waiting and they bundled their captive inside. It roared away as Dennis reached the end of the alley at a sprint. It was a dark, possibly black or navy-blue BMW X5.

"Damn these Italian registration numbers," he said out loud, cursing the small numbers that couldn't be read from very far.

Nearby was a street vendor selling hamburgers and doner kebabs from a window of his fast-food venue and Dennis noticed people queuing for a late night snack. There was a scrambler motorcycle parked next to two motor scooters at the kerb. One of the mopeds had a full-face helmet on its seat and Dennis wandered over to the bikes. He was amazed to see the scrambler's keys were in the ignition. He checked the queue of people and saw the man at the front now being served had a crash helmet in his hand. Dennis picked up the helmet on the moped and put it on. He swung his leg over the saddle of the scrambler, gently leaned his weight until the bike was upright off its parking stand. Then as quietly as he could his foot brought the stand up with a click. Not once taking his eyes of the unsuspecting rider Dennis turned the ignition key and stood up in the saddle and jumped down with all his might onto the kick starter. The engine roared into life and Dennis selected first gear, twisted the accelerator while holding the brake, spun the back wheel round in a semi-circle accompanied with a cloud of black smoke and raced off down the street as the

145

motorbikes owner turned in astonishment with tomato ketchup oozing out of the bottle he was squeezing and dripping onto his clothes.

Peter Dennis kept a big distance from the BMW X5 as it turned into the docks at Naples. He followed slowly and as the X5 turned through a gate with stop barriers he had no choice but to continue straight on. The security guards on the gate watching him as he rode past. He knew he must look out of place riding a scrambler dirt bike with a full faced crash helmet and a dinner suit and he hoped they wouldn't get suspicious. He'd followed the BMW for the 140 miles from Rome and had managed to remain undetected. The BMW had kept to the 125km speed limit which the little Honda motorcycle had at times struggled with. In his thin suit at that speed Dennis had been freezing.

He continued going straight for a distance then took the next right. There was a barrier here also, but it was unattended and down and he was able to squeeze the bike past it. He rode along this stretch of road which was lined with containers. In the gaps between them he caught glimpses of the BMW X5 running parallel to him. Beyond the BMW was a large container ship moored at the dock. As he passed the next gap Dennis realised the BMW had stopped. He shut off the engine of the very noisy scrambler dirt bike and got off it and wheeled it between two containers and propped it against one. He crept along the rows. At the end was a chain link fence at least ten feet high with razor wire atop it. Dennis kept in the shadows when he got to the fence. The BMW was a couple of hundred metres away and Dennis watched as all the doors opened and men got out. They half dragged; half carried Hutchinson whose hands were tied. A hood was placed over his head. They bundled him to a metal gangway and pushed and prodded him up it. Twice he tripped and stumbled and was yanked roughly back to his feet and forced on.

"Bastards!" Dennis said out loud.

He watched until they'd disappeared inside the ship and then took his phone out. The battery was almost dead. He selected Natalie from his contacts list and rang her and she answered almost instantly.

"Peter is that you?"

"Yes…."

"Where the bloody hell have you been?" she cut him off, "I've been worried sick."

"I haven't got long. My battery is almost dead. I've followed the kidnappers to Naples…."

"Naples?"

"Yes. Listen don't interrupt I don't have much time. They've taken Hutchinson onto a ship. I can't see what it's called but it's a large container ship. I need you to get hold of De Luca…."

"He's here now."

De Luca looked up from the notes he was taking. He and his men were going over Hutchinson's hotel room for clues.

"Is that him?" he called out to Natalie, who nodded.

De Luca clicked his fingers at Ferrara.

"Get forensics up here."

He took the phone from Natalie.

"Mr Dennis it's De Luca."

"Cesare my battery is almost dead. I've followed Hutchinson's kidnappers to Naples's port. They've taken him onto a container ship, I don't know its name, I can't see it, sorry. I'm going to try and get on board…."

"No Mr Dennis. That is precisely what you're not going to do. I will give you the address of the nearest police station once this call is finished and you will report to them and wait for me to call you again. Understood?"

"Understood," Dennis said.

The phone bleeped and he took it away from his ear to look at the screen. The battery symbol was now flashing. The display said 'insert charger'.

"My phone is almost dead."

"Okay Peter. So we don't have much time. We've received a demand from the kidnappers. They want something called the Von Brest journal. Natalie has told us all about it but she doesn't know where it is. We're assuming Hutchinson doesn't have it, though they've turned his room overlooking for it."

"It's in the safe in our room, my room."

"Natalie will look. Where is the key she's just asked."

"In the pocket of my red and white check shirt."

"She's got the key. She's just going to look."

147

"Cesare, I stole a motorbike to follow them."

"Don't worry about that Peter. I'll get my men to sort it out. Right, we've got the journal, thank you. Now Peter, I need you to…. Hello…. Hello…."

The phone was dead. De Luca clicked his fingers at Ferrara again.

"I need you to get hold of the port authorities in Naples. I want the name of whoever is in charge there. Find out the name of a large container ship moored there. There can't be that many and find out who is head of the police in Naples. I want to speak to him as soon as possible. Once you've done that get the car. We're taking a trip to Naples."

Dennis looked at the blank screen. He pressed the power button on the side of the phone. Nothing. He put the phone back in his pocket. The wind was getting up. Strong gusts had begun blowing. He looked up at the sky, the clouds were scudding across rapidly. A few spots of rain hit his face. Dennis looked down at himself, he took his bow tie off and shoved it in his trouser pocket. The rain began now, coming down hard.

Dennis looked up at the razor wire.

'There must be a way over it'.

He moved along the containers and saw that the fence ran the entire length of the docks and extended over the water. Then on his way back he noticed a container that was on its own near the fence. The doors were open on it and he peered inside. There was just a pile of smelly rubbish and some pages of a newspaper blowing about within. Dennis tested the bars of the door lock. He was sure they would take his weight and he began to climb up them. It was difficult with the wet and he slipped frequently but finally he made it to the top. He pulled himself up and knelt on the roof of the container. He rubbed the palms of his hands together. The cold wet metal had been painful to them.

The fence was eight feet from the container and two feet above it. He took his jacket off. In seconds his white shirt was soaked from the rain. Bunching the sleeves of the jacket in his fists he stepped back to the edge of the container, checked his grip on the steel roof by sliding his foot backwards and forwards over the surface, took a few deep breaths and started his very short run. He launched himself across the gap and slammed into the chain link

148

fence. The jacket caught on the razor wire and he both heard and felt it ripping. He held on with all his strength and pulled himself up. Dennis felt the razor wire begin to cut through the material and he felt his palms being sliced by the wire. He scrabbled over the top and felt a sharp pain over his ribs as he kicked his legs over and dropped to the ground. In the dark he held his palms up to his face and saw the fresh blood. He looked down at his shirt. There was a slash in it, over his ribs. He put his fingertips inside the tear. There was fresh blood on them when he pulled them out. He felt along the cut, though it was stinging it didn't feel serious. He looked up at his jacket hanging in shreds on top of the fence.

"Oh well there goes three hundred quid," he said out loud, "Nat's going to be pissed!" He looked over at the vessel, "Now I just need to get on that ship."

Keeping close to the fence which he hoped was keeping him in the shadows Dennis moved along the dock looking for a way onto the ship. It towered above him, containers stacked five and six high on its deck. The bridge was near the stern and Dennis could see people moving about in the lights. At the stern he could see the rotor blades of a helicopter on the Heli-pad. There was no way onto the ship that he could see. He looked at the thick ropes, as thick as a man's thigh that went from the dock's cleats to the stern of the ship. Now he could see her name painted in large white letters.

'Meeresbrise' Hamburg.

Dennis' German was very limited, but he translated the ship's name into 'Ocean Breeze' home port Hamburg, Germany. Then he saw the death's head next to the last 'e' of Meeresbrise.

'Now there's a surprise' he said to himself.

Dennis grabbed hold of the ropes and leaned out over the water as far as he could, turned upside down and wrapped his feet around the ropes and began to climb up hand over fist. It was difficult in the wind and rain and the further he climbed the harder it got. His strength was ebbing fast, his muscles in his arms, legs, neck and back screaming for relief. Dennis stopped and leaned his neck back to see how much further he had to go. He was almost at the ship and he glanced down at the water seventy feet below. Another six feet and he could clamber over the stern and onto the ship. Summoning the last reserves of his strength he made to move the last few feet when he froze. He could hear voices approaching and then he saw the tops of the heads of two men. Dennis waited with muscles straining. He knew at any moment that they would look over the stern and see him. He gritted his teeth against the pain and then a strong gust of wind blew at him and his feet slipped. Now he was dangling above the water. He tried to swing his legs up. Four times he failed. Then his fingers began to slip. In desperation he swung his legs up again and wrapped them around the rope just as his right hand slipped. He hung on for dear life but for the moment he was safe. His grip wasn't slipping any more. He flexed the fingers of his right hand to get the circulation flowing again. Then the two men finished their conversation, and he heard one of them leave. The other one hawked and spat over the stern and Dennis saw the thick gob pass his head by a whisper. Then not knowing if the man was still there or not Dennis adjusted his grip on the rope and began climbing again.

He was able to grab the edge of the steel where the rope passed through and pulled himself over and dropped to the deck, breathing hard. He saw the departing back of the man who'd spat and Dennis quickly moved into hiding to get his bearings.

He could now see the helicopter was an MH-65 Dolphin. The model widely used by the United States coastguard.

Directly opposite him was a door marked 'Mannschaft nur' crew only. He crossed to it and went inside, closing the door quietly behind him. He went up two flights of stairs and through another door marked crew only, again in German. He went through this door and into a nicely furnished lounge. The room was carpeted, had large sofas, chairs, tables and a large plasma television, DVD player and play station 3. Another door at the end of the lounge led him to a corridor with bedrooms off to either side. At the end of the corridor were washrooms. It was here that Dennis found tall upright lockers.

He tried a few that were locked, the names of the users written on them. The second from the right was unlocked and he was pleased to find a pile of T-shirts, two pairs of jeans and some boiler suits inside.

Kicking his shoes off he quickly took his trousers and blood stained shirt off and stuffed them into the bottom of the locker. He changed into a pair of jeans and a red T-shirt and then put a boiler suit on. It was stained and smelt faintly of diesel. He was halfway through putting his arms into the sleeves when an announcement in German came out over the internal speakers. It was repeated in English, but he wasn't listening and didn't hear it. He was just doing the poppers up on the front with his back to the door when he heard the door open.

"Didn't you hear the announcement?" a deep voice said, "Everyone is to be on deck. The helicopter is leaving soon."

Dennis turned slowly. The man was huge. On the breast of his boiler suit was a patch saying 'supervisor'

"Yes sir. Sorry sir," Dennis said as he made to move past the leviathan.

The supervisor continued to block the way.

"I thought I knew all the crew on this ship. How come I haven't seen you before?"

"I'm the new guy. Replaced the one who was sacked," Dennis lied, readying himself for the fight, hoping an element of surprise would catch his much larger opponent off guard. To his relief Dennis heard the supervisor say.

"Oh him! Yeah, well, he was warned about his drinking on duty. Now you'd better get topside," the man said jerking his thumb at the door.

Dennis went out into the corridor.

"Ahem!"

He stopped and turned. The supervisor was tapping the hard hat on his head.

"Forgotten something?"

Dennis went for a hard hat hanging on the coat hooks.

"Sorry," he said putting it on. He went to go left at the end of the corridor.

"Hey!"

"For fuck's sake now what?" Dennis muttered to himself.

The supervisor was staring at him.

"Don't tell me you've forgotten the way to the Helipad as well.

Dennis saw the sign with the helicopter on it on the wall.

"No of course not," he smiled.

At the end of the corridor, he looked back. The huge man was still glowering at him. Dennis quickly made his way on deck, relieved to be away from confrontation.

The helicopter rotor blades were already turning, getting faster and faster as the engine powered up. Dennis saw a door open and a man and woman came out. The man was of oriental origin and was carrying a briefcase and was staring at him. Dennis quickly went to the stern and checked the mooring ropes. The man took his eyes off Dennis and the journalist relaxed.

The woman was tall, in heels and an above the knee skirt and matching jacket. She stopped as the oriental man opened the helicopter's passenger door and moved out of her way. She got in, her skirt riding up, revealing shapely legs. Dennis could see as she sat down that she was beautiful. Her hair auburn or possibly ginger.

The oriental man followed her in and the helicopter's engine whined as it lifted off the Heli-pad and banked immediately and headed out over the dock towards the sea. Dennis watched until it disappeared from view. He heard footsteps behind him and turned. He just had time to see the word supervisor before the heavy adjustable spanner cracked into his jaw and his world went black.

CHAPTER FOURTEEN

When Peter Dennis came round the first thing, he knew was that he'd been knocked out. He remembered the sight of the adjustable spanner inches from his face and he, unable to avoid it. His jaw hurt and felt swollen. He rolled his tongue around the inside of his mouth and tasted blood. The lower left part of his jaw hurt and the pain made him wince. He pushed his tongue against several of his teeth. They had been jarred and felt loose. There was a lump bitten out of the inside of his left cheek and it stung to poke his tongue there. He felt warmth from the wound and knew that was where the blood had come from.

Over his head was a hood that surprisingly let in a lot of light, though he could see nothing at all. It felt like it was hessian, a hessian sack, and smelt strongly of coffee. It was loose over his head but tied with rope around his neck. Tight enough to keep it on but not to restrict his breathing. He moved his head quickly this way and that but was unable to dislodge the hood.

He was sitting on a chair, his arms tied behind it. He tried to move his hands but realised they were tied too tightly. The ropes cutting into his wrists. His fingers numb with pins and needles. His feet were also tied together but not to the chair and there was something else. A strange inaudible rumbling beneath his feet. He couldn't hear but sensed and felt it. Then he felt his stomach move from within and he knew that he was still on the ship and the strange rumbling meant that the ship had set sail. His senses told him it was turning.

"I wonder if we're out at sea," he was thinking, "And if so how far. God, I hope Hutchinson's still on board. Did I tell De Luca what I was going to do?"

He racked his memory for what had happened before he'd been knocked out.

'How long was I out for? Minutes? Hours? Days? The phone battery failed before I told him what I was doing'.

He tried to move his shoulders; they were aching. His backside hurt as well and he squirmed to try and ease the cramp. He felt the chair move under him and he was sure it was wooden. He was able to move his legs.

'So, they're not tied to the chair'.

He tried to stand but couldn't. He could rock the chair. It began to tip backwards and forwards and he used his leg muscles until they ached. The chair was getting higher and higher with each effort and then finally he felt it begin to tip. He quickly threw his weight the other way and the chair tilted past its zenith and then fell sending him crashing to the floor. Instinctively he craned his neck so that his head would avoid contact with the floor. He felt the chair crack when he landed and he wriggled about on the floor and though he was still tied to the chair he had more freedom of movement with his arms. The ropes were still cutting into his wrists, but he now found he could move his hands apart. He struggled against his bonds. Then suddenly he felt himself free of the chair. Now he was able to roll onto his back and roll himself into a ball. He brought his legs up to his chest and slowly and painfully was able to bring his hands up and over his feet and now his arms were in front of him.

Struggling to get air through the hood, breathing hard, his chest rising and falling he reached behind his neck and scrabbled at the knot holding the hood. Finally, he was able to yank the hood off and take a huge gulp of air. At first the bright light temporarily blinded him and he raised his hands up to his face to shield his eyes from the light until they adjusted.

Dennis reached forward to tackle the knots around his ankles. They were too tight. Then he felt one of them give a little, just a touch, but it was enough to give him hope. The tips of his fingers were by now numb and then the knot loosened. Dennis paused and opened and closed his fingers, flexing them. Then as some feeling flowed back to his fingertips he reached forward again and attacked the knot. Suddenly it came loose and he undid the ropes around his shins. Now he was able to roll over and get to his knees and slowly stand up. He did a quick scan of his surroundings. He was obviously in the hold of the ship. There were lights at even intervals along the walls. Running the entire length of one of the walls was a metal workbench with a large vice at one end. There were also some large tool chests fixed to the wall and Dennis rushed over to them. He opened very stiff drawers. He found some chisels and picking one up he tried to position it in his hands to cut the ropes. It was no good. He dropped the chisel and continued to rummage in the chest. Then his eyes lit up when he saw the Stanley knife. He pulled it from the drawer, slid the blade out with the little switch, turned the knife and began sawing at the ropes with the very thin blade. It was slow and difficult but eventually one of the rope cords was cut and the two ends peeled away from each other. Dennis set to work on the next one. He felt the ship turn again and he had to lean into the worktop to keep his balance. Finally, his hands were free and he pulled the ropes away.

Dennis continued searching the drawers for anything he could use. In the bottom drawer were some heavy spanners. He took a heavy two foot long one out and did a couple of practice swings with it. It would be slow but very effective.

Dennis closed the drawers gently then stopped. He could hear voices and laughter. He ran to the door and listened. The voices were directly outside. Dennis ran back to the overturned chair. He grabbed the cut ropes from the floor, picked the hood up and quickly shoved it over his head, wrapped the ropes loosely around his hands and threw himself down next to the chair. Dennis heard the hand wheel on the door being turned and the heavy door creaked open. When the four men entered the compartment Dennis was writhing on the floor and groaning.

The four stopped and chuckled when they saw him. Dennis' senses were tuned and he heard the footsteps as they got closer. Somebody said something in French and Dennis could tell by the accent that the person was a negro. Someone replied to the man and there was more laughter. Then Dennis sensed someone standing over him and rough hands grabbed the boiler suit he was wearing and hauled him to his feet.

"Did you hurt yourself when you fell off your chair?" the man said in a baby voice in English, mocking the journalist.

The others chuckled. Dennis pretended to still be groggy. The man holding him was trying to steady him. Dennis suddenly launched himself forward and head butted the man in the face. As the man fell away holding a broken nose and howling with pain, Dennis ripped the hood off and lunged at the next man nearest him hoping he still had the element of surprise. This man was also caught unawares and Dennis was able to land a few punches to this man's face. Dennis ducked as a fist came at him from the side and as the arm sailed past above his head he turned and landed punches in the man's abdomen, winding him. This man collapsed to his knees unable to draw a breath. The man whose nose had been broken was slowly getting back to his feet. With his eyes watering he was unable to see clearly. Dennis readied himself to attack him again when he was suddenly grabbed from behind, his arms pinned. Whoever held him was taller, bigger and stronger and though Dennis wriggled he was held easily. The black man with the broken nose shook his head and snorted blood and snot on the floor. Then focusing his eyes on Dennis, he bared his teeth, bellowed and rushed at the journalist. Dennis was able to push against the man holding him and he jumped up while still being pinioned. He kicked the man with the broken nose in the chest which sent him crashing away and in the same instant Dennis threw his head back and butted the man holding him in the face. This man released his grip and as Dennis fought out of the way a fist from the fourth man crashed into his temple. Dennis saw stars and he groped for the work bench. His fingers found the heavy spanner and he grabbed it, turned and swung it into the face of this man. He sank to the floor without a sound. The big man that had been holding him let out a bellow of rage and at rushed Dennis. The first two punches were swung wildly with both arms and Dennis was able to easily duck under them. He hammered his fists into the man's ribs and met solid muscle. The big man roared with rage and brought a foot up and kicked Dennis in the chest. Winded, Dennis fell against the work top. The large spanner was where he'd dropped it and his fingers closed around the handle. The big man hammered blows at Dennis with huge fists. The journalist instinctively brought the spanner up just in time with both hands to deflect the blows. Dennis heard the crunch as flesh and blood connected with the inch thick heavy steel. The man turned his knuckles towards himself and stared in disbelief at his shattered fingers. Dennis calmly took a step forward and brought the spanner up in both hands in an uppercut and connected it with the man's jaw. The big man grunted and fell onto his back. Dennis let the spanner clang to the floor. He took a few gulps of air, leaning on the work bench. The first man he'd headbutted with the broken nose was trying to get to his knees and Dennis slid over to him and crashed his fist into the side of the man's head. The man went out. Dennis got up and surveyed the scene.

The four crewmen were prone on the floor. Three appeared to be unconscious, completely out cold. The fourth, the big man, was still moaning and groaning, though he didn't appear to be with it. His eyes were open but distant.

Dennis took off the boiler suit he was wearing and wiped the sweat from his brow before throwing it to the floor. He quickly searched the men's pockets for mobile phones. There weren't any. He picked up the heavy two-foot-long adjustable spanner and dashed over to the watertight door. He checked that the coast was clear and stepped out into the corridor. He pulled the heavy watertight door behind him and closed it and began winding the hand wheel until it clicked. Then he placed the heavy spanner between the hand wheel and the door and pulled with all his strength until the hand wheel began to move. Dennis paused to get his breath. He then filled his lungs with air and held his breath and gave another supreme effort. Then just as spots appeared in front of his eyes and he thought he would pass out he felt the wheel move away from the door as the thread was stripped. He put a foot up against the door and snatched at the spanner and suddenly the hand wheel came spinning off. It clattered on the steel corridor floor and Dennis kicked it to one side. He dropped the spanner with a clang and flexed his hands from the pain of having used all his strength. The muscles in his forearms were aching. He looked at his ribs and saw fresh blood on the T-shirt. He'd opened the cut from the razor wire.

Dennis moved along the corridor to the next hold. There was another door with a hand wheel and he put his ear against it and listened. There was no sound from within. The ship lurched again violently and as he was thrown against the door and held on to the hand wheel, he realised that they must be at sea and the ship was in a storm. He looked along the corridor and saw that it was leaning at quite an angle, then righted and tilted the other way.

Dennis grabbed the door wheel with both hands and began turning it. It turned easier than he thought it would. He pushed the door in slowly and peered around it. This compartment was exactly the same as the one he'd been held in except there was no work bench or tool chests. In the middle of the floor space was a figure lying on the floor, wearing a hood, still tied to a chair. The figure appeared to be lifeless. Dennis rushed over and knelt next to the person.

"Jim," he called quietly.

The figure stirred.

"Pete is that you?"

"Yes. Stay still."

Dennis untied the rope around Hutchinson's neck that kept the hood on. Hutchinson had a large purple bruise on his forehead.

"Did those bastards do this to you?"

"I hit my head when I fell off the chair. I don't think there was anyone here with me. I'm not sure. It felt like the ship swerved or something. I don't know. I think I blacked out for a moment or two."

"Yeah, I think we're at sea Jim. They got me too. Someone hit me with something. Knocked me out. I got four of them, next door. They were going to rough me up. I've managed to lock them in and break the door lock but how long for I don't know."

Dennis had already undone Hutchinson's wrists and together they were untying the American's feet.

"Can you stand?"

"I think so."

Dennis helped his friend to stand and held him against the pitching of the ship.

"Sorry," Hutchinson said, "I'm a bit groggy."

Dennis examined the older man's forehead.

"That's quite a bump you've got there."

"Did you say you thought we were at sea?"

"Yeah. That would explain the pitching and rolling. It feels like there may be a storm. I don't know how far down in the ship we are, but it feels like a big one."

"They happen sometimes in the Mediterranean. Big storms. They can suddenly blow up from nowhere and disappear just as quickly."

"Yeah, I know. Listen, if you're up to it Jim I think we'd better try and get off this ship. Storm or no storm."

"Good idea."

Then Hutchinson said.

"Thanks for coming to get me Pete."

"Don't mention it."

"How did you know where they'd taken me?"

"I followed them."

"To where?"

"Naples."

"I see. And Nat?"

"Back in Rome with De Luca. Say, I don't suppose you have your mobile with you."

"Sorry left it in the hotel room. Kind of left in a hurry."

"Yeah of course. Listen did they say what they wanted you for."

"When I answered the door of the hotel room and they burst in they turned the place over. They were looking for the journal that belonged to Von Brest. They called me Dennis twice. I realised straight away that they'd got the wrong room number, that the journal was next door, and they'd got the rooms mixed up. I didn't tell them because I didn't want you or Nat in danger. I told them the police had it. I thought they'd just rough me up a bit and leave. I was shocked that they took me hostage. Do we still have the journal?"

"Forget about the book Jim. We just need to concentrate on getting off this ship. Are you ready?"

Dennis helped the American until he could stand unaided.

"Where is this ship heading anyhow?"

"Don't know. We need to go Jim. Now. Come on this way."

Dennis grabbed Hutchinson's hand and together they ran for the door, through it and into the corridor. As they passed the hold Dennis had been held in they could hear hammering on the door.

"We haven't got much time," Dennis said rushing along the corridor.

"What's that noise about?"

"I already told you. They were holding me the same as you. I overpowered four of them and broke the door lock when I left. That compartment was full of tools and it probably won't take them long to break out. We must hurry."

Dennis led the American on and on, always climbing flights of stairs. They paused at a corner for Hutchinson to catch his breath.

"How much further?"

"Shouldn't be far. I think we were being held in the very bottom of the ship."

They were both thrown sideways as the ship lurched again. Much harder this time."

159

"Damn Pete. This must be one hell of a storm."

"We need to find some life jackets or a lifeboat or something."

"Do you think any of these guys are armed?"

"I don't know Jim. All I've seen are the ones who brought you here and crew members who work the ship. Oh and there was a red head, beautiful, don't know who she was. She left in a helicopter back in port."

"That is interesting. Have you seen Von Werner?"

"No."

"Maybe he's not aboard. Come to think of it nobody has seen him in Italy so far, have they?"

"Not as far as I know. Now are you ready to move?"

"Right behind you friend."

They burst out onto the main deck and stopped and stared. Rain lashed at them hard stinging their faces. They both grabbed a handrail to steady themselves as forty-foot waves battered the ship's hull. Lightning streaked across the sky lighting their faces up for a moment.

"This storm's bigger than I thought," Dennis shouted over the howling wind.

They both hung on as the ship's deck rose and fell. One moment the bridge was a hundred feet above them. The next it was fifty feet below. The large stacks of containers rumbled and shook with terrifying force.

"Bloody hell!" Hutchinson said, "I thought the ship was going over then."

The Ocean Breeze heeled and lurched thirty degrees to starboard then shuddered as she righted. Then as the ship rose again Dennis saw the freefall lifeboat attached to the stern.

"Come on!"

Dennis grabbed Hutchinson's hand again.

"That's our way off!"

Slipping and sliding on the wet deck they groped their way past the Heli-pad to the lifeboat.

"How the hell does this thing work?" Hutchinson asked.

"I think we get in it and it launches."

"Let's go then."

Hutchinson rushed around the front of the lifeboat looking for a way in. A large man in a boiler suit punched him in the face which sent him sprawling. Dennis saw Hutchinson crash to the deck. Then he recognised the supervisor who had hit him before. The man wore a sickly grin. He had the large adjustable spanner in his right hand and he slapped his left palm with it in a threatening gesture. Dennis searched around frantically for anything he could use in the fight to come. The man grinned and came on. Hutchinson, on the floor, kicked out with his feet entangling the man's legs who stumbled and dropped the spanner. The ship suddenly lurched and the man was thrown over the stern. He clung on desperately while trying to change his grip. Dennis walked to the rails and stared down into the terrified eyes. He watched impassively as the man struggled for a few moments then the supervisor's grip failed and he plunged seventy feet into the sea. Dennis turned for Hutchinson and helped him to his feet and they both looked at each other as the sound of an intermittent siren sounded over the pitching deck, accompanied by red flashing lights.

"What is that?" Hutchinson asked.

"Either the ship is in danger or we've been discovered," Dennis nodded towards the bridge, "and I think it may be us."

The unmistakeable figure of Von Werner in his white suit appeared at the railing surrounding the bridge. Petrov in black military fatigues was with him and Dennis saw the Dragonuv sniper rifle cradled in the man's arms.

"Fuck!" Dennis said, "Come with me."

He picked up the dropped adjustable wrench and he and Hutchinson moved away from the lifeboat and slipped in amongst the containers.

Von Werner had a megaphone in his hand and he raised it to his lips. Dennis and Hutchinson stopped as the voice carried across the deck.

"Mr Dennis! I assume it's you Mr Dennis. You can give yourselves up."

Dennis wasn't listening. He was trying to break the seal on a container.

"Very well you had your chance," the voice came to him through the containers.

"Uh Pete! You better take a look at this."

Dennis let go of the handle on the container's door and moved to see what Hutchinson was pointing at.

"Allow me to introduce Gennady Borodinoff."

Dennis watched with wide eyes as a heavily armoured man moved slowly down the stairs towards them armed with a sidearm, grenades and a SPAS-12 assault shotgun. The man was covered from head to toe in armour. On his head night vision goggles and a Kevlar helmet.

"Pete what the fuck are we going to do?"

The only weapon they had was the spanner. Dennis got into a position where he could see Petrov clearly. The sniper seemed to be able to keep his balance despite the pitching of the ship. A single shot ricocheted off the container inches from Dennis' face. Dennis flinched away into cover. He looked up at the single container he was next to reading the labels on the side.

"Jim! Quick! Give me a hand to get this open."

"Pete he's getting really close."

Dennis peered through the gap again just in time to see Borodinoff pump the shotgun one handed to cock it. Dennis smashed down on the seal locking the container. It pinged away and he pulled the double handles to open one door.

"Give yourself up Dennis!" Borodinoff shouted.

Dennis helped Hutchinson open the other door. Borodinoff could now see them and he fired his shotgun just over their heads.

"Jesus!" Dennis shouted.

They swung the other door open just as Petrov got to them. The ship suddenly lurched again as they dived for cover. Two cages containing dozens of gas cylinders tumbled out. They burst across the deck taking Borodinoff off his feet. Dennis and Hutchinson each holding onto a container door until the ship righted, then leaned the other way. The door Dennis was holding onto banged shut and he bounced off it and went down amongst the gas canisters. They bounced and plinked around him. Hutchinson still hanging on felt the container move further than it had before and he dropped down and rolled away from it and came to his knees.

Dennis was back on his feet swaying with the motion of the ship. Borodinoff, weighed down by his heavy armour was much slower in getting up. Dennis picked up a barbecue sized gas canister and drew his arm back and threw it at Borodinoff. It hit the Russian in the head and the man was forced back down to one knee.

The ship lurched again.

"Pete that container's loose!"

Dennis rolled himself out of the way just in the nick of time as the container rumbled past him, gaining speed. Borodinoff was slowly getting back to his feet on the slippery deck. He more felt than heard or saw the container coming, spilling its contents out as it came. He couldn't move from its path and it slammed into him taking him with it crushing him against the rails, killing him. Up by the bridge Von Werner watched in silence, his knuckles white on the rail.

Dennis went slowly to the container stepping over gas cylinders. The next time the ship lurched the container moved away from Borodinoff and his body slumped to the deck. Dennis picked up the assault shotgun and checked it for ammunition. There were six shells left.

"Uh Pete!" Hutchinson said pointing.

Dennis saw four more men running down the stairs towards them. Three of them had handguns, one was carrying a machete. The gas cylinders were still rolling around on the deck and bouncing off objects. The container was still sliding about blocking their exit. Dennis backed to the rail and peered down at the black sea, the crests of the waves churned white by the storm. The sea was a long way below.

"Jim get ready to jump over the side."

"Over the side! Are you mad?"

"There's no other choice."

Dennis heard the four men taunting them as they came closer.

"When I say go Jim go. Ok!"

"Yeah sure. Whatever you say Pete."

Hutchinson was looking down at what he could only perceive as certain death.

"Go!" Dennis shouted, "Jim Go!"

As another shot from Petrov missed Dennis by a fraction, he pointed the shotgun around the corner of the container and fired. The first man was hit at almost point-blank range and the powerful blast from the shotgun threw him backwards, his chest blasted to a pulp. Dennis cocked and fired again and again. Hutchinson ran to the rail. Up on the gantry Petrov sighted Hutchinson and brought the crosshairs to focus on the American's head. He put his finger on the trigger and pulled it back. The container suddenly filled the scope as it once again slid across the deck in front of Hutchinson. Jim heard it coming. This time it was heading straight for him and would crush him as it had Borodinoff. Hutchinson turned, climbed the waist high railing and jumped. He landed with a heavy smack in the churning sea. His head broke the surface and he turned around to face the ship. Ten feet of the container had gone through the safety rail and was now balancing over thin air. Then twelve, then fifteen, now twenty. At twenty-five feet it began to tilt. Hutchinson began frantically kicking away from the ship, but the next waves brought him closer. The container suddenly tipped and crashed into the sea not far from him. It disappeared for a moment under the waves, then came back up, the front rising out of the water, then it righted and appeared to be staying afloat.

Dennis, now the container was gone, was fully exposed to Petrov and his sniper rifle. He turned and fired the SPAS-12 twice at the gantry. Von Werner ducked as pellets whined and smacked off the rails. Petrov hadn't moved and he calmly pulled the trigger just as Dennis turned and ran. The bullet from the Dragunov whined harmlessly into the wet deck and ricocheted away. With one cartridge left Dennis pointed the shotgun over his shoulder at the centre of the gas canisters and pulled the trigger a moment before he dived over the side. The resulting explosion shook the ship as gas canister after gas canister erupted causing a chain reaction which threw Von Werner and Petrov to the floor.

Dennis' head broke the surface of the water in time for him to see the massive fireball the explosion had caused.

"Pete! Over here."

A large wave pushed Dennis towards the container and together he and Hutchinson clung to it. An ominous creaking and groaning sound came from the ship and they watched in amazement as four stacks of containers six high leaned out over the side and then toppled into the sea one at a time.

"Fuck!" Dennis said, "Did I cause that?"

"Uh-huh," Hutchinson replied as the ship moved further away.

On the gantry by the bridge Von Werner and Petrov slowly picked themselves up. Von Werner found his small round spectacles and put them on. He brushed his white suit down with his hand, a strange smile on his lips.

"Do you want me to go after them sir?" Petrov asked, the Dragunov rifle resting across his chest.

Von Werner shook his head.

"They won't last long in that sea."

Inside he was thinking, 'I hope you do survive Mr Dennis. I hope to see you again real soon'.

He turned and went back to the bridge.

Dennis and Hutchinson were still watching the ship. Within minutes it was a quarter of a mile away. Dennis pulled himself up out of the cold water and onto the top of the container. He instantly turned, held out his hands and helped pull Hutchinson out of the sea also. Together they collapsed onto the hard steel surface.

"What a night!" Dennis said.

"Do you think this thing will stay afloat?"

"I hope so."

"What do you think is in it?"

"I don't know. Why don't we open it?"

"Ha funny!"

The rain was still lashing at them. Hutchinson turned on his side.

"Pete there are lights on the horizon."

Dennis rolled over to look. With the rising and falling of the container in the churning sea Dennis could make out the lights. One particularly large wave lifted them high enough to see more lights.

"I think it's Naples Jim."

"How far out do you think we are?"

"Don't know. Five miles. Ten. But I think we're slowly being swept in."

"Oh good," Hutchinson said, "I've always wanted to see Pompeii."

Dennis looked at him for a moment then threw back his head and roared with laughter.

"I sure could use a cold beer," Hutchinson added.

"Yeah, me too," Dennis agreed as the waves brought them closer to   land.

CHAPTER FIFTEEN

Dennis and Hutchinson woke to a chilly dawn. They had spent a cold, uncomfortable night drifting on the container in the Tyrrhenian Sea towards the city of Naples. Dennis guessed that they were a couple of miles out and he thanked their luck that they'd not drifted out to sea. A passing ship had spotted them and alerted the Italian navy who had sent a patrol boat out to pick them up.

After being given dry clothes, food and drink, they were detained under house arrest until De Luca had driven to Naples with Natalie to pick them up.

Hutchinson had slept in the car during the drive back to Rome and Dennis had told of their story.

When Sonnenburg saw them walk into his office his face split into a large grin.

"Welcome back to the Vatican," he said, "And may I say how pleased I am to see you both still in one piece," he said to Dennis and Hutchinson, "Though I see you are both sporting some nasty bruises. Have you seen a doctor?"

They both nodded.

Sonnenburg gestured towards the large screen on the wall.

"You'll be interested to know that we have received correspondence from the British military intelligence service. You will probably better know it as MI6...."

Dennis nodded.

"We are no longer working with Interpol but with respective military authorities on this matter. This means that progress may become a little slower regarding the warrant for Von Werner and his group. His acts have now been classified as terrorism and therefore will merit military intervention. I can tell you that his container ship, the one you were on, the 'Ocean breeze' was boarded by Interpol agents accompanied by Italian navy seals. Von Werner had already left the ship. It was found to only contain crew members and none of his mercenaries. Six crew members were arrested, two released and four detained. The ship itself was allowed to continue on schedule because of the itinerary of its cargo. It will be docking in Agadir in Morocco in one week."

Sonnenburg brought up images on the screen.

"Thanks to British intelligence we now have known acquaintances on five more of Von Werner's associates. For instance, this man."

"Anatoly Petrov," Hutchinson read the name on Sonnenburg's screen.

"Yes. Former Russian agent, ex-military. First gulf war. Served in Afghanistan, Kosovo, virtually anywhere the Russians have been involved in in the last twenty-five years, Petrov has been a part of it. Rose to the rank of colonel. In charge of a task force in Iraq he began working for the other side, supplying weapons to various terrorist factions. Has disappeared until now."

"Sounds like a real nasty piece of work," Hutchinson said.

Dennis leaned in closer to the screen.

"Mr Dennis, do you have something you wish to add?" Sonnenburg asked.

Dennis studied the face casting his mind back to the sniper on the Ocean breeze.

"I think he was on the ship."

"You are sure?"

"It was raining hard. It was dark and the ship was rolling and pitching but I did get a good glimpse of him for a split second. I think it was him."

Sonnenburg clicked on the next picture. This name Dennis did know.

"Gennady Borodinoff," Sonnenburg began, "Served under Petrov in Iraq. Wanted for war crimes against humanity…."

Dennis raised his hand.

"Yes."

"He was crushed by a container on the ship."

"Crushed?"

"Yes. There was a container that come adrift. It killed him."

Sonnenburg began typing on his laptop.

"We'll need confirmation of course."

The next picture showed Sergei Danilov. A red banner across the image read 'deceased'. Natalie looked into the eyes and shuddered. The next image was of a man with oriental features with very scarred cheeks. Possibly caused by acne as a child.

"This we believe is Kim Li Choi. He's North Korean, a former North Korean army lieutenant. His father is a colonel in the North

Korean army. Kim was court-martialled from the army in disgrace. His father disowned him and he was believed to have moved to Russia, became involved in drug dealing and is wanted in connection with the murders of two policemen in St Petersburg, Russia. Has a taste for fast cars, could possibly be one of our Hummer drivers."

"He was on the ship," Dennis said, "He handed a briefcase to her," Dennis added as the image of the redhead appeared next.

"We're not sure about her. Her name and details are unknown."

"She was on the ship. She left in the Dolphin helicopter with the Korean," Dennis said moving closer to the screen. He looked at the picture of the beautiful redhead getting into a black car. She was wearing dark sunglasses, but Dennis was sure it was her.

"You are sure?" Sonnenburg asked the journalist.

"Definitely. She took the briefcase and left just before they took me hostage."

"Have you any idea of what was in the briefcase?"

"Sorry."

"Where did all this intelligence originate. I mean why weren't we shown these before?" Hutchinson asked.

"I already told you we got this information from MI6. The man you captured in London Mr Dennis has decided to talk," Sonnenburg brought the man's image up on the screen. "His name is Ireneusz Stancyk. He is a Polish national. Not much is known about his background as yet. It seems the British offered him 15 years off a prison sentence if he was willing to talk, and he did."

"Ah well, I'm pleased to see that my evening of getting my arse grilled by the metropolitan police paid off."

"Where does Von Werner get his people from?" Hutchinson asked quietly.

"Physco's-r-us," Dennis offered to a stern look from Sonnenburg.

"Sorry," he said, he grimaced at Natalie who was trying to keep a straight face.

Sonnenburg chose to ignore them and turned back to his large screen on the wall. The team stayed with him for a further hour helping him with his enquiries. Then Sonnenburg put a large white envelope on his desk.

"You are booked onto a flight to London tomorrow morning at

nine o'clock. My officers will pick you up at your hotel at 7am," he extended his hand for them to shake, "I would like once again to thank you for everything that you have done to help us in this case. I am sorry that it concluded without a conviction, but we did everything we could."

Dennis shook the offered hand.

"So, is that everything then?" he asked.

"Yes."

"I'm not in trouble for anything I've done."

"No."

"I stole a motorcycle."

"It's been dealt with."

"Caused an explosion on a ship."

"Of the twenty-five containers that fell from the Ocean breeze two were recovered. The one you were on and another. The rest sank. The company or companies who own them will be insured. This is Italy Mr Dennis, not Britain. Here the criminals are in the wrong."

Sonnenburg shook Hutchinson's and Natalie's hands.

"On behalf of my government thank you for your assistance. Have a safe journey home."

The three of them sat in the departure lounge at the Leonardo Da Vinci airport waiting for their flight to Gatwick.

"I'm kinda sorry we're going home," Hutchinson said, blowing on his hot coffee.

"Yeah, me too," Dennis replied, "After all we've done in trying to help them apprehend Von Werner all we get is our marching orders."

"Well, I for one will be glad to get home," Natalie said, "My life was quiet until I met you. I was a simple marine archaeologist working in Greece...."

Dennis stared at her open mouthed.

"Then I get dragged all around Europe. Nearly killed God knows how many times. Almost raped, been shot at. Thought I'd lost you God knows how many times...."

"Are you serious?" Dennis asked.

".... Nearly been blown up," she continued.

Hutchinson chuckled.

"It's been fun though Nat hey?"

She smiled.

"Absolutely. I didn't realise just how boring my life was until I met you."

Dennis puffed up his cheeks and blew out his breath.

"Thank God for that. I wasn't sure where you were going with this."

"Has your life always been like this Pete," Hutchinson asked, "Always getting into the thick of it."

"Actually, it has."

"I'll be honest though," Hutchinson continued, "It's a shame to let them get away with what they've done and not bring the spear back with us."

"I'm sure the authorities will bring them to justice Jim," Natalie added.

"Yeah, but gee…. I'd love to have seen the spear perform its magic. You know it's said that whoever possesses the spear would be invincible."

Natalie and Dennis looked at each other and then at the American.

"We know," they said together.

Hutchinson was staring into his coffee.

"Were there any clues in that journal Pete?"

"To tell you the truth, in all the excitement of the last few days, I haven't even looked at it."

"You've still got it though."

"Yes. It's in my hand luggage."

"Can I have a look at it?"

Dennis put his rucksack on the seat next to him.

"Of course."

He got the old leather-bound journal out and unclipped the popper. Hutchinson began flicking through the pages. He paused briefly over the ones with Alexander the great's sarcophagus on them. Then moved on. He went another four pages and paused again. There were some drawings here of Chinese lions and some writing he didn't understand. He could read and speak Latin fluently but these days it was an almost dead language. Something on the next page caught his eye.

"Hm! What's this?"

Dennis turned the book slightly to see better.

"This is to do with Sir Francis Drake searching for the lost city of El Dorado."

"Now that is interesting," Hutchinson said studying the drawings.

Dennis reached across and turned the page.

"Moving on!"

"What?" Hutchinson said, "A guy can't broaden his horizons."

"Are you interested in the spear or not?"

"Of course."

"Then let's look for that. Wait a minute what's this?"

There were four different drawings of spear heads. There was a sketch of Christ on his cross being speared in the side by a Roman soldier.

"And that I presume is Longinus stabbing Christ to death."

"Looks like it," Dennis said, then his tone took on a darker note, "You know Jim there are those who say that Longinus is still alive. That he still walks the earth. His punishment to dwell neither in heaven nor hell for what he did that day."

Hutchinson looked up from the page he was studying.

"What?"

"There is a legend about Longinus which often gets confused with that of the wandering Jew."

"It's what? I'm sorry, say again."

Natalie cut in.

"it's said that as a punishment for what he did Longinus was cursed to walk the earth in perpetual immortality. The wandering Jew is of a legend about a man who taunted Christ on his way to his crucifixion and was then cursed to walk the earth until the second coming of our lord. The two stories very often get confused."

"I thought we discovered back in London that Longinus himself was beheaded."

"He was," Dennis replied, "He was beheaded in front of a king who was blind and the king's sight was restored when he was splashed by the blood of Longinus. Or so the story goes. Like we said, it's only a legend."

Hutchinson was studying the four spears again. The Schatzkammer one was the only one sketched with a shaft.

"Now this is interesting," Hutchinson said, "The Vienna spear is the only one depicted as having the shaft attached."

Dennis and Natalie both craned their necks to see.

"Do you suppose the shaft is needed. Maybe that's the missing piece of the puzzle. Maybe it's not relics at all. Would it still exist?"

Dennis saw a sign on the wall announcing free wi-fi. He picked up Hutchinson's permanently left on laptop.

"Mind if I have a look?"

"Be my guest."

Dennis got the answer in less than a minute.

"The shaft is in one of the four pillars of st Peter's church."

"Why didn't they go for it then."

"Probably they knew it would be impossible," Natalie said.

"Or without the journal you're holding they didn't even know of its existence."

"Hey. Apparently, legend has it, that another spear shaft exists in Israel or Palestine. The whereabouts is unknown."

"That's not much help," Hutchinson said studying the drawings of the spear and shaft both separate and then joined together. The joined drawing had a halo around the spear head.

"It would seem that Doctor Von Brest knew that the spear was magical only when complete and joined to the shaft, Hutchinson tapped the leather-bound journal, "That would now explain why Von Werner was desperate to get this back,"

"And kidnap you for it."

Hutchinson turned another page. The creature sketched was hideous.

"What the hell is this?"

Dennis and Natalie leaned in again for another look. The creature drawn had its hands held up to its face and was screaming. The fingers were long with long fingernails like talons. The teeth were long and pointed, sharp fangs to rip at flesh. The jaw was also long and frayed in the sketch, where the jaw ended couldn't be seen and yet, strangely, the creature was wearing what appeared to be Roman armour. There wasn't enough of the shoulders and torso drawn to verify it but the armour definitely looked to be Roman. Next to the sketch were the words 'Casca Loggius'

"Casca Loggius," Hutchinson said, "Is that the name of a place.

Like city of the dead or something."

"No," Dennis shook his head, "It's him. Longinus. Von Brest has misspelt the name. Or got it confused with someone else. These are very common names in ancient Rome."

"Longinus? Don't tell me you believe the story that he still walks the earth."

Dennis looked at the foul creature in the sketch.

"If that's anything to go by. I hope not."

Hutchinson turned the next page, glad to be rid of the foul monster. On the next page was a sketch of the church of the holy Sepulchre in Jerusalem. He flicked back a few pages to Christ on the cross, his side pierced by Longinus. Dennis was taking a swig of his coffee. Natalie had taken over the laptop and she suddenly looked up.

"I think I've found our missing link. There is a second possible location for the spear shaft," she said spinning the computer screen around for them to see.

"Where?" they both asked excitedly.

Natalie brought up a map and zoomed out slightly.

"Qumran?" Dennis asked, "Where or what is that?"

"It's the caves in Palestine where the dead sea scrolls were discovered," Hutchinson answered, "It's always been rumoured that they were linked to Christ himself. They're certainly from the same time period. The Vatican on the other hand dismisses any evidence of Christ and the scrolls though."

Natalie looked for more clues on the web page.

"Anything else?" Dennis asked.

Natalie read on. There were more clues and she read them out one at a time. Hutchinson listened intently. He continued to flick backwards and forwards between the pages of the journal.

Then he looked up.

"How sure are you that Von Werner is trying to heal himself?"

"I'm certain of it."

He flicked through one last time and then snapped the journal shut. Natalie and Dennis still had their faces shoved into the lap top screen. Hutchinson suddenly jumped to his feet.

"Give me your tickets."

They did as they were told. The American dashed off to find an official.

"What's going on?" Natalie asked.

"I Don't know."

Hutchinson was taken to a desk and a customs official came out to speak to him.

"I need to cancel these tickets." he said, "I need three tickets for the next flight to Tel Aviv."

The customs man picked up his telephone.

"Peter?" Natalie said.

"I think we're still in the game," he replied.

CHAPTER SIXTEEN

CITY OF RAFAH, SOUTHERN GAZA.

Natalie looked across at the Mediterranean Sea just four miles away and twinkling in the sunshine. It was a warm late October afternoon. The sky overhead clear. The sound of Israeli fighter jets never far away.

For the first time the team of Natalie, Dennis and Hutchinson had entered a war zone. From Rome Hutchinson had intended for the three of them to enter Israel directly but Dennis had persuaded them the easiest and best way to enter the Palestinian territories, currently closed to tourism, was through Egypt and the Rafah border crossing.

They had needed special permission to enter Gaza, as all visitors do, and during a three day stay over in Alexandria, Egypt, Hutchinson had managed to go to his office and make a phone call to a contact from the international solidarity movement for human welfare, otherwise known as the ISM, to invite them in as guests. Dennis' status as a freelance journalist helping to speed up the normally three-week waiting period process for the invite. Hutchinson had managed to arrange important archaeological permits to accompany them.

Dennis had acquired the 1994 Land Rover defender they were travelling in from someone he knew in Alexandria and the vehicle was perfect for what they needed. He had paid a fair price for it and had removed the black UN lettering from the white paint.

"Wouldn't it be better to leave those on?" Hutchinson had asked.

"No," Dennis had replied, pulling the last of the black stickers off. Their outline could still be made out as the paint around them had discoloured over the years, "Trust me they'll only draw the wrong sort of attention to us and as westerners we are targets for kidnapping as it is," he glanced at Natalie in the rear-view mirror, "It might be a good idea to get rid of your 'I love NY' hat,"

He threw her a black and white Keffiyeh, the traditional head scarf worn by Arabs, "Put that on instead."

"I thought only men wore them," she said, tying it in place.

"Some women wear them. In some countries they've become a fashionable item."

She concealed her blonde ponytail in it and caught a glimpse of her reflection in the window.

"I quite like it," she said.

"I don't understand why we couldn't have just flown into Gaza this morning," Hutchinson said as they passed a sign for the Yasser Arafat airport.

"I told you," Dennis said, "The airport was destroyed in 2001 by Israel and the other airport simply known as Gaza, two miles from the city of Khan Yunis is currently blockaded by a no-fly zone controlled by Israel. Nothing can land or take off."

"So, everything has to come in and go out this way?"

"Pretty much. Though of course there are other border crossings. One is at the other end of the strip known as Ezra and the others are Karni, Kerem Shalom and Sufi, and these are cargo terminals."

"Are they all as painfully slow as Rafah was?"

"Pretty much. Though of course a lot of it depends on the mood of the border guard on the day. It probably doesn't help that certain governments have declared the Hamas government as a terrorist organisation."

"Which governments?" Hutchinson asked, expecting the UK and US to probably be spearheading it. He wasn't surprised at the answer.

"The US and the UK," Dennis replied, "The EU, Canada, Japan and of course Israel."

"Are there any friendly nations?"

"The Arab nations, Iran, Russia and Turkey."

"And what do you think?"

"I don't get involved in politics. But I will say I've always been treated fairly by Hamas. Remember I lived and worked out here before the coup."

Hutchinson let his mind drift back to their morning's events. Crossing from Rafah in Egypt to Rafah in Palestine had been painfully slow. The city was split between the two countries with a no man's land in the centre.

They had arrived at Rafah at 9am when the border had opened. The Egyptians currently controlled the border and only allowed five to seven hundred Palestinians in and out per day. The border was only open on five days of the week. They had entered the small airport style terminal building and had handed over their passports and Egyptian permit letters. It had taken nearly an hour for these to be authenticated. Hutchinson had become frustrated by the delay and got annoyed. Dennis had sat with Natalie with his baseball cap pulled down over his eyes, presumably sleeping. Hutchinson got further annoyed at the noisy, smelly, local people around him. One small boy had decided to stand in front of the American archaeologist and stare while he picked his nose and put his fingers in his mouth. Hutchinson looked at the parents who were also staring at him. Finally, he could take no more and he shooed the child away. The parents continued to stare.

Finally, after another hour and a half their names were called out and Hutchinson jumped to his feet. They joined the queue of pedestrians and got their passports stamped with their Egyptian exit stamps. Once outside they climbed aboard the waiting coach that drove them to the Palestinian side of the Rafah crossing. They had left the coach and entered the building. Hutchinson had stopped at the door to look back as Natalie went on in.

"Congratulations," Dennis patted him on the back, "You've just left Egypt. Welcome to Palestine."

"To tell you the truth Pete. It's a lot scarier than I thought it was going to be. Are we going to be alright?"

"Trust me. I lived here for four years."

"Only four?" Hutchinson asked. He couldn't imagine surviving four weeks.

"Yeah, I covered the Gaza war in December 2008."

"The Gaza war? What was that?"

"It was a three-week conflict between Israel and Palestinian militants."

"What was it about?"

"Palestinian militants were firing rockets into southern Israel and hitting civilian targets. Israel responded with operation 'cast lead'. They attacked police stations, military targets and political and administrative institutions. On January 3rd, 2009, Israel began a ground invasion. A UN mission headed by Richard Goldstone accused both sides of crimes against humanity and following international criticism for the growing number of casualties, Israel withdrew on January 21st."

"How many were killed Pete?"

Dennis had covered the story and the figures had shocked him.

"Thirteen Israelis."

"Is that all? How many Palestinians?"

"Over fourteen hundred."

A policeman standing nearby overheard their conversation and he now turned and stared in their direction.

"Listen we'd better shut up. No more politics from now on okay. They're a bit touchy about it."

"A bit?"

"Very then."

They caught up to Natalie who was at a table having her luggage searched.

"What were you two talking about over there?" She'd seen the policeman's scowl.

"Don't ask."

Natalie watched as the border guard took a long time in rummaging through her underwear, too long for her liking. She reached towards her personal items but froze as he barked at her in Arabic and shook his head at her.

"What is he looking for?" she asked Dennis.

"Restricted items. Alcohol and pornography mainly."

"That's just great, isn't it?" Hutchinson whispered into the journalist's ear, "We're being checked by a terrorist organisation. Shouldn't it be the other way round."

Dennis rounded on him.

"Jim. From now on you really need to be very careful with what you say. Believe me you don't want to get arrested for making political statements out here. Your government would be unable to help and you're making me really nervous."

Finally, the guard finished with Natalie's hold-all and he grinned at her as she took it back. He jerked his thumb at her towards another table where another customs man waited to ask her routine questions about her visit. She bit her lip at the obscenity that she wanted to shout at him and went to the next table. The first guard watching her bottom in her jeans as she walked away. Dennis and Hutchinson were processed in turn and then finally the three of them stepped outside. Their land rover was waiting for them, itself having received a thorough going over. Hutchinson had brought along some cases that had fragile archaeological artefacts on them and he was annoyed to see that they'd been opened also. He checked the contents and then resealed them.

"What are they?" Dennis had asked back in Alexandria before they had left.

"You just never know when they'll come in handy," was the reply.

Now the three of them were heading back into the city of Rafah.

"So, who is this guy we're going to see?" Hutchinson asked.

"His name is Khalil Al Massri. He's a sort of a friend, kind of an old acquaintance," Dennis replied.

"And is he the reason you wanted twenty thousand dollars in cash?"

"Yes."

"And er! What does he do?"

Dennis put an indicator on and pulled the defender to the side of the road.

"He's a smuggler and arms dealer."

Hutchinson rolled his eyes and focused on the ceiling.

"I thought so."

Dennis knew Hutchinson was always touchy on the subject of guns. Natalie was staring at Dennis in the rear-view mirror.

"Look we're going to need to arm ourselves out here. I've already said that the fact that we are westerners puts us at risk of kidnapping. Also, if we're right about Von Werner coming here, well, you've seen his private army of military contractors, I don't think we'll get away with it next time. Remember Naples?"

Dennis knew Hutchinson wouldn't be happy but to the journalist's surprise the American said.

"Will he have a good selection?"

Dennis grinned.

"We'll have to see what he's got."

"What do you mean smuggle?" Natalie asked, "Smuggle what?"

"Food mainly. But anything he can get his hands on. Ninety per cent of what you can buy here in shops has been smuggled into Gaza in one form or another."

"Smuggled from where?"

"Egypt mainly. Some does get through from Israel but not much. In Rafah, which is where I'm taking us now, there are smugglers

179

tunnels that go deep into Egypt. Everything is brought in through them."

"Including weapons?"

"Yeah probably. Though they'd never admit it."

"What if the government found out?"

Dennis raised his eyebrows at her.

"Oh, I see. They already know."

A police car going in the opposite direction slowed to almost a stop as it passed them. All three officers in the car were staring at them. Dennis glanced across at them.

"You see, we're already drawing attention to ourselves."

The next time he looked over the driver appeared to be getting ready to perform a U-turn in the road and come over to them. Dennis quickly put the defender into first gear and re-joined the road.

Thirty minutes later Dennis turned off this road and began heading towards the Egyptian border again. The tarmac road ended and turned to sand; terrain more suited to the land rover. Ahead they could see the beginnings of ruined buildings, houses, huge mounds of earth, large earth moving vehicles and the tarpaulins of makeshift camps.

"Where the hell are we now?" Hutchinson said.

"It looks like a building site," Natalie added.

"More like a refugee camp," Hutchinson put in.

"You're both wrong," Dennis said stopping the land rover next to a man in a green khaki army uniform and carrying an AK-47 Kalashnikov. Dennis wound his window down and greeted the man who looked through the windows at Dennis' companions. He and Dennis exchanged a few sentences in Arabic then the armed man nodded and stepped back. Dennis did his window up and then turned to Natalie and Hutchinson.

"Welcome to the smuggling capital of Gaza."

They drove on past buildings several storeys high, some just ruined hulks of masonry, many exposing the scars of bullet holes and fire damage, others, amazingly looked finished, complete with doors and windows. Ahead was a tall guard tower proudly displaying the Palestinian flag.

"There are over twelve hundred tunnels here," Dennis said as they drove past row upon row of tents, "The tunnels burrow under the border and into Egypt. The Egyptian government has, since 2009, been trying to close them but they're fighting a losing battle. For everyone they are able to destroy another ten open up. They are mainly under the tents and tarpaulins. Some are under the floors of houses. There are also loads of them out under those olive groves over there."

Natalie and Hutchinson were amazed at what they saw as they drove through what was clearly a huge well organised, precise, operation, on a massive scale.

They passed a black Mitsubishi warrior pick-up truck filled with police.

"Uh Pete," Hutchinson said, pointing out the officers.

"Relax. This is state sanctioned smuggling. There is nothing secretive about what goes on here. Every one of the smugglers pays a tax to Hamas to keep his tunnel open."

"It's absolutely unbelievable," Hutchinson said.

"It's a fight for survival. For some it's their only way of life. On average three a week are killed by Israeli or Egyptian attacks or just tunnel collapses."

"Why do they do it?"

"For them the money is good. A successful smuggler can earn twenty-five dollars per day. Without the risks they take and the smuggling Gaza would die."

Dennis brought the land rover to a halt by a large block of houses with armed guards with machine guns patrolling outside. A large dog ran up and started barking at Dennis as he got slowly out of the vehicle. The dog ran off in the opposite direction. Natalie and Jim joined him. The guards were watching the three. Dennis waved at one of them and the man put his hand up in response, his manner not unfriendly. Dennis took the briefcase containing the cash from Hutchinson.

"Stay close to me," Dennis said to his companions. He could see that Natalie was nervous, but she smiled at him and followed a few paces behind. Hutchinson couldn't take his eyes off a boy of about eight years old who was running around playing a game with other boys while brandishing a handgun.

"Jesus," Hutchinson said, "I hope that thing isn't loaded."

To his relief it wasn't. He watched as the boy caught another about the same age and pinned him against the wall, levelled the gun at the other boy's head and pulled the trigger. The gun was then lowered and handed to the other boy who now became the 'you're it' as the game of tag continued and the children ran off laughing.

Dennis greeted the armed men at the door, exchanging pleasantries with them before he was allowed in. The three of them were quickly patted down for concealed weapons while one man watched. Dennis opened the case briefly to show the guards what was inside and he was allowed to pass. Natalie and Hutchinson followed him in. The man who had watched leading the way.

The interior of the large house was plain, the walls whitewashed. They passed many rooms that had beds in them. They climbed a flight of stairs. There were two armed guards at the top and they moved out of the way, their faces stony. They turned a corner and entered a large lounge, the entire floor space of the first floor. There were huge French doors that led out onto a large balcony and patio area. Armed guards paced up and down the well-furnished patio.

A large rug covered the centre of the lounge floor, on it a large coffee table. Three large sofas filled the room, large enough to seat five people each. There were only three sitting though. Two men sitting opposite each other were smoking cigarettes. On the sofa with its back to the French doors sat a huge man wearing a red beret and British army woodland camouflage. His eyes were concealed by a very expensive pair of ray ban sunglasses. The lower part of his face was concealed by a huge bushy black beard with flecks of grey in it. In front of this man, on the coffee table, was an AK-74M Kalashnikov assault rifle equipped with a GP30 40mm grenade launcher attached.

All conversation on the sofas stopped as the three visitors approached. The two men facing each didn't move. They both wore ammunition belts around their waists and both had handguns within easy reach in holsters on the hips. One sat casually with his arm draped over the back of a sofa and he nodded at Dennis and grinned at Natalie exposing a mouth of gold teeth.

The big man in the camouflage suddenly jumped to his feet and strode around the table to greet Dennis.

Dennis spoke first, aware of the certain etiquette required.

"Salaam Alaykum," he said using the Arabic greeting.

Khalil Al Massri towered over Dennis.

"Salaam," the big man replied using the lesser greeting. Then he looked to Dennis' companions and smiled at them both.

"This is Natalie Feltham and Jim Hutchinson," Dennis said introducing them.

"Salaam," Hutchinson greeted Al Massri.

"Salaam."

Natalie not understanding the etiquette involved just said.

"Hi."

Al Massri flashed her his strong white teeth. He was keen to find out what Dennis wanted but he put this aside to continue the Arab custom of welcoming someone into his home.

"Would you care for some mint tea?"

"Yes, thank you," Dennis answered for them all.

Al Massri spoke rapidly to a man lurking by the door who nodded and left to make the sweet tea that should never be refused when offered. The two men on the sofas were dismissed and they got up and moved to an opposite wall each and stood with arms folded and watched. Al Massri had decided to wait for the tea to arrive before getting down to business. He invited the visitors to sit, taking his sofa to himself.

"So, tell me my friend. How long has it been?"

"Almost three years," Dennis replied.

Al Massri nodded slowly, casting his mind back.

"Perhaps I should explain," Dennis said to his companions. Natalie focused on him. Hutchinson couldn't take his eyes off the machine gun on the coffee table. Hutchinson had worked in hostile countries for most of his life, had often worked huge archaeological sites that required armed guards but had never been so close to a weapon like this. A weapon that could cause so much death and destruction.

"I mentioned to you both before that I reported on the three-week war between Palestine and Israel. I was working here and based in Rafah where I was staying. I was here with a film crew and Kim Nguyen. You remember her from London?"

"I remember her," Natalie said.

"I had been covering the war for its first week when I was contacted, or should I say, invited by Khalil to meet with his faction. At the time we had no idea as to what they wanted only that they wanted to talk to us. What they wanted to say we didn't know either. They gave us no clue. So, we met them not knowing if we were being led into a trap. When we did finally meet in an obscure location, they told us of their story. That they were a military faction that Khalil had founded. They had been active since early 2002 and were funded by a much larger group. They wanted to tell us about themselves which I documented without names or locations. Each of them wore balaclavas every time the cameras were on. Khalil's group were responsible for rocket attacks and strikes against Israel. They even took us on a mission which we didn't film."

Al Massri said something in Arabic and Dennis replied.

"Khalil said that what I've told you so far is sufficient and that you do not need to know more."

Natalie and Hutchinson both nodded at the man in camouflage. The sweet mint tea arrived, served traditionally in the little clear glasses. The friends each took one from the tray offered. Al Massri took his last. Natalie never having tried the drink before sipped it. Though incredibly sweet it was very refreshing.

"You like?" Al Massri asked.

"Yes. Thank you," she replied.

He nodded and smiled, then his attention turned to Dennis.

"Now perhaps you are ready to tell me why you have arranged to visit me."

Dennis reached down by his feet, brought the briefcase up and rested it on his lap, entered the codes for the locks, opened the case towards himself, put it on the table and spun it around to face Al Massri who's eyes widened.

"There is twenty thousand American dollars there. We would very much like to buy some guns."

Al Massri reached forward and picked up a banded wad of notes.

"It's all in used fifty's," Dennis said, "Almost impossible to trace."

"Do you need any documents? Passports? Permits?"

"No, I've already taken care of that," Dennis said trying to avoid Hutchinson's questioning stare, "Do we have a deal?"

Al Massri grinned at the journalist.

"We have a deal. What type of weapons would you like?"

Dennis looked at his travelling companions then back at the Arab.

"What have you got?"

Al Massri got up and picked the Kalashnikov up from the coffee table.

"If you are ready."

Natalie quickly finished her mint tea. Dennis left some of his. He closed the briefcase and took it from the table and offered it to Al Massri who took it and gave it to one of his bodyguards.

"The price of weapons has increased greatly since the three-week war. Do you wish to spend all twenty thousand?"

"Whatever it takes," Dennis replied.

"Where are we going?" Natalie asked. She instantly regretted her slip of manners.

"You wanted to buy weapons. I don't keep them here. Don't worry it's just a short walk."

They stepped back out into the warm sunshine. A small girl of about six was playing near the steps that led into the house. She had a naked Barbie doll that was missing one arm and a plastic Russian fighter jet. Al Massri stopped to talk to one of his men and Natalie went over closer to the little girl who was holding the doll up and flying the jet fighter at the dolls head and veering the plane away at the last moment accompanied with the sound of machine gun fire coming from the little girl's mouth. The child continued to play her game as she looked up into Natalie's eyes.

"Hello," Natalie said, "You're pretty."

No reply.

The little girl flew the plane in once more.

"Your dolly is very pretty. What is her name?"

No answer.

Al Massri turned to look in their direction.

"My name is Natalie," she pointed at her chest, "Natalie."

Still nothing from the child.

"She doesn't speak," Al Massri volunteered.

"No," Natalie said, looking from the bearded man to the child.

"No. Her name is Fatima," he said, "She is....," he made a swirling motion with his finger to his temple, "She is.... I don't know the English," he struggled, "She hasn't spoken since her parents were killed in front of her."

"Traumatised," Dennis corrected him.

"Yes. This is it. Trauma….as you said."

"Traumatised."

"Her family were killed?" Natalie asked.

"Yes, in an air strike on her family's house. She was pulled from the rubble. She spent two days with her father laying across her. His head was crushed and his brain had come out of his head."

Natalie brought her hand up to her mouth. Hutchinson was shaking his head. Dennis remained impassive. During his time in the middle east, he had seen far worse.

"You poor thing," Natalie said, taking her hand away again. She turned to Al Massri again.

"Can I give her a gift?"

He waved his hand expansively.

"Yes."

Natalie reached around behind her neck and undid the small clasp on the heart shaped pendant and gold chain she always wore. She put it around the little girl's neck and let the pendant down gently onto the little chest. Fatima dropped her toys and reached up and held the pendant in her fingers, twisting it this way and that.

"There you are. A pretty necklace for a very pretty little girl." Suddenly the child dropped the gold heart and she threw herself forward and hugged Natalie tightly. Natalie put her arms around the tiny back and held Fatima equally, her eyes closed. Then the little girl released her grip and smiled at the beautiful woman.

Al Massri watched on.

"There are many thousands of children here in Gaza just like her."

He nodded at one of his men who moved to the child.

"Come on little one," he said, "Let's get you away from the house."

The child followed him towards where she lived on a small makeshift bed under a large tarpaulin.

"We took her to an orphanage, but she came back. She seems to like it here. She can stay, where she will grow up to hate my country's enemies."

Natalie re-joined them. Tears were running down her face. Al Massri finished talking to his man then led them on. Hutchinson was still puzzled at something Dennis had said in the house. He caught up to the journalist and grabbed his arm to slow him down.

Al Massri, unaware, moved further on ahead flanked by his bodyguards.

"Pete, I don't like this one bit. Are you sure we can trust him."

"He can be trusted. He would give his life for what he believes in."

"What didn't he want us to know when he stopped you from explaining any more about him?"

"His group has used torture on its enemies. Torture and suicide bombings."

Hutchinson could only imagine the horror.

"I'll be honest Pete. I'm petrified of him; of the power he holds." Hutchinson had watched as Al Massri had walked up the road with his machine gun slung carelessly over his shoulder and people had called out to him.

"What was that about not needing passports. Already taken care of. How are we going to get guns through Israel and into the west bank?"

Dennis knew that the time had come. He reached into his jeans back pocket and pulled out three passports, opened them one at a time and handed one to Hutchinson who looked at the writing on the front.

"These are Australian?"

Dennis nodded and pointed at his girlfriend.

"Meet the new head of the British red cross in Palestine. Miss Natalie Feltham."

"What?"

"Natalie is travelling under her own name but now she is a top aid worker with the red cross."

Hutchinson couldn't believe his ears. He knew he wasn't going to like the next answer.

"And we are?" he asked looking at his own photograph in his forged passport.

"We are private military contractors or PMC's as they're known for short. We are working for an Australian security company called utility resources group. We are based in Dubai. We're her bodyguards and because I speak Arabic, I am also her interpreter."

Hutchinson was speechless. Dennis knew his plan was brilliant. Finally, Hutchinson asked.

"How were you able to arrange this without us getting wind of it?"

Before Dennis was able to answer the American said.

"That afternoon in Alexandria, when Natalie said she wasn't feeling well and you said you had business and were gone all afternoon. You did it then didn't you."

Hutchinson suddenly saw red.

"You're going to get us fucking killed!"

Dennis grabbed his arm and pulled him in close.

"Do you want to keep your voice down," Dennis said looking anxiously at Al Massri.

The bearded man had heard and had stopped and was now facing back in their direction.

"Is everything alright."

Natalie had almost caught up to Al Massri and she looked back, shielding her eyes from the bright sun.

"Yeah fine!" Dennis yelled back.

"For fuck's sake don't do this now Jim."

"I wish you'd include me in everything Pete."

"I didn't want to tell you back in Egypt in case you reacted as you just have. I didn't want you to pull out."

"We probably should."

"No way. We are in way deep. Remember the spear. That's what we've come after. Don't forget that."

"I haven't forgotten and I'm not going to quit. From now on I want to be included in everything okay. No more secrets."

Dennis shook Hutchinson's hand.

"From now on. I promise."

Al Massri was still watching them.

"It's alright!" Dennis shouted, "We're just discussing the deal."

He waved to show all was alright. Al Massri glanced at Natalie.

"I can't stop thinking about that poor child," she said.

"There are thousands like her."

"I expect Israel has just as many."

She hadn't meant to say it out loud and she cursed the slip. She saw Al Massri's face flush with anger.

"I'm sorry I meant no disrespect."

His voice was flinty and cruel.

"Do you know how many children have died because of Israel?

188

Tens of thousands," he said before giving Natalie a chance to answer. "Do you know how much land Israel has stolen from my country since 1948. Or how many refugees have been created? Over one million people have been driven from their homes, their lands, their livelihoods. My own grandfather used to work in Israel, for thirty years he worked there. Then one day he was kicked out and a wall was built. He died a poor, broken man...."

"I'm sorry. Please forget what I said."

Al Massri knew the girl would never understand. He felt some of the anger leave him.

"Because this is your first time here and you are ignorant of our problems you are forgiven."

Dennis and Hutchinson re-joined them. Dennis saw the look on his girlfriend's face.

"Everything alright?" he asked.

"I was just telling your friend about the conditions in the refugee camps here in Palestine."

"Horrible places," Dennis agreed.

Al Massri ordered them onward. After a few minutes more they approached a large, covered area. It was swarming with men wearing a variety of camouflage, some green, some desert, some mixed, green jackets and desert trousers or the other way round. More than once, Dennis saw an American or British flag on a sleeve. Every man here wore a black balaclava that completely covered their face, leaving only eyes and noses exposed. Some wore, on their foreheads, green banners with white Arabic writing. Each man wore a military tactical assault vest over their jacket that held large knives, handguns, flashlights, spare ammunition and grenades. All carried AK-47's. Three carried RPGs slung across their backs. They all greeted Al Massri as a group.

"Jesus Pete. These guys look serious."

"You'd better believe it," Dennis moved closer to Natalie and said in a low voice so as not to be heard, "You went pale earlier. What did he say to you?"

"He was saying about how his people have suffered and I just said I'm sure Israel has too."

Dennis winced.

"I didn't mean anything by it. Just that there are two sides to every story and that surely Israel has one to tell also. Doesn't it?"

"Yes, it does," Dennis made sure both Natalie and Hutchinson could hear him, "I warned you both to be careful about what you say. People have died for less. Remember we're only alive still because he respects the work I did here. Offend him and he'll have our throats cut as soon as look at us."

"I thought you said he was a kind of friend," Hutchinson added. Dennis shook his head.

"His religion does not allow it. He will trade with us because trade is for the good of all but that's as far as it goes. We cannot be friends; it is not permitted. I think it would be best from now on if you only asked relevant questions about the guns. Okay? Leave the talking to me."

Al Massri led them in under the large canopy, which was a dozen tarpaulins tied together. There was a large square table in the centre and a man was opening boxes of communications equipment and inspecting it. It was hot under cover and Dennis felt the sweat trickling down his back. The air was thin and a constant trail of dust drifted past. Al Massri threw out his arms.

"What do you want?"

"We need a machine gun each, sidearms, vests...." Dennis looked Hutchinson up and down, "He needs clothes. Do you want a sidearm?" he asked Natalie. She shrugged. "Give her a sidearm. Oh and we'll want some thigh holsters. Flashlights. Let me think a minute. We brought some food with us. We'll think about provisions in a minute. Let's start with weapons."

Al Massri grabbed a crowbar and began opening some crates.

"For assault rifles we have AR-15's, FN FAL's, AK's...."

"AR-15," Dennis said, "Give us two of those."

Al Massri took two of the American machine guns out of the crate and threw one to Dennis and one to Hutchinson, who hefted it in his hand.

"Not too heavy," he said, "Is it a good weapon?"

"Very," Dennis replied.

"Extra ammunition?" Al Massri asked.

"What do they come with?"

"One clip each of thirty rounds in an extended mag."

"We'll take two hundred rounds each."

Al Massri nodded at one of his men to sort the extra ammunition.

"Sidearms?"

"Something easy to use."

Al Massri threw a gun over. Dennis caught it and turned it over in his hand.

"Sig-pro! Nice," he said inspecting the German-Swiss made handgun, "These are used by police forces around the world."

He tossed it to Hutchinson who passed it from hand to hand.

"Nice and light," the American said. He handed it on to Natalie who looked at it and went to hand it straight back.

"It's yours," Dennis said to her," I suggest you tuck it into the waistband of your jeans so you can get to it easily."

She did as she was told. The feel of it was reassuring to her.

"We'll have thigh holsters for ours."

Al Massri sorted two out. Dennis attached his to his jeans straight away. He stopped Hutchinson from doing his.

"Hang on Jim. We're going to sort your attire out."

"RPG's?" Al Massri asked.

"No," Dennis answered. His t-shirt was now completely soaked from the heat under the tarpaulins. "We could do with some flashlights though. The type that clip onto combat jackets."

Al Massri sought out three.

"What else do you want?"

"I don't know. Are we still in budget?"

"Still in budget?" Hutchinson said, "That was twenty grand."

"I told you prices have gone up. Before 2008 an AK-47 was less than a thousand, now they're probably two. Plus, the percentage Hamas takes for itself."

"Grenades?" Al Massri asked.

Dennis looked at his companions, then at the bearded man.

"No," then a thought struck him, "Have you got any trackers?"

"Personal trackers? Of course."

"Magnetic ones?"

"All types. What do you want to track? People? Vehicles?"

"Probably both."

Al Massri spoke to the man sitting at the table. He was still opening small boxes. He hadn't spoken since they'd got there. Now he beckoned Dennis over. He opened a box and took two personal trackers, the size of a large cigarette lighter, out and activated them. He handed one to Dennis and the other to

Hutchinson.

"One more," Dennis said.

The man nodded and opened another box. There was a brief discussion between himself and Al Massri. The faction leader had the final word and the man shrugged.

"They come in pairs. I told him to let you have the other one so now you have a spare."

"I'm sure it will come in very handy," Hutchinson thanked him.

"So how do we track ourselves?" Dennis asked.

"The signals can be picked up by computers, laptops and smart phones."

The man handing out the trackers gave Dennis the codes for each personal tracker. Dennis found it on his I-phone and was impressed to see a red dot appear on the GPS map on his screen.

"It's working?" Al Massri asked.

They each checked with their phones. Each had a red dot.

"You had better turn them off again," Al Massri ordered," I hope Israel is not already picking up the signals."

"I wouldn't have thought so," Dennis replied.

"Let us hope not."

"Do you want us to switch our phones off now."

"It might be better if you did."

Al Massri felt a little more relaxed once their phones were off. He should have insisted when they'd first arrived.

"Now," he said, "A weapon for the woman."

"AK-47," Dennis said instantly, "Something lightweight, easy to use."

Al Massri selected one and tossed it to Dennis who caught it mid-air.

"This is a great weapon," he said, "Designed in 1949 by the Russian general with the same name. Mikhail Kalashnikov. Still being used around the globe. Over 75 million rifles built. Weighs a little over ten pounds. Doesn't freeze or stick in any condition. Even if you get sand in it."

He took the AK-47 and handed it to Natalie. To her the weapon felt heavy and cumbersome but she took it and held it across her waist.

"Are you okay with it?"

"Yeah, I'll be fine," she answered, already getting used to the weight of the gun.

"You could have it without the stock, but I think it's better for you with it. It'll be easier to control."

"Is that everything?"

"We need a couple of those vests your men are wearing, but not new ones. They'd stand out. We need to look like we've been doing this for a long time."

While Al Massri went to sort out the vests, Hutchinson spoke to Dennis, while keeping his voice low.

"Pete, I don't think I can do this."

"Of course, you can."

Dennis looked at his friend. Hutchinson, despite the weapons, the handgun and the thigh holster, still looked like an academic.

"We just need to make you look the part."

Dennis reached forward and removed Hutchinson's spectacles.

"Hey! I need those for reading."

"How bad is your eyesight?"

"I can see fine. I need them to be able to read at a distance."

Dennis spun around, looking for something for Hutchinson to focus on.

"Can you see that six-wheeler lorry over there being loaded?"

"Yes of course I can."

"Can you see what it says on the driver's door?"

"I can see it. I can't read what it says. It's too far away. I'd need my glasses for that."

"But you can see."

"Yes. I can see as far as the horizon allows. I just need glasses for reading."

"That's good enough."

Dennis put the spectacles in the older man's shirt pocket. Then he reached up and ruffled the older man's hair. Hutchinson took a step back.

"Pete!" he said reaching a hand up to smooth his hair over again. Dennis grabbed the hand to stop him.

"Don't! Trust me! You look better like that. More rugged."

Hutchinson looked to Natalie for approval. She nodded.

"I like the look, Jim."

"Really?" he asked, convinced he looked like a senior citizen yob.

"Really," she affirmed.

Dennis took a step back and looked Hutchinson's attire up and down.

"Khalil. Have you got any cargo style trousers and possibly a denim style shirt? Oh and two keffiyehs. I'd better wear one too."

Fifteen minutes later and Hutchinson was looking more like a private contractor. His clothes were now casual, more military like.

"Hold the gun across your chest like this. Gun muzzle pointing down. Finger on the trigger. That's it just there. Hold that pose."

"That's quite a transformation," Natalie said, "Wow. You do actually look the part."

"Yeah, you do," Dennis agreed. "Just try to look tough all the time."

Hutchinson took a stance which made Natalie laugh.

"No don't raise your eyebrows," she chuckled, "Try to look serious. That's it. You've got it."

"I must admit," Hutchinson said, "I do now feel that I can pull this off."

"Good," Dennis said, "Just a bit of confidence is all that is needed. Now we just need to see if you can shoot. Khalil! A few practice rounds."

The big man nodded. He took a handful of extra ammunition clips and once again led the way.

"I must say," Hutchinson said as he and Natalie walked alongside Dennis, "That you have a really good knowledge of guns. Are you also a good shot?"

"I have a small confession to make."

'What is he going to come out with now' Natalie was thinking.

"You know when I told you and the metropolitan police that I did some training with the SAS," he looked at them both for confirmation, "I lied. I learned to shoot with these guys."

"What?" Hutchinson said, "You mean you were one of them. A terrorist."

"Will you stop using that word around here," Dennis said glancing nervously about, "They prefer the term 'freedom fighter."

"Freedom fighter. Terrorist. Isn't that the same thing?"

"That depends on which side you're on."

Natalie was genuinely interested.

"What did you do?" she asked.

"I went out with them on a few nights. Only as an observer though. I want you to know and understand that. I didn't have any weapons, nor did I engage in anything other than report their story. We didn't use cameras. I was only permitted to use a Dictaphone."

"Did you take Kim whatshername with you?"

"No. It was too dangerous for her. Just me and my cameraman Greg. We went out onto the beach here at Rafah. I should explain that the entire beach area here though used by Palestinians for leisure is also a no-go area. Israel has a blockade on the entire coast. Khalil's group took me out on more than one occasion and they set booby traps on the beaches for any unsuspecting Israeli marines that come ashore. On some nights if they weren't triggered, we would go out and reset them elsewhere."

Hutchinson was horrified.

"Did they kill anyone?"

"Not in the time I was there. I went out with them every night for a week."

"Doesn't that make you a terrorist as well?" Hutchinson asked.

"In the eyes of Israel maybe, or maybe our own governments, but at the end of the day I'm a journalist and I will do what is needed to get my story out."

"I suppose so," the American said.

Natalie just smiled at Dennis. She had gotten to understand with him that the story always came first. No matter the risks.

"Come on," Dennis said, "Let's see if either of you can shoot a gun."

Khalil Al Massri led them to an area away from the main road where there were sandbags piled higher than a man. Here, driven into the ground were wooden posts on top of which were targets. Some were roughly drawn outlines of people. Others just circles painted with a bullseye. Dennis was up first and he took aim with his AR-15 and splattered the body of a drawn target with a clip of bullets. He then let his machine gun drop to his chest, held by the straps, and pulled out the Sig-pro handgun from his thigh holster and holding it with both hands he emptied a clip into the target's head.

Al Massri watched on, a little impressed.

"I see you have forgotten nothing," he said as Dennis holstered the handgun.

"It's just like riding a bike."

"You," Al Massri gestured at Hutchinson.

The American stepped up to where Dennis had stood. He raised the AR-15 to shoulder height, sighted down it and fired. He wasn't prepared for the powerful kick it produced and it caused him to miss the target. Small puffs of sand erupted from the sandbags. Hutchinson stopped firing. Al Massri moved to him and put a hand on the gun.

"Hold it here like this. Tighter. That's it. In closer to your shoulder. That's better. Now sight down the barrel, line up with the sight at the tip. Now fire."

The first bullet hit the target in the shoulder.

"Aim a bit lower, to the left. That's it. Fire."

Hutchinson hit the target in the chest.

"Good," Al Massri said, "That would kill your opponent. Try again."

This time Hutchinson hit the target easily. He emptied the clip into the chest. Then when the bullets ran out he turned to his companions with a big, beaming grin.

"Your sidearm," Dennis said.

"Oh yeah right."

Hutchinson reached down for the Sig-pro, brought it up and in his haste shot the target in the throat.

"Ouch," Dennis said, "That would do the trick."

Hutchinson aimed higher with both hands and emptied the gun into the targets face.

"Nasty," Dennis said, a little impressed.

"You," Al Massri said to Natalie.

Natalie stomped up to where the other two had stood, leaned her AK-47 over at an angle, flicked the safety switch to semi-automatic fire, levelled the gun at waist height and fired single shots at the target. Every bullet found its mark. Then she flicked the safety to auto, raised the gun to shoulder height and emptied the rest of the clip into the wooden target. She then lowered the gun again and turned to Dennis who was watching her open mouthed.

"Any good?" she asked.

Dennis got up and approached the target, still open mouthed. He examined the bullet holes she'd made then turned to look at her.

"Where the hell did you learn to shoot like that?"

"Believe it or not I do listen to what you say."

"Yeah, but even so," Dennis looked back at the target.

Then Natalie laughed. Then he laughed. He grabbed her around the waist and pulled her close.

"Seriously baby. Watching you fire that gun was fucking hot!"

He was about to snog her when he remembered that Al Massri and his men were present and that such an outward show of affection in public would not be appreciated. Then he was letting go of her and they all spun around and everyone was looking up into the sky as a Hercules transporter plane roared past very low. On its wings were red crosses but there was no mistaking the death's head skull on the tail. The plane was descending and obviously heading for the ruined airport.

"Hey Pete, I thought you said nothing was allowed in or out. That nothing could land," Hutchinson said.

"That's right. Nothing can."

"Well, someone, somewhere, has obviously got clearance."

Dennis watched as the plane banked and then dropped more height and disappeared behind buildings and tarpaulins. Then, Dennis was running for the Land Rover.

"Come on!" he shouted at Natalie and Hutchinson, "Let's go."

CHAPTER SEVENTEEN

Dennis opened the driver's door of the Land Rover and jumped in. He thrust the key into the ignition, started the engine, slammed the door shut, selected first gear, released the parking brake and swung the vehicle round in a wide arc. Stones and dust were kicked up from the tyres. Dennis roared up to where Natalie and Hutchinson were. He jumped out and grabbed the equipment Al Massri was carrying. He shook the big man's hand.

"Thank you."

Al Massri nodded at his men to load the Land Rover with everything they'd bought.

"Military vests, two hundred rounds each, handguns, spare bullets, trackers, three automatic assault rifles."

"Where are you going?" Al Massri asked Dennis.

"The people in that plane are searching for something that is very dear to us. We would very much like to get to it first."

"Is that the reason for the guns?"

"Yes. They have tried to kill us on more than one occasion."

"Where are you headed?"

"We think Galilee."

"Are you going to enter Israel?"

"We must. There is no other choice."

Al Massri moved away from the Land Rover.

"I wish you luck."

"Thank you. Ma Salama. Goodbye."

"Ma Salama."

"Better keep the weapons out of sight," Dennis said to his companions. He engaged first gear and the defender roared away.

"We didn't get any extra food," Hutchinson shouted above the noise.

"We should have some left," Dennis shouted back.

Natalie leaned over the back seat and rummaged through the items they'd brought in from Egypt.

"We've still got some cheese, chocolate, water, some biscuits. That bread we bought is going hard though."

"It'll be enough. Might just need it for a night. If all goes well, we'll be in Israel tonight or tomorrow."

"And where are we going now?"

"Look that plane should not have landed here. Nothing can and if Israeli forces didn't shoot it down then it must have permission to land. And if that's the case I want to know why and what they're doing here."

"And we're going to just drive straight in there are we?"

"No. I'm going to see if I can get a tracker on that plane."

"That is precisely what I was worried you were going to say."

Natalie, Dennis and Hutchinson watched the activity around the Hercules from a distant vantage point. Behind them was Rafah. It was growing dark and Dennis glanced at his watch again. Natalie was starting to shiver at the cool evening air.

Dennis was laying on his front while peering through a pair of binoculars. He had watched as netted pallets of cargo had been unloaded and reloaded into the large belly of the transporter by a forklift truck. There were currently pallets and crates scattered nearby as the forklift driver sorted them.

The Hercules was stopped on the smooth desert terrain where cones marked a landing strip. The badly damaged runways had long since gone, ripped up many years before by civilians who, after the airport was destroyed in 2001 by Israel, had used the tarmac and foundations for building materials elsewhere in Rafah.

The three had been watching the activity for some hours now. The only visitor had been a large black Mercedes saloon flying Palestinian flags from its front wings. Men in suits with short stubby machine guns had got out of the car along with another man in a suit who had appeared to be unarmed. Then as Dennis had watched, the stunning redhead he had seen on the ocean breeze and the unmistakeable figure of Von Werner had descended from the open ramp at the back of the Hercules. The redhead moved to stand by him.

Dennis watched as they'd conversed for several minutes and then Von Werner surrounded by his armed men had handed over a large briefcase, clearly payment for something.

The two men had shaken hands. Then the man from the Mercedes shook the hand of the redhead, turned and had gotten back into the saloon which sped away.

Now Dennis focused on the tall redhead. She was clearly saying something to Von Werner, then together, they turned and he placed an arm around her shoulder as they headed for the severely wrecked airport buildings.

Dennis watched for a further few minutes as the forklift truck continued to drive crates up the ramp into the back of the Hercules. He counted all the men on the ground with guns. There appeared to be twelve in all. Then he saw Petrov standing with two others. The Russian appeared to be giving orders. Then he too headed for the buildings. Dennis had seen enough. He scrambled back to where Natalie and Hutchinson waited, crouching by a large rock.

"I'm going down there."

"How did I know you were going to say that?" Hutchinson said.

"You don't think it's too dangerous?" Natalie asked, knowing he wouldn't.

"If I can get a tracker on one of those crates we can find out where they're going. Then all we need to do is follow. They'll lead us straight to where they hope the spear will work. Maybe we could even collect the bounty on Von Werner."

"Or get killed in the process," Hutchinson put in.

"I'll be fine. I'm just going to plant a tracker and I'll be out."

"Okay. We'll be watching," Hutchinson said, "The first sign of trouble and I want you out of there."

"No worries. I'm going to take the AK-47. Maybe I can pass as a local if I'm seen. They'd probably shoot first and ask questions later, but I've got to try."

Dennis kissed Natalie on the lips.

"Wish me luck."

"Good luck."

Dennis checked that the Kalashnikov was loaded, put it over his back, wrapped his keffiyeh around his head and covered all but his eyes with it. He gave his companions a cheery wave and set off towards the destroyed airport.

To begin with he moved fast because there was no cover. Once he stopped and ducked behind rocks as vehicles rumbled past him. He looked back to where he'd left Natalie and Hutchinson. He couldn't see them in the failing light, but he knew they'd still be watching his every move.

Dennis had a quick check around him then moved off again. He kept low, almost running over double. Natalie feeling the cold now got up from her crouching position, her joints stiff.

"I'm going to get something warm to put on," she said, remembering she had an extra hoodie in the land rover.

"Okay," Hutchinson said, not taking his eyes away from the binoculars.

She got back to the land rover and opened the rear door. She rummaged around on the back seat until she found her hooded top and put it over her head. She pulled it down her face and stopped.

A convoy of army lorries was heading towards her, their headlights ablaze. She instinctively ducked down out of sight as they thundered past the white land rover. She was able to see out of the back window that there were four of them. Their drivers paid no heed to the parked vehicle. Natalie waited until they'd disappeared from sight before getting back out of the Land Rover. She ran back to Hutchinson.

"Jim did you see the trucks?"

"Yes. Did you see what was in them?"

"No."

"Shit," he said, watching Dennis through the binoculars, "I hope they're not heading in Pete's direction."

Dennis had made it undetected to the first of the ruined airport buildings. These concrete structures showed the scars of battle. There were no windows left intact and the walls were peppered with bullet and shell holes. Von Werner's armed sentries patrolled nonchalantly as the forklift continued to bring crates down from the Hercules. Dennis watched and waited for an opportunity to break his cover and as soon as he saw two of the guards meet with their backs to him, he made his move. He dashed across the open ground and the now sand runway and slid into cover behind some crates. He resisted the urge to cough at the dust he'd kicked up and stole a quick peek around his cover. The forklift driver was continuing with his work, completely unawares. The two sentries were now walking away from each other.

Now for the first time Dennis looked at the crate he was hiding behind. It had red crosses on white backgrounds stamped all over it.

'What the fuck is Von Werner up to?' Dennis asked himself.

From where he was laying with the binoculars Hutchinson could see two men approaching where Dennis was crouching.

"Shit Pete! Get out of there," he said out loud.

Natalie looked on anxiously.

Dennis moved to the end of the crate to see if there was anything else stamped on it to give away its contents. He heard the voices of the two men approaching and stole a quick glance. He shot his head back behind the crate. Two men carrying machine guns across their chests were fifty metres away. Dennis reached down to his thigh and unclipped the holster around his leg and pulled out his Sig-pro handgun. He would have to take the two of them out with one shot each if he was discovered. He pressed the gun against his face and readied. He peered around the crate again. The two men were almost on top of him and he couldn't believe in the half-light that they hadn't seen him. Then suddenly they were spinning around as the four army trucks rumbled onto the sand runway. The two men began walking back the way they'd come. Dennis was now able to lean out to watch. He took his attention off the two men as he saw Von Werner and the redhead come out of the building and stand side by side. The lead truck stopped in front of them and the passenger door opened and a man in camouflage jumped out. He strode up to Von Werner and the two shook hands. The man then shook hands with the redhead. They appeared to be discussing something then Von Werner led the man in camouflage to a nearby crate. Von Werner clicked his fingers at one of his men who came forward with a crowbar and prised the lid off the crate. The man in camouflage reached in and took out an AK-12 assault rifle. He held it up, pulled out and replaced the magazine, flicked the safety switch and sighted down the gun and fired a few practice bullets. Then, pleased, he put it back in the crate. He shook hands with Von Werner again then turned and gave an order. His men jumped out of the four trucks and began loading the crates into the backs of the lorries. One man approached the trio carrying something in his arms. The man in camouflage took it from him and presented it to Von Werner. From where Dennis was watching he couldn't see what was being offered. Von Werner appeared to unwrap something and the redhead moved forward to examine whatever it was. She gave her approval and now Von Werner completely uncovered it and held it in both hands examining it. Dennis still couldn't see what it was. It appeared to be a large, long stick or pole or something similar in nature. Dennis fished around in his pockets until he found his mobile phone. He selected Hutchinson's number and rang it.

Still laying on his front with the binoculars Hutchinson found his phone and answered it.

"Jim!" Dennis called in a loud whisper.

"Yes Pete."

"Are you still watching and seeing this?"

"Yeah."

"What has Von Werner been handed?"

"It's a wooden pole or something. It doesn't look to be anything special. It's quite ordinary sort of.... Holy shit Pete! I think it's the shaft of a spear."

"A spear..." then the realisation of what he was witnessing sunk in, "Hey! Do you think it's a Roman spear shaft?"

"Could be," Hutchinson replied, "You mean like the shaft of Longinus' spear."

These words hit home for Dennis.

"Yeah, could be," then the doubt set in, "No it can't be can it? What would someone, a terrorist, soldier, mercenary, or whatever he is be doing with such a relic here in Palestine. No, it can't be."

"Well, it seems pretty important."

"Yeah, important enough for Von Werner to be paying in brand new Kalashnikov AK-12's. Those things only came out this year."

"Yeah, I saw that.... Shit Pete look out!"

A shadow fell across Dennis. He turned and was able to roll out of the way just in time as a machine gun butt crashed into the crate where his head had been a moment before. He kicked out with his legs and this made the other man stumble long enough for Dennis to get to his feet. He wasn't quick enough and the other man was on him, grabbing him by the throat and pulling him close. The grip was death like and Dennis was already struggling to breathe. The man was mocking Dennis in a language that was guttural, the teeth bared. It sounded Russian to the journalist's ears. Dennis brought his hands together and chopped at the man's pressure points by the side of the neck, but he met tough, heavy, Kevlar. It numbed his hands. Incredibly the man squeezed Dennis' throat harder and he felt his face go red. He wriggled and fought and scrabbled at the man's clothing. His opponent was heavily armed and armoured. Dennis' fingers found a handgun but in the fight he couldn't free it from the holster across the man's chest. Then his fingers brushed against the handle of a large, very sharp, combat knife. Dennis managed to unclip the knife and pull it out. The other man head butted him hard twice in the face while still choking him. Dennis felt the knife slip from his fingers and fall to the desert floor. He now felt his face turning purple and he began to cough. Frantically he searched with his fingertips for anything he could use against his assailant. Then his fingers found grenades on the man's combat vest and he felt a ring pull. His fingers entered the ring and he pulled the pin out and held it up to the man's face. The Russian let Dennis go who groped away drawing his first breath in over a minute. The man was frantically patting his equipment over, looking for the live grenade. Dennis jumped up and drop kicked the man who staggered back half a dozen steps. Dennis threw himself face first into the sand and covered his head with his hands as the Russian shouted something and then exploded. A smoking boot landed next to Dennis' head and he opened his eyes and moved his hands away from his head. Where the Russian had been there was now a large black mark on the sand and the entire area was soaked in blood. Large lumps of meat were raining down around the journalist. Dennis heard voices shouting and he turned and saw men running towards him with guns ready.

"Fuck!"

Dennis took the AK-47 from his shoulders, slung it round in front of him and loosed off a volley at the approaching men. He hit one who went down flat on his face which sent other men diving for cover. Dennis ducked back behind a pallet and continued to lean out and fire random bursts. He changed mags and leaned out again. The men he was firing at were moving up on his position, drawing closer. In the background he saw Von Werner and the redhead running for the Hercules, its engines now running.

"We have been compromised!" Von Werner shouted at the man in camouflage as he and the redhead raced past and ran up the ramp and into the Hercules. The man in camouflage watched them go then turned, drew his handgun and began walking slowly after his men.

Every time Dennis leaned out from cover to fire the Kalashnikov he was alarmed to see his enemies had moved even closer. He fired another burst at a man who was trying to flank him. The man was hit in the legs and went down groaning and holding his knees. Dennis sent another burst and the Ak-47 suddenly stopped firing. He pulled the trigger again but now there was only a click. He took the magazine out. He was out of bullets.

"Damn!"

He slung the Kalashnikov over his back and took out the Sig-pro again. He leaned out of cover and shot one man straight in the face. The man went down without a sound, a look of surprise on his face. Bullets now sprayed the pallet of crates Dennis was crouching behind. He waited until they stopped, leaned out and hit another man four times in the chest. This man went down also. Dennis turned to his right and shot another man who was trying to flank him dead. Something heavy landed in the sand near him and he saw it was a grenade and instinctively dived out of its way. It exploded two seconds later so close it caused ringing in his ears. For a second, he was stunned and he shook his head not yet knowing if he was hurt or not. He fired the Sig-pro again and again but missed his targets. Then this gun stopped also and Dennis knew he was out of bullets and that he was now living the last few moments of his life. He looked at the Sig-pro and pursed his lips, accepting his fate. He looked on as the men advancing on him had stopped running and were now walking slowly towards him, their weapons trained on him, calling out, taunting and jeering him. Dennis saw the man in camouflage at the back of his men, fury written all over his face. The forklift had picked up the last pallet and was now heading for the loading ramp of the Hercules, Von Werner at the top of the ramp still shouting orders.

Dennis had resigned himself to his fate and was now stood with a smirk on his face as the two men closest to him began instructing him to drop to his knees with his hands on his head. Slowly he sank to the sand. One man let his machine gun fall to his waist by its straps and drew a vicious looking hunting knife, his mouth grinning. He spun suddenly in surprise and died under the wheels of the land rover defender being driven by Hutchinson. The second man turned with his machine gun to fire at the vehicle just as it collided with him with force and threw his body twenty yards away, the sand staining red with his blood. The other men pursuing Dennis now dropped to one knee and began firing at the land rover. Natalie threw open the rear passenger door while ducking from the bullets splattering the bodywork.

"Peter get in!" she shouted.

Dennis jumped up and sprinted to the land rover. Hutchinson sped away as Dennis dived through the door. Hutchinson ran two more men down as others dived out of his way.

The Hercules was now moving slowly along the sand runway, the ramp slowly raising. Von Werner's men running after it and jumping in one at a time. Dennis picked up an AR-15 from the back of the defender, pointed it out of the window and killed three of the men in camouflage.

"Catch up to that plane," Dennis shouted.

"You got it," Hutchinson said, looking into the rear-view mirror at the gunmen now being left behind.

The land rover was gaining on the Hercules which was now also gaining speed.

"What are you going to do?" Hutchinson asked.

"I didn't get a chance to get that tracker on board. Try and catch up to it before that ramp fully closes."

"I'm on it!" Hutchinson yelled above the noise of the screaming land rover engine.

The Hercules was now approaching take off speed and Hutchinson pushed the land rover to its limits. Dennis climbed over into the front passenger seat and got a magnetic tracker ready. Hutchinson was directly behind the Hercules now as it kicked up a cloud of dust from its wheels.

"Whatever you're going to do you'd better hurry," the American said looking at the speedometer which was hovering over the sixty miles per hour mark, "I don't think this thing can go any faster."

Dennis opened the passenger door and began to climb out.

"Pete! What the fuck are you doing?"

"Just get me closer."

Dennis was holding onto the door, his feet still inside the vehicle, the ground beneath him whipping by in a blur. The land rover hit a bump and he was nearly thrown out. Hutchinson grappled with the steering wheel and brought the vehicle back to his control. Dennis readied the tracker by switching it on. He waited for the optimum moment to throw, then drew back his arm and launched it. For a brief moment Dennis thought it would miss. The ramp was almost closed and he saw with relief as the tracker entered the space between the ramp and the fuselage and disappear from view just as the ramp fully closed. Dennis climbed back into the defender and slammed the door shut.

"It's in!" he shouted, "I just hope no one saw it."

The small tracker had shot through the small gap left as the ramp was closing. It had struck one of the six pallets that had been loaded and had bounced off and settled underneath another pallet.

Hutchinson brought the land rover to a stop and Dennis searched for the tracker on his I-phone. The Hercules got up to take off speed and lifted off the desert. It took a minute and Dennis shouted excitedly as a red dot appeared on the smart phone's screen.

"We've got them," he said, watching as the Hercules was climbing into the evening sky.

Hutchinson looked into the rear-view mirror. Men were running up the runway towards them. Dennis turned and looked out of the back window. He saw the running men and behind them the four army lorries turning and heading towards them. The gunmen running alongside and jumping up into them as they passed.

"We'd better get out of here," Dennis said, "There's a place in the city we can hide. I'll show you the way."

CHAPTER EIGHTEEN

The land rover bumped and jarred its way along the road across the desert. For once Natalie was at the wheel. Dennis was riding shotgun with her and Hutchinson was trying to have a short nap on the back seat.

They had spent an uncomfortable night in the land rover in an area of abandoned factories that were derelict to the north of the Gaza strip. Dennis had gone out alone armed with a screwdriver and had returned over an hour later with two number plates he'd stolen from a car parked in a residential area of the nearest town.

"What are they for?" Hutchinson had asked as the Englishman had set to work removing the front plate from the defender.

"In case our number was taken and reported," he'd replied.

"Do you think it will be?"

He shook his head.

"No, I don't think so. I'm ninety nine percent sure Von Werner was in Gaza illegally and whoever he was supplying guns to certainly isn't going to complain and if they did, they'd have to complain to Hamas who would almost certainly confiscate everything and jail them or worse."

"And how are we going to explain the bullet holes?"

Dennis stopped to scratch his head with the Philips screwdriver.

"It was like it when we bought it."

"And do you think we'll get away with that?"

"I hope so," Dennis had replied.

They had woken to a chilly morning and stiff necks and after a small breakfast of now rapidly hardening bread and cheese they had moved onto the border crossing at Erez. They had been allowed into Israel without any difficulty. Something that had surprised Dennis. It had actually been too easy.

"What are you complaining about?" Hutchinson had asked once they'd cleared customs, "Maybe lady luck is going to start running in our favour."

"No," Dennis had replied, "It's not luck. It's never that easy to get in or out of this country. It's almost as if it was a set up."

Dennis had been expecting Mossad, the Israeli national intelligence agency, and the whole of the Israeli military to come crashing down on them at any moment.

"Well, we're here now," Hutchinson had said, "Just need to find where that tracker is."

The small tracker Dennis had thrown into the back of the Hercules was still transmitting, giving its position sixty miles from their current location. Dennis tried to bring the map on his phone up bigger. Then the tracker stopped moving.

"It's stopped," he told them.

Hutchinson suddenly jumped up from the back seat. He'd been unable to doze and was fully awake.

"Where is it?" he asked excitedly.

"Just getting a fix on its location."

It took a couple of minutes for the position to lock, then Dennis confirmed.

"The tracker is currently in the southern Hebron mountains."

"Just north of Bethlehem?" Hutchinson asked.

"Yes. Why, do you know it?"

"I think so. Or at least I hope so. There's an old crusader castle up there built on the ruins of one of Herod's palaces. It was once thought to contain a very important tomb, believed by the knights templars to have been the final resting place of the Messiah himself, Jesus Christ."

"Why the bloody hell haven't you mentioned it before?" Dennis asked.

"Why? Because it's just a myth. An easily disproved myth. Learned scholars will tell you that Christ was buried in Jerusalem Pete!"

"Well, it looks like Von Werner may have heard of your myth too. Though there's no mention of it in Von Brest's journal, and why a crusader castle. That doesn't make sense."

"The crusader's often built castles over ancient sites to protect their identity."

"Oh boys," Natalie said, "I think we've got company."

Dennis and Hutchinson looked out of the windscreen at the Mitsubishi Pajero that was broadside, blocking the road. One man in Arab dress was frantically waving them down while another had his back to them and was working away under the raised bonnet.

"Shall I go round them?" Natalie asked.

Dennis looked into his mirror. The road behind was empty. The road ahead beyond the Pajero he couldn't see. The vehicle was blocking the view.

"Shall I go round," Natalie asked again.

Dennis watched the man who'd been waving start to walk towards them. He didn't appear to be in a hurry.

"Peter. Should I go round them?" Natalie asked for a third time.
Dennis unclipped the holster on his thigh and put his hand on the butt of the Sig-pro ready to draw the weapon.

"Pete something doesn't feel right here," Hutchinson said.
The Arab was almost at the defender now. He had a red keffiyeh on his head which was covering his neck and one shoulder. He was wearing large dark sunglasses and had a week's stubble on his chin.

"Please friend. Push!" he said. He gestured with his hands, "Push!"
Dennis eased his hand off his sidearm and answered in Arabic. The man gestured again for a push.

"Come on Jim. He wants a push to the side of the road."
Dennis and Hutchinson got slowly out of the defender. The man who'd asked for help was walking slowly away from the pair.

"Leave the engine running," Dennis instructed his girlfriend.
They hadn't gone more than a few paces when Hutchinson nudged Dennis' arm and pointed at the Arab's feet. Dennis looked but didn't notice anything. Then he saw the British military issue boots.

'What the fuck is going on' he was thinking.
The man stopped near the Pajero.

"Push! Push!" He said in a heavy accent.

"Yeah! Push. Push." Dennis replied.
The man under the bonnet turned suddenly and pointed an Ak-47 straight at the pair.

"Hands up!" he yelled.
Dennis and Hutchinson put their hands on their heads. The other man produced an AK-47 from under his robe. He levelled it at the windscreen of the defender and strode towards Natalie. Dennis could see the terror in her eyes.

"Bastards! If you hurt, her?"

"Shut it!" the man covering them said. He took their handguns from them then told them to sit. Reluctantly they obeyed.

The other man opened the driver's door of the Land Rover.

"Step out of the vehicle please Miss."

She did as she was told. He lowered the gun.

"You can join your friends."

As she walked towards Dennis and Hutchinson, he rifled through their belongings in the Land Rover until he found what he was looking for. He climbed into the driver's seat, started the engine, and drove the defender to the Pajero and switched it off. He got out and kept the AK-47 pointing at the ground.

"If this is a carjacking it's pretty sloppy."

"Just keep quiet can you," the man covering them said, "Miss you sit there please."

"You're English," Dennis challenged him, "Would you mind telling us what the fuck is going on."

"In about thirty seconds I will mate."

He spoke into his collar and Dennis now noticed this man's gun was also pointing at the ground, no longer threatening. A low humming sound could now be heard. It got closer and louder. They could all now see a black dot in the sky that was getting bigger. It came in low, barely feet off the desert floor. As it got closer Dennis could see it was a Boeing MH6 little bird helicopter, also known as a killer egg because of its shape. Now he knew for sure who was detaining them.

"British special forces," he said to his companions.

The little bird touched down on the road and the four men who were sitting half in half out of the small helicopter stepped out and walked swiftly towards the vehicles on the road. The helicopter lifted off again almost instantly and was soon just a speck in the sky again. One man clearly in command approached ahead of his men. None of their weapons were pointing in a threatening manner. The man who'd got Natalie out of the Land Rover came forward and handed over passports. They were quickly thumbed through. The man glanced at each face as he found each photograph, comparing the likenesses. Then he nodded at the man who been under the bonnet of the Pajero. This man slung his AK-47 over his back and offered his hand to Dennis to pull the journalist up.

"Sorry about that mate."

Dennis swatted the hand away and got up. The passports were

offered.

"Mr Peter Dennis."

"Yes," Dennis replied snatching the passports.

"Those fake Australian passports are very good."

"How do you know they're fake?" Dennis asked, knowing the copies were perfect.

"Because if our intel is correct, you are Peter Dennis and Natalie Feltham, both British nationals and Jim Hutchinson of the United States. We've been tracking you since you entered and left Egypt. Mossad has been tracking you since you entered Gaza. We are with the British SAS. I'm Tosh. That there's Deano, Smithy, Tommo, Richie and the jock with the ginger goatee is Angus."

"What are your real names?"

"Those are our real names."

Dennis smirked. Then asked.

"Where did you come from. I know that little helicopter has a range of over two hundred miles but there isn't a base near here."

Tosh now smirked at Dennis.

"Like I said. We've been tracking you since you left Egypt."

"Did you say Mossad were watching us?" Hutchinson asked dusting the palms of his hands off. Natalie looked into the back of the Pajero and saw a pack of mineral water on the back seat. She opened the door and helped herself to a new bottle.

"Do you mind?" she asked the two who had been introduced as Deano and Smithy.

"Not at all darlin'," Smithy replied eyeing the beautiful archaeologist up. Dennis chose to ignore it.

"Yes, Mossad are tracking you also. They know about your meeting with Khalil Al Massri. They were watching you via satellite and were preparing to take you out with a single rocket strike. MI6 were able to convince them that you were working for us and that you were operatives in an undercover mission. Israel of course questioned your Australian passports and we were able to convince them that it was part of your cover. You should have been allowed into Israel without a hitch."

"We were," Dennis confirmed, "I knew there was something funny about that. Didn't I say it was too easy?"

"You did," Hutchinson replied.

"Well, it's bought us some time," Tosh continued, "But not

much. Israeli forces are planning to capture and arrest you anytime now."

"How did they? You? Know that we visited Al Massri."

"You were being tracked on your mobile phone signals. They now have a lock on Al Massri's position. For all we know he may be dead already. Israel is using air strikes to eliminate insurgents."

"So, I may have sealed his fate."

"Maybe mate. That's for Israel to decide. Not up to us. Britain doesn't get involved in that one, Israel's problems I mean."

"Only because they can't," Hutchinson said.

"I'm sure your government is itching to have a go though mate isn't it."

Hutchinson ignored the sarcastic comment.

"So, what do you want with us?" Dennis asked.

"The British government want the German count Otto Brest Von Werner under the terrorism act. You were leading us to him but with the impending action by Israel, MI6 has decided that we come in as an extraction team. Our mission here is to locate you, apprehend Von Werner, alive, if possible, dead if necessary and get out before we're discovered."

"Could we not just take him to the Israeli authorities for extradition?" Hutchinson asked.

Dennis looked at his friend.

"You really don't know anything about Israeli politics do you."

"We're not exactly here legally either mate," Tosh added.

"What?" Hutchinson didn't understand.

"Our presence here is not exactly known. Deano and Smithy have been out here for a couple of months now providing intel on various terrorist organisations, but we've just nipped in over the border to complete our mission."

There was a distant sound of Israeli fighter jets.

"And our helicopter was probably picked up on radar. It won't be long before they come looking for us. Let's get ready to move out. Deano, Smithy, Tommo, Richie, Pajero. Mr Dennis, Hutchinson, miss Feltham, Angus and I are in the land rover with you. Oh, and by the way," Tosh said stopping the three of them, "Sorry for scaring   you."

CHAPTER NINETEEN

The Pajero and the Land Rover had been climbing steadily into the Hebron mountains all afternoon. Captain John 'Tosh' Mackintosh of the British SAS had been receiving intel on the area from the British tri forces base in Cyprus via his wireless headset. He and his team of British special forces had flown in earlier that day by helicopter from a British warship patrolling the eastern Mediterranean.

Their mission to capture the international terrorist Count Otto Brest von Werner. To capture or kill his army of private mercenaries and to evacuate the journalist Peter Dennis and archaeologists Jim Hutchinson and Natalie Feltham before a diplomatic incident between Britain and Israel developed.

Tosh finished loading all the data he'd received into the Panasonic tough book on his knees. Then, finished, he thanked the person on the other end with whom he was in direct contact with. He turned the tough book screen towards Hutchinson and Dennis who were sitting behind him.

"Now Jim if you could help me to learn the layout of this place. Intel is a little sketchy on such an unimportant site."

"What do you want to know?"

"Whatever you remember."

"I haven't been up there since the 70's. I think it became something of a tourist attraction."

"Not anymore. Since Hamas took control tourism has been almost at zero. The only people up here are religious pilgrims. According to my people nobody has been up here in years, decades even."

"If there is anyone up there these maniacs would have killed them already."

"That's a possibility. Just be prepared that when we get in there, there may be casualties already and it may not be pretty."

"Don't worry," Dennis answered for them, "We're getting used to Von Werner's methods. We've seen what he's capable of."

"If I can remember the site exactly," Hutchinson put in "And it's been almost forty years, but the whole site sits in a large depression in the mountains but also on its own large plateau. A bit like Macchu Pichhu in Peru."

On the tough book screen was a slowly, spinning, cut away computer image of the site.

"These are the remains of a crusader castle built on top of one of Herod's lesser palaces, a palace that is relatively unknown."

"Relatively unknown?" Angus said, "It's supposed to be the final resting place of Jesus Christ."

"That's never been proved," Hutchinson said, "Never been discovered. There are over forty tombs in ancient Jerusalem along with the inscriptions for Jesus on them. The thing is Jesus Christ and his family were poor. They would not and could not have afforded to bury him in Jerusalem."

"So, are you telling us that you believe the tomb up here is the real one?" Dennis said.

"Like I said the tomb up here has the inscription for Jesus on it but it's never been proved. The templars who occupied this region opened it centuries ago and removed the contents or destroyed them. I have to tell you though that Jesus was then, as it still is, a very popular name."

"Sorry to break up the history lesson. As interesting as it surely is," Tosh said, "But I need to know what the layout is."

"Of the crusader castle there are only walls left. Centuries of earthquakes reduced it all to rubble. Most of Herod's palace is below the current land level. What the locals haven't stolen or should I say 'recycled' is now buried."

"So where is this tomb located?" Tosh asked.

"In the subterranean levels. The entrances to the subterranean levels are here, here, here, here and here. The tomb is here," Hutchinson pointed to the location on the map. "These four entrances here are flooded by an underground river at this time of year. That is they used to be. The course of the river may have changed over the decades, if it still runs that is. The entrances are three levels down. The last remaining entrance leads into a very narrow pass that men have to squeeze through. This point here ends in a deep shaft thought to be a well that the Templars either discovered or dug themselves. It is fed either by the river or an underground spring. They were just starting to investigate it when I finished working there all those years ago. I would imagine that nothing of importance in this site has ever been discovered."

"Why do you think that?"

"Because as an archaeologist I am sure I would have heard of it if it had."

The red dot on the tough book was very close now.

"It's just ahead. We'll ditch the vehicles in the next half a mile," Tosh said, "From there we'll be on foot."

They parked the vehicles off the main road and out of sight and climbed an old track that led up into the Hebron mountains. Tosh kept the pace steady enough for Hutchinson, who was twice the age of most of them, to be able to keep up.

"It's probably been decades since anyone climbed this," Natalie said looking at the scrub growing on the path.

"Maybe centuries," Dennis said, "Von Werner's people didn't come this way."

Tosh, at their head, suddenly stopped. The red dot on the tough book was just ahead.

"Just over this next rise."

Tosh motioned for everyone to get down, then he his men and Dennis crawled forward to the top of the ridge. They could all see the Hercules was parked on a long flat piece of desert near the ruins. Tosh put the tough book aside and raised his binoculars to his head. He saw two of Von Werner's men looking at something that they were holding close then he saw one of them drop whatever it was and stamp on it. The other one crushed it with his heel. Tosh looked at the tough book screen just as 'signal lost' flashed up.

"They've discovered the tracker."

Tosh continued to watch as one of them tapped the comms head set by his ear. He tried again then shook his head and waved his arms at his companion.

"They've got comms, but it looks like he's not getting an answer. Now's our chance. Deano, Smithy, you're up. Get down there. Get yourselves into position. Angus will take out the two guards once you're ready. Secure the pilots, we need them alive."

Deano and Smithy moved down the hillside keeping in cover as much as they could. They used the unloaded Hercules cargo as cover and moved into position. The two guards hadn't seen them.

Up on the hillside Angus had set up an L96 sniper rifle, favourite of the SAS. He screwed on the suppressor and adjusted the sights.

"Hold," Tosh said into his headset at the two men on the ground, "Angus take the shots."

Angus took the first of the guards out with a head shot. The other man gaped in astonishment at the suddenness of the killing then his brains too, splattered the earth.

"Both targets down," Tosh said, "No more targets. Secure the Herc."

Tosh watched as his men subdued the two pilots and zip tied their wrists and forced them to sit.

"Plane secured," Smithy said into his headset.

"Hold your ground," Tosh said, to the others he said, "Let's move."

They entered the ruins and moved slowly, using the walls as cover. Tosh and Angus leading, Natalie, Hutchinson and Dennis in the middle, Tommo and Richie bringing up the rear. They encountered a sentry and Tosh gave the signal for them to stop. He put his C8 assault rifle on his back and drew out his large hunting knife and advanced on the man slowly and silently. He grabbed the man from behind, clamping his hand over the mouth and plunged the knife into the man's neck, and pulled it free. He heard the hiss of air and knew the windpipe had been severed along with the main artery. The man would be dead in seconds. Tosh let the body to the ground gently, then crouching over it while looking around for other signs of activity he slit the throat. The man twitched in his death throes and then fell still. Natalie averted her eyes as she passed the brutal killing. She knew if she looked, she would probably be sick. She stepped around the growing pool of blood and pushed on following those in front.

They continued on and then down steps that had been cut out of the very rock. They passed through huge iron barred gates, installed years before to keep intruders out. There was a large rusting metal sign in Arabic and English explaining that it was forbidden to go beyond this point. The gates had been closed and locked with a large rusty chain and padlock which now lay on the ground, kicked into a corner.

Lights were mounted on the walls which gave off just enough to see where you were going but little else. Ahead the passage appeared dark.

They continued down getting deeper and deeper, the air smelling fetid and dank. Their way was now also lit by portable halogen floodlights presumably placed by Von Werner's men. Somewhere there would be a generator as cables snaked away into the darkness.

It was getting darker now and the SAS men turned the lights on their guns to see in the dark. Then the ground levelled out and they found themselves in a large, pillared chamber. Dennis and Hutchinson flicked on their flashlights and moved the beams around the chamber.

"Archaeologists believe that this was once Herod's armoury," Hutchinson said.

"It's pretty big," Dennis replied.

"Roughly one acre," the American said.

"Impressive. It's cut out of the solid rock, even these pillars," then the beam of Dennis' torch caught something on the wall and he went over to investigate.

"What is it, Pete?"

Hutchinson had joined him, Tosh standing just behind. Dennis shone his torch up. Gouged into and around the corner were deep scratches in the hewn rock. There were four of them. Dennis put his fingertips into them and was surprised to see that they were as deep as his entire fingernails.

"What the hell caused them?" Hutchinson asked.

"Uh Sir. You might want to take a look at this," Tommo said crouching over a body.

Tosh went over to the body. It was dry and emaciated and had been dead for many years. The eyes were gone, now just dried sunken holes in a face that was parched. The skin was so tight that the cheek bones were protruding through it. The teeth were mildewed. The throat had been ripped out. The body was twisted and deformed as if it had been broken before death. The only other flesh exposed were the hands and the skin was so tight and dry they were almost skeletal. Dennis bent down next to the body and patted dust away from the jacket. There was an embroidered patch on the left breast. The uniform was dark blue, the lettering gold.

"I guess he was the security guard," the journalist said.

"What the hell happened to him?"

Hutchinson touched the hand which began to crumble.

"I don't know. A wild animal perhaps."

"A wild animal? What is there out here that could do that to a man."

"No idea. But I hope it's long gone."

"How long do you think he's been here?" Natalie asked, "He looks like he's self-mummified."

"That self-mummification," Hutchinson replied, "Is due to the dry air down here. No moisture preserves bodies. He's been here for years, twenty, thirty. Who knows. You saw how rusty that chain at the gates was."

Dennis moved his torch.

"Look. There are more of those scratches here. On the floor and this pillar."

They followed them with the torchlight. The walls and floor were scarred with them.

"All that was done by just one animal?" Natalie asked, her fear evident.

Tosh moved closer to them.

"We need to move."

They left the armoury and descended deeper into the caverns. It became colder the further they went. Then Dennis said,

"What's that?"

"Running water," Hutchinson answered with a smile, "It runs right through these mountains. It's never been explored so we don't know the extent of it."

Suddenly there was a distant rumbling and the whole cavern shook.

"What the bloody hell was that?" Hutchinson was looking up at the cavern's ceiling.

"Earthquake?"

"No," Tosh replied, "it sounded more like an explosion."

"An explosion. Down here?"

"Come on. Let's move."

Further on, the passage became very narrow and they had to squeeze through the gap in the rock in single file. Incredibly there appeared to be light ahead, daylight. Another explosion rocked the cavern. Then the gap widened out again. Hutchinson went to the edge of a deep crevice.

"This drops down…."

He didn't get to finish what he wanted to say as another louder explosion rocked them again and Hutchinson had to cling to the wall. Dennis grabbed him to stop him going over the edge and the American's torch slipped from his grasp and fell into the crevice.

"You alright?"

"Yes. Thanks," Hutchinson replied, "Lost my bloody torch though."

They looked over the edge for it. It was falling fast into the darkness, lighting up the wall as it fell. Just as the torch disappeared from view it lit something up. Something that was white and moved. It happened so fast they were unable to see what it was but Dennis felt the hairs on the back of his neck rise. Whatever it was he was sure it had looked up at him. Hutchinson had seen it too.

"Pete! What the fuck was that?"

Dennis shook his head.

"Don't know," he flashed his own torch down there into the dark and listened. There were no sounds, no movement, nothing.

"It was nothing. Just the light playing tricks on us."

"If you two have finished playing pat-a-cake," Tosh said, "We really need to get moving."

The muzzle of a gun jammed into the SAS captain's neck. The sound of many guns being cocked filled the cavern.

"Drop your weapons," a Russian voice ordered in English.

"Shit."

"Hands up."

They were outnumbered two to one.

CHAPTER TWENTY

Poked and prodded at gunpoint the team were pushed forward into a large chamber that opened out. Daylight fell in a wide beam from high up in the ceiling. Ropes trailed down from it as men abseiled back down to the ground below. The daylight fell onto a huge stone sarcophagus in the centre of the floor. At the edge of the cavern water trickled and ran off into another deep crevice.

Count Otto Brest von Verner, still terribly scarred, paced around the stone tomb rubbing at it here and there with his hands clearing away years of dust and cobwebs.

"Ah! There you are," he shouted, stopping his pacing and beaming a smile at the group, "So good of you to join us," he continued, his manner seeming genuinely friendly.

"Those explosions were you, weren't they?" Dennis asked, as Von Werner's men stripped, he and his group of all weapons and equipment including their phones.

"It was necessary to blow a hole in the ceiling to allow the extraction of this," he gestured with his hands, "The final resting place of our saviour, the lord Jesus Christ. In a few minutes I have a helicopter coming which will winch this, the greatest treasure in history, to safety. But first there is something I must do…."

Von Werner gestured to the beautiful redhead who came forward.

"I need to heal myself of these terrible wounds. Have you met my daughter Katja?"

"Well, you know what they say. You can't choose your family." The beautiful woman looked Dennis straight in the eye.

"It must be terrible love. Having a father like that."

Katja smiled at him, ignoring his remark.

"That's very funny Mr Dennis. Very funny indeed. Always the comedian aren't you. And speaking of friends who have you brought along with you?"

"I am captain John Mackintosh of the British SAS. These are my men. Count Otto Brest von Werner you are under arrest. You are returning to the UK to stand trial…."

Von Werner held up a hand to cut him off.

"Really Captain. I doubt that very much. However, I may have a use for you. I can't say the same for your men though."

Von Werner made a gesture at Tosh's men. Petrov moved to them with a silenced handgun. Their deaths were quick and painless. Tosh kept his cold stare on Von Werner.

"You murdering bastard."

"And how many men have you murdered in your lifetime Captain?"

"That's different."

"Is it? Because you do it for queen and country. You know you and I are very much alike."

"I am nothing like you."

Dennis had had enough.

"If you're going to kill us, why don't you do us a favour and save us the bullshit and get on with it."

"Kill you Mr Dennis! Oh lord no! What would I do without you? You are the thorn in my side. You have thwarted all my plans. By the way you owe me for twenty-five containers and their contents."

Dennis patted his pockets.

"Sorry. Must have left my wallet at home."

"Very funny Mr Dennis," Von Werner held his hand out, "But I will have my grandfather's journal back."

Dennis reached into the back pocket of his jeans and took it out and lobbed it to Von Werner who caught it one handed. The sound of an approaching helicopter filled the cavern.

"Thank you. And now if you are all ready?"

Katja opened the briefcase she was holding and Von Werner reached in and took something out wrapped in the Nazi flag. He unrolled it and held up the 'spear of destiny'.

".... It's time for a miracle."

Hutchinson watched the Nazi Flag that Von Werner had dropped as it settled on the ground. Von Werner now picked up the spear shaft he'd been given at Rafah.

"There won't be a miracle," Hutchinson suddenly said, catching the German Count off guard.

"What?"

"There won't be a miracle here today. Once again, my dear Count you have got it wrong. This is not and never was the tomb of Jesus Christ."

"Of course, it is."

Dennis now shook his head.

"We have read your grandfather's journal. He makes no reference of it."

"Ah my grandfather's journal. Yes, in all the excitement I must admit I forgot to look in it. But no matter. He wasn't always correct. Now if you'll excuse me. I have healing to be done."

Von Werner placed the spear head onto the shaft and pulled it down until he felt it connect fully. Then he pushed the two metal pins into place and they locked. He laid the spear down gently on top of the sarcophagus. Then he undid and removed his trademark white jacket. Next, he rolled up the sleeves of his dark blue shirt revealing the extent of his burns. Katja handed him a small vial and he took it from her.

"From the church of Santa Croce," he offered to his audience, "You remember it don't you."

No one answered him.

"This small vial has not been opened in two thousand years. It is Christ's blood."

He un-stoppered the tiny glass bottle and raised his hands to the hole in the ceiling of the cavern.

"Lord Jesus Christ," his voice boomed over the steadily growing noise from the helicopter approaching above, "Yours was the power and glory to give forever and ever. Amen."

He tipped the vial up and allowed the contents to drip out and splash the spear head. Hutchinson, Dennis and Natalie watched on in morbid fascination. At first nothing happened then the spear appeared to change colour. The gold remained but the base metal took on a bluish tinge. Then small sparks began to dance over the head. They grew bigger and stronger. Von Werner reached down and took the spear head in his hand. The blue sparks got stronger still and began to lick at his flesh. They grew steadily over his fingers and began moving up his hand and now up his forearm. They became almost white in colour with their intensity and now Von Werner threw his head back and opened his mouth and roared with pain. Petrov rushed forward to help him, but Von Werner put a hand out to stop him.

"NO!" he roared.

The sparks had consumed his entire arm and now came from under his shirt, moving up his neck and onto his face. His roaring intensified and then suddenly there was one massive surge of energy and a blinding flash of light and he was flung through the air to land twenty feet away near the edge of the deep crevice where the water tumbled. A resounding shockwave boomed around the cavern. The spear clattered down onto the sarcophagus with a metallic ringing sound. The little blue sparks fizzled and went out.

Then everyone looked at Von Werner who was slowly getting to his feet. He ripped his shirt open. The veins in his body had turned black and were visibly throbbing just under the skin. Then as he watched they turned red and then green and back to normal.

"My God!" Hutchinson said as Von Werner's skin lost its scars and it too went back to normal.

Strange animal growling noises began rising from the crevice and filled the cavern. The men with guns began shifting about nervously. Pointing the guns around them searching for the sounds.

"Von Werner," Dennis said, "You need to step back away from the edge."

The German count was running his fingers over his new skin. He looked up at Dennis.

"What?"

"I said, you need to step away from the edge. There is something down there. Something not of this world."

Now for the first time Von Werner heard the strange animal sounds coming from the chasm. He rushed to the spear and snatched it up just as the first of the creatures reached the lip of the crevice. White hands ending in long talon like fingers reached over the edge of the gap. The fingernails like claws. Then their heads appeared, hairless with black eyes. Their mouths demon like, the teeth long and pointed. Von Werner backed away from the edge and moved closer to Dennis. More and more of the creatures came over the lip. Dennis counted over twenty of them. They moved towards the sarcophagus and spaced themselves out, snarling at the intruders. They stood crouched, ape like, their hands down by their knees. Some wore stained loincloths, grey compared to their pasty white skin. Others were wearing rags of red clothing.

They stood menacing, their upper bodies rising and falling with their laboured breathing.

"Wait! Don't shoot!" Von Werner shouted as he saw Petrov about to fire. All eyes of the creatures snapped to him.

"What the hell are they?" Von Werner asked.

"Pete! Look at the red clothing."

"They're the remains of togas," Dennis said, "Holy shit! These things were once Romans!"

The creatures remained standing where they were, low groans coming from the lips. Then there came another animal sound and still snarling they moved apart clearing a space in the middle of them. Another pair of white hands appeared over the lip and then the head appeared. This creature stopped and looked at the humans with red eyes. Then this creature also came over the lip and moved near the sarcophagus. From the way the other things moved from this one's path all who watched realised its importance to them.

"It must be their leader or whatever the hell it is," Hutchinson said.

Dennis was staring at the red eyes.

"Holy shit! It's him!"

"Who?"

"Longinus!"

"Longinus?"

"Yeah. Remember in legend he had pink eyes."

The creature was studying them. Then the red eyes fell on the spear. The creature moved to it and picked it up. Instantly the blue sparks returned and as they watched the white skin turned to flesh colour and the eyes returned to normal. The creature suddenly lunged forward but Hutchinson, the only one present who spoke Latin, suddenly moved forward.

"Is your name Longinus?" he asked in the ancient language.

The man now in front of them stopped.

"You speak the language of the emperors," he asked.

"Yes," Hutchinson said. He took a step closer to the creature. Natalie grabbed his arm but Hutchinson gaining confidence pulled her hand away. Von Werner encouraged now stepped forward as well, eager to be part of this unfolding miracle.

"You are the one called Longinus?" Hutchinson asked.

"I am Gaius Longinus. Loyal servant to the emperor Tiberius,"

Longinus answered.

"Do you know what year it is?" Hutchinson asked.

The creature stared at him puzzled. Then its eyes focused on the spear again. Hutchinson clearly forgotten.

"You have been alive for two thousand years," the American said in perfect Latin.

"I serve the empire for eternity," came the answer.

"Your empire is dead," Von Werner said, placing his hand on the spear, "It has been dead for fifteen hundred years."

Hutchinson looked puzzled at the German Count, who smiled.

"I too speak Latin. Or did you think you were the only educated man here?"

Longinus was no longer listening. He suddenly snatched the spear away from Von Werner's touch. Von Werner grabbed it and tried to pull it back, but the Roman was too strong and Von Werner was losing the fight. Petrov suddenly stepped forward.

"Enough of this," he said.

He flicked the safety off his AK-74M and fired a burst at Longinus hitting the creature in the chest. Longinus yelled and crashed to the ground.

"Petrov No!" Von Werner shouted.

The other creatures snarled and moved menacingly closer. Longinus turned over slowly on the ground and began to get up. He then said something short and swift in Latin. The creatures near the men with guns suddenly pounced. One sunk its teeth into the throat of a Russian mercenary and ripped it out. Dennis shoved Hutchinson back towards the way they'd come in. he grabbed Natalie's hand, ran forward a few paces and grabbed Katya's hand and shouted,

"RUN!"

CHAPTER TWENTY-ONE

Dennis shoved Natalie and Katja towards the narrow pass in the rocks. Hutchinson had already gone through. Katja was struggling to run in her three-inch heels and she took them off and kept them in her hand, refusing to let go of a pair of shoes that had cost her five hundred euros.

The cavern was filled with the sound of gunfire and the howls of men and the white skinned creatures that had so long ago been Roman legionaries.

As the women rushed for the gap Dennis turned to a scene of carnage. He saw one of Von Werner's men firing from the hip when one of the creatures dropped down on him from the wall above. It slashed at the man's throat with its long fingernails, then it grabbed the man's head and twisted, breaking the neck. Slowly it turned to look at Dennis with its teeth bared dripping blood. Then it was sent crashing sideways by a burst of bullets and it roared in anguish and bounced off the wall and knelt shaking its head and growling. Dennis rushed to the dead mercenary and snatched up the fallen man's Kalashnikov. He fired the AK-74M at the creature and was relieved to see that the bullets which struck it in the head appeared to kill it. With a last howl it slumped against the wall and stopped moving.

"Shoot them in the head!" he roared.

He saw one mercenary grappling with one of the monsters when the pair of them exploded. The mercenary's grenades having somehow been pulled in the struggle. A rain of blood and flesh rained down.

Von Werner was trapped near the edge of the crevice. He was between the sarcophagus and Longinus who was still holding the spear. Petrov was working his way towards his boss. He was firing a Remington 870 assault shotgun he'd taken from one of the SAS men he'd murdered. Firing from the hip he was blasting the creatures. Now he was almost on top of Longinus and he blasted him in the side. Strangely no blood came from the wound and he saw the black pellet holes heal in front of his very eyes. Longinus turned towards Petrov and roared his defiance. Petrov blasted him three more times in the chest and Longinus staggered backwards towards the edge. Petrov pumped the shotgun once more and fired again. Longinus dropped the spear and stumbled backwards into open air and fell from sight. Petrov suddenly yelled in agony as one of the white skinned monsters slashed the back of his head and neck. He turned with the shotgun and fired but the creature had already bounded away. Another creature grabbed the shotgun and yanked it out of Petrov's hands and threw it away. Petrov fumbled for his handgun and drew it and fired twice at the vile being. He hit it in the throat and it roared away clutching the wound. Then it snarled at the Russian marksman and leapt at him. It knocked the handgun out of his hand and he was able to move out of its way enough to draw out his large hunting knife. The creature leapt at him again and he drove the eight-inch blade straight into the white torso. The sharp blade slid in to the hilt. The creature howled and spat its foul saliva into Petrov's face. Then it ripped at his face with its wicked talons. Despite the pain and being almost blinded Petrov was able to pull the knife out and slash the monster's throat. It fell away clutching the gaping wound.

"I can't hold them off much longer," he yelled at Von Werner, "Save yourself Sir."

Another white skinned monster jumped at him and landed on his back knocking him to the floor. The one with the slashed throat, still horribly alive and unfazed by its injury, slashed at him and then another dived on him and Dennis watched as the three of them tore him to pieces.

Dennis shot one of them and then another in the head. They fell where they were and were still. The third bounded away before he could fire and Dennis aimed the Kalashnikov at Von Werner's head. The German Count stood slowly to his full height and stared down the barrel at certain death. Then Dennis lowered the gun.

"You need to get out of here."

Von Werner stared at him incredulously.

"You're letting me go?"

"You need to help Katja. Your daughter should not die here today in this God forsaken place. Go!"

Von Werner nodded once at Dennis then bent down and snatched up the spear. He ran towards the narrow gap in the cavern where Natalie, Hutchinson and Katja had run. Dennis fired at another creature knocking it into the wall then set off after Von

Werner. Tosh was firing single shots from a handgun while backing one step at a time towards the gap.

"You should have killed him when you had the chance. Always take the shot."

"We wouldn't have been able to take his body with us," Dennis said, "And besides we're not out of this yet and may need him."

Dennis pressed himself into the narrow gap.

"Go!" Tosh ordered, "I'm right behind you."

He followed Dennis into the neck of the gap. Tosh pulled the pins on three grenades and lobbed them back into the cavern. The resulting explosion was deafening in the narrow space as Dennis and Tosh rushed after Von Werner. They could hear the creatures rushing into the narrow gap behind them.

"Go on!" Tosh shouted. He stopped and turned back. The creatures were slowed by the narrowness of the passage and Tosh shot the first one as it appeared around the bend in the head. It crashed to the ground and the one behind stumbled over it. The SAS Captain emptied some rounds into this one as well. He loaded a new clip then heard a roar from above and one of the creatures dropped down on him slashing at his head. Tosh felt the excruciating pain and he shot the creature dead. He wiped the blood that was running into his eyes and groped after Dennis who was waiting for him as the narrow cut widened again.

"Come on," Dennis yelled, grabbing the man and helping him, pushing him on after the others.

Natalie, Katja, Hutchinson, Dennis, Tosh, Von Werner and the remainder of the mercenaries burst through the iron barred doors, up the stairs and into the bright sunlight. They could hear the creatures bounding up the steps behind them. When the white skinned beings burst out into the light, they threw their hands up in front of their eyes, snarling at the bright sunlight as they were blinded for a moment.

Back in the cavern Longinus climbed over the lip of the crevice. His eyes had gone red again and his skin white. He stood with his chest rising and falling heavily and then with an animal roar he bounded ape like towards the cut in the rocks.

Outside Deano and Smithy heard the shouts from the people and heard the animal roars and began running towards the danger.

"No!" Tosh roared at them, "Cut those pilots free! Get that

fucking plane in the air now!"

They rushed to obey his commands.

Running flat out Katja lost one of her shoes and she tried to stop to go back for it.

"No! Keep moving," Dennis yelled at her, "We need to get on that plane."

Dennis pushed them on and turned and dropped to one knee and killed another creature with the Kalashnikov. He heard a loud animal roar and looked back at the entrance to the subterranean levels and saw Longinus burst out into the afternoon sun. The creature stopped and roared as the bright sunshine hurt his red eyes. Then he shook his head, snorted, saw Dennis and roaring with rage set off at a fast run straight for the journalist.

Deano and Smithy cut the pilots loose and pushed them to the plane. Creatures were running straight for them and the two SAS men took them out with precise shots. Tosh was running as fast as Von Werner could allow. He had his hand on the German's neck pushing him on towards the Hercules. Running hard with the two women Dennis was suddenly aware that something was about to flank him. He glanced right and saw it was Longinus. The creature so much bigger and stronger.

A Bell Huey helicopter banked from the mountains and swung in low. Tosh made it to Deano and snatched the younger man's headset off his head and held it to his ear and mouth.

"Base. This is delta echo. Delta echo. Are you receiving?"

"Delta echo. This is base. Major Cochoran receiving you."

"Base there is an inbound helicopter. Is it one of ours. We request immediate evac. Repeat immediate evac."

"Delta Echo we have you on screen. Inbound chopper is not one of ours. Repeat not one of ours. Helicopter is unfriendly. Treat as hostile."

"Fuck!" Tosh let the headset go.

Dennis saw the Bell Huey coming in to land. It hovered just feet above the ground and Dennis saw the Gau 17a minigun mounted in the doorway. The north Korean Kim Li Choi at the gun.

"Everyone down," Dennis yelled pushing Natalie and Katja behind a pallet of cargo before diving behind it himself. He put his arms around the pair of them as they covered their ears with their hands. The Gau sprayed the ground kicking up sand and stones. Where the pallets and crates were hit splinters erupted off them and showered the air. Dennis saw one of the creatures out of the corner of his eye. It stopped near them and was literally cut in half by the deadly fire. Choi stopped firing to allow the rotating barrels to cool. Dennis looked up as the firing stopped. The creature at his feet wasn't Longinus and he searched for him knowing he couldn't be far.

"Peter!" Natalie shouted.

Dennis turned. Katja was running for the Huey. One of the creatures that was running flat out parallel to them suddenly changed direction and bounded after Katja. The minigun had cooled sufficiently but Choi now couldn't fire without the risk of hitting the redhead. He drew a handgun and fired shots at the monster, hitting it in the shoulder, which only angered it and didn't slow it. Dennis aimed down the sights of his AK-74M and shot the creature in the back of the head. It crashed to the desert floor and was still. The helicopter touched down briefly as Katja got to it and Choi grabbed her hand and pulled her in. She threw herself into a seat and put the lap belt around her waist. As the Huey lifted off again Choi gave Dennis a mocking salute. Katja smiled at him and then the helicopter was banking away and climbing, gaining height and speed.

'Fuck! She's hot' Dennis said to himself.

"Pete! Natalie! Come on!" Hutchinson shouted. He was now on the loading ramp of the Hercules. The ramp was six inches off the ground and the plane was moving slowly and turning. Tosh bundled Von Werner into the back of the plane as Deano and Smithy gave covering fire. Dennis grabbed Natalie's hand and together they sprinted for the Hercules. There were still a few of Von Werner's men on the ground shooting at anything that moved. Suddenly Smithy was hit by a stray bullet and went down clutching his throat. Deano called out and ran to his aid as one of the creatures side swiped him knocking him down. As Deano tried to get back to his feet, he was swamped by two more of the creatures and he went down under them. Dennis and Natalie jumped onto the ramp of the Hercules that was now gaining speed fast for take-off.

Tosh put his hand on the button to close the back up when Hutchinson said.

"Captain. Your men."

Tosh looked out and saw the creatures that had killed Deano bound away. Smithy was unmoving on the desert floor. The sand soaking up his blood.

"They're gone," Tosh said.

He smacked the button and the ramp began to close.

The pilots levelled the Hercules out at 1000ft. Natalie was tending to the deep scratches on Tosh's head and back of his neck while the SAS Captain kept the handgun trained on the billionaire Count. Inside the Hercules was a pallet of munitions and a Mercedes Benz G class open top 4x4 on skis.

Von Werner still had the spear of destiny in his hands and had it clutched to his chest lovingly. The shaft had been snapped off and now only a few inches of wood jutted from the spear head.

The pilot turned around and shouted back into the hold.

"Sir the Israeli military have scrambled fighter jets. ETA five minutes. Our instructions are to follow them and land and surrender ourselves into custody."

"Ignore this!" Von Werner said, "Change our heading for Gaza."

"No!" Tosh shouted, "Tell them that we are a British red cross mission and will proceed to Shaheed Mwaffaq air base in Jordan where we will land. We have British nationals on board and will seek the help of the Jordanian government," Tosh turned back to Von Werner, "you no longer give the orders here Count."

The pilot relayed the new message.

"The Israelis are refusing," he shouted back, "They have re-issued their warning to us. We are to follow them to Tel Nof air force base. Our refusal to follow these instructions will result in military intervention. I think they mean to shoot us out of the sky."

"Repeat my message to them," Tosh shouted. He turned to everyone in the aircraft, "Does anyone have a cell phone?"

Hutchinson shook his head.

"His lot took them. Remember," the American said nodding at Von Werner.

"I have mine."

The German Count took his phone from his trouser pocket. Tosh opened the screen up.

"No service. That's just bloody brilliant. Without comms I can't get help from my unit."

Tosh turned his attention back to Von Werner.

"And now my dear Count It's time to hand that over," he extended his hand for the spear.

Von Werner didn't move so Tosh waved the pistol at him.

"Now!"

"Tosh look out!" Dennis yelled as Natalie screamed.

Tosh spun around at the sound of snarling. Longinus had risen up behind him. Tosh stared into the white face with red eyes. The long sharp teeth were bared. He attempted to bring the gun up but Longinus was too quick. The creature rushed forward and sank its jaws into the trapezius muscle at the side of the SAS Captain's neck and ripped them free. Tosh slumped to the floor of the plane, his blood pumped out thickly and he tried to speak but only managed to cough up blood. Longinus spat the large lump of flesh out and then with his jaws dripping it focused on the spear again. He reached Von Werner in two steps and snatched the spear from him. Von Werner shrank away and as all watched Longinus' face and eyes returned to human again.

"Longinus," Hutchinson called in Latin. The Roman turned towards the American as Hutchinson said, "Let us help you."

Longinus held the spear in his hands as the blue sparks danced over his fingers.

Dennis spoke in a low voice.

"Nat. get ready to open the ramp when I say."

Von Werner placed his hand on the spear head. He smiled at Longinus.

"This truly is the work of God," he said.

Longinus' eyes travelled up to look at the German Count before him. Then his face contorted into rage and his eyes turned red again and his face white. He lashed out and backhanded Von Werner which sent the man flying.

"Now!" Dennis shouted.

Natalie went for the button that opened the ramp. The creature saw her move and blocked her. She shrank back. Von Werner wiping blood from his face suddenly threw himself forward and hit the button. The ramp began to open quickly and the wind rushed in. Dennis had picked up Tosh's handgun and fired again and again hitting Longinus time and time again. The creature stumbled backwards and fell getting tangled in the netting of the ammo crate. The spear fell from its grasp and rolled towards the end of the ramp. Von Werner lunged after it and managed to wrap his fingers around it just as the netting ripped free. The pallet of weapons began sliding backwards towards the rear.

"Von Werner that crate!" Dennis yelled.

Von Werner managed to move out of its way as it slid past and fell out of the back of the Hercules. It's parachutes opening the moment it cleared the plane. It ripped the netting as it went and now this hung outside the aircraft in shreds dragging Von Werner and Longinus with it. Dennis ran and dived for the rear of the plane when he saw Von Werner hanging on for dear life. He reached out his hand and then his eyes widened as he saw Longinus right himself and lunge at Von Werner. The creature roared and dived on Von Werner's back clawing and slashing at him. Then it reached the spear and snatched it out of the German's grasp.

"Hey asshole!" Dennis shouted.

Longinus looked up and Dennis pulled the trigger on the handgun and shot the creature right between the eyes. The contorted face took on a peaceful look for a moment then Longinus fell backwards and out of the Hercules. The netting suddenly ripped and Von Werner was dragged outside the plane now and hung on desperately as the powerful wind twisted and turned and bumped him against the turbulence. His eyes were wide with fear. Dennis wrapped his foot around some of the netting and reached as far out as he could with his hands. Von Werner was still desperately holding on to the spear. Dennis strained his muscles as far as he could and Von Werner's outstretched hand was only inches away.

"Try to reach my hand!" Dennis yelled above the howling wind.

Von Werner tried to move up the netting, but the power of the wind was too great and was pulling him back.

"Let go of the spear."

Two Israeli fighter jets whooshed past. Dennis saw them out of the corner of his eye. Time was running out.

"Let go of the spear."

"No. I cannot," Von Werner shouted back, he felt his strength starting to fade against the buffeting, then he looked Dennis in the eyes, "Thank you for saving my daughter."

Then his grip slipped and he was gone. Dennis watched his body as it spun faster and faster gaining speed uncontrollably as it fell. Dennis closed his eyes and punched the floor of the plane.

Hutchinson grabbed Dennis and pulled him back away from the edge.

"Pete. Those Israeli jets have a missile lock on us."

Dennis jumped to his feet.

"Quick! Get in the Mercedes."

Natalie, Hutchinson and Dennis climbed in the open topped 4x4. Then with a last look at Tosh who was slumped against the side of the plane in a pool of his own blood, dead, Dennis pulled the release and the Mercedes slid backwards out of the cargo hold as the parachutes deployed and they were pulled out into the open air. The car snatched as it swung down underneath its chutes and they were descending slowly now. The Hercules was leaving them behind and they ducked as missiles struck it and it exploded in mid-air and the blast shattered the windscreen of the Mercedes. Burning debris rained down and Dennis looked up nervously to see if their parachutes were on fire. To his relief they weren't.

The Mercedes bumped the earth and Dennis turned the ignition key to start the engine and drove from the skis onto the sand of the desert.

"Where do you think we are Pete?" Hutchinson asked.

"I'll drive up to the top of that dune to get our bearings. There must be a road around here somewhere."

He stopped the Mercedes at the top of a dune and the three of them scanned the surrounding desert. Behind them was the backdrop of the Hebron mountains. In the far distance they could see a road snaking through the yellow sand. Natalie saw something glinting in the sand.

"What is that?" she pointed in the distance.

"I think I know," Dennis said. He turned the steering wheel on the Mercedes and drove down the side of the dune towards what was sparkling in the sun.

Halfway there they came across the body of Longinus still in his red toga. Dennis stopped the 4x4 by the side of the body. The face had returned to its human form and the eyes were open and normal. The bullet hole evident in the forehead.

"I'm sorry I had to do that," Dennis said.

"It's a real pity that we weren't able to save him. Imagine if we could have done. To bring home someone who lived two thousand years ago during the time of the Caesar's," Natalie said.

"What a find that would have been," Hutchinson added.

"He was just pure evil," Dennis said, "Over the two Millenia his body and soul were transformed into that creature we saw. I only hope he finds peace now."

He took one more look and then put his foot down and drove the Mercedes on towards the glint in the sand. He pulled up near a road just a few metres from Von Werner and stepped slowly from the vehicle, Hutchinson following.

"Is he dead this time?" the American asked.

Dennis looked down at the broken body. Blood was dripping from every opening. The spear was still clutched in the dead hand. Dennis reached down and plucked the spear from the fingers.

"He is this time."

Dennis passed the spear to Hutchinson. The sparks had gone now, the metal ordinary.

"We'd better get this to its home," Hutchinson said, "If we go that way it will take us to Jordan. Don't fancy Israel now do you?"

"No."

They got back into the Mercedes. Dennis put his hand on the ignition key then paused. He looked down at the Count's broken body.

"You know even after everything he has done, I was going to save him."

Dennis started the engine. Natalie leaned forward from the back seat and put her arms around his neck.

"You're a good man Peter Dennis," she said.

Hutchinson in the front passenger seat looked at his friend.

"You did save his daughter."

"Yes," Dennis said, selecting first gear and turning onto the tarmac road for Jordan, "And I've no doubt we'll be seeing her again."

EPILOGUE

Dennis, Natalie and Hutchinson walked out of the building at Shaheed Mwaffaq Military airport in Jordan and onto the tarmac. The C130 Lockheed Hercules that would take them to the British military base in Cyprus for a flight back to England was just a short distance ahead. Jordanian soldiers stood at intervals around the buildings and plane on guard.

Dennis carried both his and Natalie's small cases. Hutchinson wheeled his. Natalie carried a rucksack over one shoulder.

"I don't know about you," she said looking at her chipped fingernails, "But I'll be really glad to get home. I need a manicure."

"I'll treat you to one," Dennis said, "What about you Jim?"

The American was slightly ahead of them and he turned his head.

"What's that?"

"Will it be good to get home?"

"Well, I've been thinking...."

Natalie and Dennis stopped and gave each other knowing looks.

".... About this Francis Drake, El Dorado thing."

Dennis rolled his eyes and put the cases down. Hutchinson continued walking while speaking over his shoulder.

"Who was it who first went in search of it?"

"El Dorado was named after a Muisca king who covered himself in gold dust and threw himself into lake Guatavita. It later became known as the lost city of gold. Two Spanish conquistadors, Gonzalo Pizarro and Francisco Orellana set out from Quito in Ecuador in 1541 in search of the legendary city. They discovered the Amazon basin and were the first to navigate the Amazon River. El Dorado's existence has never been proved Jim."

"And Drake searched for the city?"

"Many explorers have."

"Lost city of gold, eh?"

"Please don't tell me you're seriously considering it," Dennis turned his attention to Natalie, "He's not, is he?"

She shrugged and put her sunglasses on against the bright sun.

"Well, a man's got to do something around here to make a living," Hutchinson continued quietly, muttering to himself. Neither of his travelling companions heard him.

"There's always Alexander's sarcophagus," he turned to them, "We never did finish that project."

"No!" they both shouted at the same time.

Hutchinson shrugged and continued towards the plane. He said something over his shoulder just as the Hercules' engines started up. His reply drowned out.

"To tell you the truth," Dennis said to his girlfriend, "I'm thinking of quitting my job at the newspaper."

Natalie lowered her sunglasses to peer over them.

"What?"

"All this action-adventure stuff has got me hooked. How about Peter Dennis fortune hunter...." he gestured with his hands, imagining his name in lights.

"No."

"Oh okay. How about Peter Dennis treasure hunter?"

Natalie picked her suitcase up from the tarmac and made to walk off.

"That's the same thing."

"Oh okay. How about Peter Dennis husband?"

She stopped and peered over her sunglasses again.

"What did you say?"

Dennis held his hands out by his side.

"I said, Natalie will you marry me?"

Her mouth dropped open.

"Are you serious?"

"Yeah. Why not. Come on what do you say?"

She removed her sunglasses and looked him up and down for a few moments. Then she came over and whispered her answer in his ear. Then, leaving him open mouthed this time, she turned and followed Hutchinson. At the plane she turned back. Dennis hadn't moved. He was staring after her.

"Well, are you coming or not?" she called.

Half smiling to himself he picked his suitcase up and followed her to the waiting Hercules.

THE END

NOW READ THE NEXT IN THIS SERIES
'DRAKE'S GOLD'

Printed in Great Britain
by Amazon